Queen of Night's Promise

Queen of Night's Promise
1st Edition

Story concept, text, and compilation by © 2025 Arian Niwl.

Editing, print preparation, formatting, back cover summary, cover and interior design provided by Page Turner Books, Inc.

Books may be ordered through popular, online retailers, the publisher's online store, IngramSpark, or by contacting the publisher at:

Page Turner Books, LLC
222 N. Lafayette St., Suite 11
Shelby, NC 28150

Visit our website at www.ptbooksinc.com or contact us via email at contact@ptbooksinc.com.

Page Turner Books, Inc. name and imprint are the trademark and copyright of Page Turner Books, Inc.

978-1-965788-98-1 (iBook & ePUB)
978-1-967289-00-4 (Hardcover)
978-1-965788-99-8 (Kindle)
978-1-967289-01-1 (Paperback)

Library of Congress Control Number: 2025934417

Printed in the United States of America.

First printing: November 2025

QUEEN OF NIGHT'S PROMISE

ARIAN NIWL

SHELBY, NC, USA

QUEEN OF NIGHT'S PROMISE

ARIAN NIWL

SHELBY, NC USA

TABLE OF CONTENTS

CHAPTER 1..1

CHAPTER 2..23

CHAPTER 3..47

CHAPTER 4..65

CHAPTER 5..75

CHAPTER 6..94

CHAPTER 7..102

CHAPTER 8..124

CHAPTER 9..141

CHAPTER 10..152

CHAPTER 11..164

CHAPTER 12..173

CHAPTER 13..181

CHAPTER 14..193

CHAPTER 15..209

CHAPTER 16..218

CHAPTER 17..228

CHAPTER 18..243

CHAPTER 19..261

CHAPTER 20..272

BONUS CHAPTER..287

ABOUT THE AUTHOR..1

Chapter 1

HOUSE WARRAQUIM

ALLYNDRA

The sky blazed as a gigantic fireball swept overhead, its brilliance dimming the Queen of Night's Promise. Allyndra instinctively ducked her head as the flaming object passed so close she could feel its heat. The boom and concussion that followed nearly knocked her from the air.

The stone that has been circling the world for the past few days has finally come down!

She steadied herself and gained altitude, gazing after the rapidly fading object as it curved toward what might be an island in the distance. The light vanished from sight.

Wouldn't an object that large explode on impact, whether it struck the sea or the land? I wonder what it all means.

She climbed higher, wings straining, to see what she could. Squinting, she thought she saw a faint glow far to the west. She hovered, watching for any further sign, before realizing that

O'lathe, Mother of her House, was likely already calling for her at the Guild House. *I'm supposed to be in the archives, not out here dancing over the ocean. She'll be upset with me again!*

Allyndra took a deep breath, knowing there was nothing more to be done for now. She descended toward the beach, where a long, ankle-length dress lay neatly folded on the sand. Stripping off her light flight dress, she frowned. She would have to leave it—no doubt the Mother would want her to search the library for any record of this strange event.

Odd is the least of it, she thought. *The flame vanished, but from what I've read, this stone traveled opposite the usual course of heavenly bodies. And it's been visible for days in the night sky.*

As she landed, the sounds of the night resumed. A humid breeze stirred the lush foliage, and above her the Promise—the rings that encircled her world—filled the heavens with silver light reflected from the suns, stretching from horizon to horizon like a titanic rainbow.

The Twins will be rising soon. I've wasted another night.

She slipped into the heavier Guild dress, tying the straps behind her neck, and placed a rock atop the flight dress she would soon abandon. She hesitated before sliding her damp feet into her light slippers—there was no time to dry them.

Ah well, they're worn anyway. Time to think about a new pair.

Allyndra ran, lifting the hem of her long dress as she bounded into the air. The four ankle-length, translucent wings on her back blurred almost to invisibility, leaving only flashes of light to mark their presence. She climbed swiftly, then leveled her flight across the bay toward the Guild House.

Soon, the tall white, spiral-shaped tower of Warraquim came into view. The air grew warmer as the Twins began to lighten the eastern sky.

As she neared the structure, she angled upward in a near-vertical ascent.

I hope the Mother will forgive me. She knows I love to water dance but thinks I spend too much time at it.

She overshot the balcony leading to the Mother's apartment before gliding gently down. Her shoes touched the stone pavers with the softness of a leaf kissing the ground. The two large infertile males standing guard tensed at her sudden appearance but relaxed when they noticed the embroidery on her gown marking her as one of high rank.

"Mother?" the one on her right asked.

He glanced at her, then at the symbol on her gown. His tone shifted, and he bowed deeply.

"Mother!"

His companion quickly followed suit.

"I apologize for my unusual entrance," Allyndra said. "I thought I should come as soon as possible from the archives."

Her black hair, streaked with metallic blue and tangled from flight, might give the House Mother other ideas.

There was no time to comb it. Hopefully, she won't notice.

The speaker turned to his companion and instructed him to inform the Mother of the House that a high one had arrived. As he disappeared behind the curtains that separated the balcony from the chamber, Allyndra studied the remaining infertile male. Like the others of his kind, he was tall—easily two heads above her height—with broad shoulders and well-muscled limbs.

A fine specimen for the Iresmia House, she mused. *Still, this post outranks that one, though it's far duller in its duties.*

He kept his eyes lowered, careful not to meet hers directly—such a look would be considered disrespectful.

His companion returned, holding the curtain aside before bowing respectfully.

"Mother, the Guild Mother awaits you."

Allyndra dipped her head in acknowledgment and passed between the two into the Guild Mother's private apartment. The moment she entered, oppressive heat struck her like a physical blow. It was so stifling she thought she had stepped into a furnace. Braziers lined the walls, their flames flickering in the dimness. The room was otherwise dark, and she had to wait a moment for her eyes to adjust.

When they did, her hearts sank. Mother O'lathe sat propped in a dark, intricately carved wooden chair before a matching table—both heirlooms, gifts from the House of Artisans long ago. The figure slumped in the seat barely resembled the commanding woman Allyndra had always known. O'lathe was thin, her frail body little more than flesh stretched over delicate bones. Her face and hands were deeply wrinkled, her once-streaked hair now entirely white, and her eyes had faded almost to colorlessness.

"Ah, Allyndra, please—come, sit. There's much to discuss." O'lathe's gaze sharpened. "I'm glad the heralds found you so quickly... or did they?"

Her voice was still strong, though everything else about her was failing. The realization that the Mother's time was nearly upon her made Allyndra's throat tighten. She bowed deeply, forcing back tears and holding her composure.

"Come, child. There's no time for crying or woe. Much must be done. Sit, sit."

She pointed one thin finger toward the chair opposite her and called out, "Attendants! Bring chilled Blood Flower juice, please! In that heavy dress, she's liable to overheat!"

Several female attendants in light flight garments hurried to obey.

Allyndra sank into the embroidered, deeply cushioned seat, but her focus was not on comfort or ceremony—it was on O'lathe, the woman who had guided every step of her life. The Mother who had nurtured her into adulthood, encouraged her studies, arranged her marriage, and comforted her when her husband and children had perished. She leaned forward and gently took one of the withered hands in hers.

"Mother O'lathe, I knew the age had begun, but I didn't realize how far it had come upon you. My hearts ache to see you so."

Her voice, usually steady and clear, trembled with the emotion churning inside her.

O'lathe patted her hand gently, a faint smile touching her lips.

"Oh, child, you know we all come to this point eventually. If I had the time, I'd love to hear you recite one of the old tales you learned from the books. Unfortunately, that's not to be. The stone descending from the sky has changed everything."

The Mother tilted her head and peered sharply at her.

"Though you wear a House dress, your hair is tangled. You've been water dancing again, haven't you? Not in the archives, as you're supposed to be."

Allyndra closed her eyes. *The body may be failing, but her mind is as sharp as ever.*

"Yes, Mother."

She dipped her head slightly and waited for the inevitable scolding.

"I can't help but wonder, daughter, if you should have been sent to the House of Artisans," O'lathe mused. "Ah, but your wonderful mind would have rebelled without the challenge of the ancient texts, even if most are unreadable. No—I stand by my decision. Warraquim is where you belong."

Allyndra chuckled softly.

"You know me all too well, Mother."

"Indeed I do. Come now, daughter," O'lathe said, freeing her hands. "You must have seen the stone in the sky if you were out dancing."

The shift in topic helped steady Allyndra's emotions, though she still fought to keep tears from falling onto the table. *I must show restraint before the House Mother.*

"Yes, Mother, I saw it. It was strange—it came from a different direction than most objects, at least from what I've read in the books. Curiously, there was no explosion, no sign of impact. I can't explain it at all."

"Ah! Very interesting. I'm sure there is more to hear, but thanks to your information—and that of others—there are now matters that must be addressed."

O'lathe turned in her chair and beckoned.

"Alekelia, come, daughter. You need to be here and take part in this as well. There's much you must know, and you have a role to play, being so highly placed within the House."

Alekelia stepped from the shadows as if summoned by a spell, the brazier smoke curling around her like drifting veils. Allyndra studied the woman who had been her rival throughout their student years. Alekelia was slender, though less athletic than she. Her hair, black like Allyndra's, was streaked with fiery red-orange that reminded Allyndra of molten lava flowing down a volcano's side.

Some say it suits her. She's impulsive and volatile at times. Not always honest, and ethics were never her strong suit. Still, I can't fault her for having a strong will.

Many of the males found Alekelia's fine features captivating, but it was her eyes that truly unraveled them—rare, emerald green, faceted and sparkling like a finely cut gem even in the dim light.

"Mother. Allyndra."

Alekelia inclined her head as she took one of the seats at the table, then turned her attention to Allyndra.

"Why am I not surprised to hear you were off water dancing? If it had been up to me, I would have sent you to the Artist Guild ages ago."

Her lips curved in a sneer.

"Oh! I almost forgot—your husband was of that guild, wasn't he? He wouldn't have been your husband then, would he? As you know, fertile males are always mated outside their Guilds. So you'd have had no husband to lose... no children to mourn."

O'lathe's finger struck the table sharply.

"Alekelia! Watch that tongue of yours!"

Alekelia dipped her head.

"Yes, Mother."

She acted contrite, but the tone of her voice remained defiant.

"Everyone knows, Mother, that Allyndra is either buried in the old books or off at the ocean water dancing. I don't think she's ever put that loss behind her, and it still clouds her judgment."

Allyndra clenched her teeth to keep from replying.

O'lathe shook a finger sternly at Alekelia.

"And perhaps, daughter, if you had shown more interest in the males at the dances, marriage might have settled you down—and given you children to occupy your time instead of throwing accusations around!"

Alekelia's jaw tightened, and for a moment it looked as though she would argue.

"Enough, Alekelia!" O'lathe's tone left no room for protest. "There are more important matters to attend to, and little time remaining."

She paused as attendants entered, carrying cups and a pitcher beaded with condensation as the warm, humid air met the chilled surface. They arranged everything neatly before stepping back to stand along the walls.

"Help yourselves," O'lathe said. "I know it must feel like standing on the suns in here, but I'm always cold these days. That's why I allow my attendants to wear flight dresses instead of those heavy House gowns."

Allyndra nodded—it made sense. The attendants' light, almost sheer, above-the-knee dresses were far more suitable for the heat. The infertile males wore only breechcloths, as if they worked in an Iresmia house. Alekelia, unlike the attendants, was not wearing a House dress; only she and Mother O'lathe still had theirs on.

The air was stifling, and Allyndra longed to pant for relief. The sweet, fruity scent of the juice made her mouth water, but she declined.

Alekelia, of course, helped herself.

"Ah, a wonderful vintage, Mother."

O'lathe ignored her.

"Something has happened. The object that circled the world has come down—"

Alekelia lounged back in her chair and waved her cup dismissively.

"This has happened before. Usually such things fall into the sea. What does a rock from the heights have to do with the House of Knowledge Keepers and Gatherers?"

O'lathe's face pinched as she focused on Alekelia.

"Perhaps if you hushed and listened first, you might actually learn something."

Alekelia gave an obligatory nod, though, to Allyndra's eye, she didn't truly accept the Mother's rebuke.

O'lathe settled back in her chair.

"Yes, objects have fallen before—but members of this House, whose duty it is to study the heavens, observed that this one behaved oddly. It changed direction several times over the course of days, and it slowed considerably before circling the skies multiple times."

"I've been researching—or trying to," Allyndra said. "There's nothing in the archives about anything like that. It did seem to slow before curving toward the world, but there was no sound or flash of impact. That's highly unusual."

O'lathe nodded thoughtfully.

"Is there anything more in the old books that might prove useful?"

Allyndra considered what she'd managed to decipher.

"No, Mother. I still haven't made much progress. I can only use a few reference fragments to parse the language and symbols. At best, I've formed a few guesses about their meaning."

"What! The A'ksu is stymied?" Alekelia sneered.

"Alekelia!" O'lathe's voice cracked like a whip—firm, edged with anger. "You will never use that term in my presence, or anywhere else. Do you understand?"

Alekelia inclined her head slightly, but O'lathe was not satisfied.

"I said," the words came out slow and firm, "do you understand?"

Alekelia set her mug down, stood, and dropped into a deep curtsy. Allyndra felt no satisfaction—only sympathy. The posture was demanding, designed to make breathing difficult. She knew

Alekelia would remain there until the Mother granted permission to rise—or until she fainted from lack of air.

Allyndra's attention shifted as O'lathe turned her full focus on her.

"Daughter, it is known that you possess a gift for swift learning—the ability to make great intuitive leaps. Or at least, you once did. I trust it's still there."

Her tone carried no question, only quiet certainty.

Allyndra fought to hide her discomfort at the mention of the trait. Few knew she bore the mark of the A'ksu. *And every student is taught that the A'ksu nearly destroyed the world long ago—no wonder the gift is viewed with suspicion.*

She drew a steadying breath.

"I will go to the archives immediately and see what I can discover. I shall redouble my efforts."

Her gaze flicked briefly to Alekelia, who was already gasping for breath.

O'lathe raised a thin finger in gentle reprimand.

"No, daughter—not now. I have another task for you. There is a skyship at the docks, and I have instructed the captain to delay departure. You will board that vessel and sail to the place where this object came down. Determine what it is, if you can, and decide what further action must be taken—for the good of the House and the world. Do you understand?"

Allyndra dipped her head in acknowledgment but couldn't help noting the wording. *Why would I decide what to do? That's the task of the Mother of the House. True, Mother O'lathe's health is failing—perhaps that's it. I may have to make a quick decision on her behalf.*

She began to rise.

"Yes, Mother."

O'lathe gestured for her to sit again.

"Not yet. There is more to be done, and it requires both of you."

Her gaze shifted to Alekelia, whose labored breathing was now clearly audible.

"Now, Alekelia, you may stand and take your place at the table once more. You have an important role to play before this night is over."

Alekelia steadied herself with one hand as she rose. She swayed briefly, breath ragged, before resuming her seat.

"Yes, Mother," she managed in a hoarse voice.

To Allyndra's eyes she still looked pale, though the familiar glint of defiant pride had not faded.

"Good," O'lathe said. "Another skyship awaits you as well—one I've also ordered to delay its departure. You are to inform the other Houses that House Warraquim is investigating the strange stone from the sky. Tell them the Mothers of the Houses must be gathered to the Council at once. You may also inform them that we have our finest scholar on the task. Do you understand your duty?"

"Yes, Mother."

The reply sounded sincere—without a hint of sarcasm.

Perhaps she's learned her lesson, Allyndra thought. *Right— and perhaps I'll see the Twins rise in the West.*

Mother O'lathe appeared satisfied with the answer.

"Very good. As such, Alekelia, I am naming you the Voice of Warraquim."

Allyndra's hearts skipped a beat. To be named the Voice to the other Guild Houses was no small honor—it meant speaking with the authority of the Mother herself. *It's one of the most prestigious positions in the House.*

O'lathe motioned to the attendants and waited as they gathered.

"Allyndra, and all present, hear my words as Mother of House Warraquim. You are witnesses to my testament in naming Alekelia illm Warraquim as the Voice of the House."

Allyndra, along with everyone else, bowed her head in acknowledgment.

"Very good," O'lathe continued. "We'll have my words transcribed and entered into the official records shortly."

Alekelia straightened, her eyes gleaming. She paused a moment, visibly restraining herself, before bowing her head.

"Thank you, Mother, for placing your trust in me. I will carry out this duty to the best of my ability."

I think she actually means it this time, Allyndra thought.

"Voice of Warraquim," O'lathe said, "you must pack quickly— if at all—for the captain has kindly delayed her sailing at my request, and your journey is long. You may go, and may the gods be with you, my daughter."

Mother O'lathe extended her hands.

Alekelia took them briefly, then sank into a deep curtsy.

"Yes, Mother."

As the exchange unfolded, Allyndra couldn't help thinking, *As if any skyship captain would dare refuse a direct order from the Mother of a Guild House—especially from the most powerful one. Still, O'lathe has never abused her position. She is both humble and wise.*

"Mother," Alekelia asked, "what ship do I seek?"

"Pa'hole's Breath," O'lathe replied, "under the command of Captain R'lyain. Now go. Time is of the essence."

Alekelia made another deep curtsy, brief this time, before turning to carry out her task.

O'lathe watched her go, then shook her head and exhaled softly.

"She's impulsive—that's one of her failings. Now, Allyndra, as for you—once we're finished here, you must make your way to the *Wind Dancer*, under the command of Captain Hila'ar. The ship is small but swift, or so I'm told. Unfortunately, there will be no time for you to pack either. I feel it in my aching bones—time is of the essence. I don't yet know what this object is, nor how it will affect us, but I fear I'll soon pass into the arms of the gods. When that happens, the task of guiding the House will fall entirely to you."

Allyndra nodded automatically, before the meaning of the Mother's words struck her. She blinked several times.

"Mother? What do you mean—the task will fall to me?"

O'lathe's thin lips curved into a faint smile.

"I am naming you Mother Named, Allyndra. I trust you more than Alekelia to guide this House. Oh, I'll be honest—Alekelia is intelligent, well-traveled, and far more socially engaged than you. But as you've seen, she's impulsive and rarely takes time to think deeply. You, on the other hand, reflect before you act. I'm aware of your failings, yes—but it seems to me you've simply lost your way. I know that when the Twins kissed all those years ago, the event brought you great sorrow—the loss of your husband and children. But now, I'm giving you a new purpose—to reengage with life and serve as Mother to this entire House."

I am to be Mother of the House?

The thought staggered her. She grasped the edge of the table as her vision dimmed, swaying under a wave of dizziness.

Taking several deep breaths, she steadied herself and managed to whisper, "Mother!" She paused, forcing calm. "I'm not sure I'm ready for this, and well…" She glanced around the room before lowering her voice. "You know as well as I do that I bear the trait. I'm A'ksu."

O'lathe's expression grew solemn. "None of us are ever truly ready, daughter. I wasn't. In fact, the very act of questioning one's readiness convinces me I've made the right choice. You are my chosen successor to lead this House.

"As for the rest—call it a feeling, an intuition perhaps—but I believe we may yet need some of the old talent in the days ahead. This strange stone frightens me, Allyndra. As I've said, the task will soon fall to you. You will have to guide not only our House, but perhaps all the Houses, in the times to come."

It wasn't only the near-insufferable heat in the room but also the weight of what had just transpired that made Allyndra feel as though her feet were bound to the floor.

"Yes, Mother," she managed at last.

Though the air was stifling, a shiver ran through her.

O'lathe beckoned to her attendants.

"Excellent! Servants—everyone! And bring the guards as well! I want all with eyes and ears to stand before me!"

It took several minutes for everyone to assemble. The large infertile male guards exchanged questioning glances. They were seldom summoned, holding as they did the lowest position in the House's hierarchy.

"Very good. All attend and listen," O'lathe commanded. "I, Mother O'lathe, Mother of House Warraquim, hereby name Allyndra illm Warraquim as Mother Named. Should she not return from her investigation, the title of Mother Named shall pass to Alekelia illm Warraquim. You will all bear witness to this and ensure it is recorded once I have finished with my daughter here."

Those present responded with deep curtsies, and the infertile males bowed low—first to O'lathe, then to Allyndra. The gesture struck Allyndra as strange. Though her rank warranted deference, this level of reverence was reserved for the Mother herself.

She has named me Mother! How am I to fulfill such a task? Am I truly worthy of her decision?

The thoughts scattered through her mind like droplets of water skittering across a hot griddle.

O'lathe dismissed the gathering, then turned her full attention back to Allyndra.

"May the gods bless and protect you, Mother Named, and may you return to guide this House."

Her tone softened, shifting back to that of the old teacher Allyndra remembered.

"Now go on—get, fly if you must! I know how much you love it! I've kept the skyship here overlong, and haste is needed!"

She shooed her away with both hands.

"Mother! I don't know what to say!"

"Nothing—only focus on what must be done. Now go! You are not the Mother yet, daughter!"

Allyndra stood and made her courtesy before turning toward the balcony. Grasping the hem of her dress once more, she ran forward and leapt effortlessly over the parapet. She dropped briefly before snapping her wings open, angling herself toward the single skyship still moored at the dock. The other vessel was already lifting into the air and turning eastward.

Alekelia has wasted no time.

Moments later, Allyndra landed lightly on the deck. A heavyset woman stood waiting, arms crossed and a frown creasing her face. Her limbs were corded with muscle—more like one of the infertile males than the captain of a ship.

The woman's gaze was sharp with scorn.

"I'm guessing you're the daughter of House Warraquim—the one whose Mother has ordered me to re-task the *Wind Dancer* to her will. Captain Hila'ar."

Allyndra bent her knees in a respectful half-curtsy.

"I am. Allyndra illm Warraquim, Mother Named of House Warraquim. Please forgive my tardiness."

The words *Mother Named* felt strange on her tongue.

The captain blinked, then offered an awkward curtsy of her own.

"Mother Named of Warraquim? Forgive me, Mother. I didn't mean to be disrespectful."

Allyndra made a calming gesture with her hands.

"You couldn't have known, and truthfully, I'm still getting used to the title myself. Thank you, Captain, for altering your course at such short notice. Time is critical. We should depart as soon as possible—I'll explain everything as we go."

"Yes, Mother Named."

Captain Hila'ar looked past her and called out to the crew—mostly females, with a few infertile males among them.

"Get us aloft and full sail, as fast as you can!"

She paused, then turned back to Allyndra with respectful deference.

"And our course, Mother Named?"

"For the crew's sake, please—just Allyndra," she replied. "We head west, to see if we can find where the skystone came down. It seemed to me it fell near, or perhaps upon, an island in that direction."

"Very good," the captain said briskly. "Set course for Ca'halia! There's water there and no other island for a stretch. Come on, you quicklicks—move! Show me you've got more brains and spirit than you look!"

She turned back to Allyndra.

"If you'd like, I can show you your quarters—or you can stand by the prow. I'll join you once we're fully underway."

Allyndra held back a smile at the captain's colorful insult—*quicklicks* being the name of a notoriously sluggish animal.

"Watching where we're going will be perfect, Captain."

She moved forward, occasionally using her wings to steady herself as the ship began to rise.

Captain Hila'ar offered a quick grin and strode across the deck to assist her crew.

A working captain, Allyndra thought. *One who leads by doing, not just by ordering. I'm already impressed.*

Reaching the prow, she took hold of the railing lightly. Falling wasn't her concern—her wings would save her—but the embarrassment would not.

The ship lifted smoothly as the dock lines were cast away and the gas within the hull buoyed the wooden vessel into the sky. Crew members shouted orders back and forth as the sails caught the wind and filled. The *Wind Dancer* turned westward, and Allyndra knew the captain would soon find one of the high rivers of air and ride it toward their destination.

As the ship climbed higher, the full heat of the Twins warmed her face while the vessel swung to its new heading. Allyndra shaded her eyes to glimpse the two suns—one golden, the other red—burning brightly in the morning sky. Silently, she prayed for the safety of the ship, her House, and her world.

Once the *Wind Dancer* had settled into its course, Captain Hila'ar came to stand beside her, expertly managing the vessel's subtle adjustments as the air currents brushed against its hull.

"The message from the Mother of your House made this task sound important," the captain said. "She invoked Warraquim's authority over the other Houses—a rare thing. So what exactly are we sailing toward, Moth—ah, Allyndra?"

Allyndra rolled her shoulders, her translucent wings rustling softly.

"I don't know for certain, Captain. An odd stone from the sky came down—not crashing like others before it, but maneuvering, almost as your ship does. When I observed it, it appeared to settle on an island to the west. What it is, none of us in the House knows. That's why we must find it—and determine whether it poses any danger."

Captain Hila'ar frowned and nodded slowly.

"Still, it seems strange that the Mother of your House would send her Mother Named, regardless of what the object is. Why not another scholar?"

Allyndra kept her gaze fixed ahead.

"Because I'm A'ksu."

Her voice was calm, without inflection.

The captain looked sharply at her, then blinked.

"I thought that bloodline had died out long ago."

"The trait persists," Allyndra said quietly. "It's faint in most, but in some, it shows fully. I am one of those few."

"I see." The captain shook her head. "Then this must be something truly important, if the Mother of your House has sent both you and her ship on the task. I'll be discreet. A Mother Named and an A'ksu aboard the same vessel—yes, the crew doesn't need to know unless it becomes necessary."

She gestured broadly to their surroundings.

"In any case, we're making fair speed. The gods are with us."

"Let's hope they stay with us." Allyndra turned to glance back.

The House of Warraquim was already vanishing behind them as the ship gained speed. She shaded her eyes against the glare of the Twins reflecting off the sea and murmured, "*A lila mākou a lapalapaie ho'omklamklama ika pouli.*"

The captain's head snapped around.

"That sounds like the old language. What does it mean?"

"We will be a flame to light the darkness."

"You know the ancient tongue?"

Astonishment etched itself across Hila'ar's face.

"Only a little—nowhere near enough to be useful," Allyndra admitted. "There's very little left that I could read."

She managed a faint smile.

"Well then, Captain Hila'ar, let's see if we can illuminate this mystery, shall we?"

The captain leaned against the railing beside her, returning the smile.

"Aye. A mystery to be illuminated—that sounds like a fine adventure indeed. We're making excellent speed. I'd say we'll reach it by morning."

Allyndra nodded faintly, though unease lingered beneath her calm expression.

A mystery I'm terrified of, she thought. *Mother O'lathe's intuition was never wrong.*

***

There was a pounding on the cabin door, and Allyndra awoke with a start.

"Yes, Captain?"

"Good, you're awake," came Hila'ar's voice. "I came to rouse you—the day is breaking, and we're coming up on the island. I figured you'd want to be on deck. I'll bring some Bloodflower juice for us."

Allyndra thanked her. She considered washing her face to refresh herself but decided against it. She wanted to see what awaited them with her own eyes.

Leaving her cabin, she walked down the narrow corridor, passing the large bags of lifting gas that kept the ship aloft, and climbed the steps to the deck. Warmth struck her immediately; the suns were rising.

High Summer, she thought. *The days will soon grow much hotter.*

Finding her balance easily—like she was water dancing—she made her way to the prow.

I remember Hila'ar's surprise when I told her I practiced that art.

On the horizon, an island came into view, and something glinted strangely—metallic, bright, and unnatural.

Hila'ar joined her at the front and handed her a mug of chilled Bloodflower juice. Allyndra took a sip, savoring its cool sweetness and feeling the sugar stir her senses awake.

"What do you make of that, Mother? A rock from the heavens?"

Allyndra gestured toward their destination with her cup.

"From the stars, perhaps—but it shouldn't gleam like that."

Hila'ar shaded her eyes, squinting at the horizon.

"I can't make out the details from this height or distance. It looks large—and the beach below seems churned up. Is that usual?"

"Rocks from the heavens normally cause fires. I don't see any smoke—and they shouldn't look like that, not from what I've read."

Allyndra narrowed her eyes toward the gleaming object.

"Captain, keep the *Wind Dancer* a safe distance offshore. I'll fly in and take a closer look. I've got an odd feeling about that thing."

"Danger, you think?" Hila'ar asked.

"Let's be... judicious."

"I'll go," the captain said firmly. "I wouldn't risk the Mother Named of Warraquim."

"No," Allyndra replied. "The task falls to me. And if something *is* amiss, it will be up to you to carry word to the others. Stay offshore, stay safe, and report what happened—not only to my House, but to the entire Council. The current Mother has already named a backup, just in case."

Hila'ar frowned.

"I wish all Mothers were as wise as yours. It's a sound precaution. Still, I'll hold position here. May the Twins protect you."

"And to you and your crew." Allyndra nodded toward the island, where the metallic shape glimmered through the broken vegetation. "Now, if there's anything resembling a flight dress aboard, I'll change and investigate this phenomenon."

"We've no true flight dresses," Hila'ar said, "only what the crew wears while working aloft—but that should suit your purpose. I'll have someone bring you a few options. I've got to bring us to a stop and set the sea anchor."

The captain bent her knees slightly in a respectful gesture before striding off, barking crisp orders. The crew sprang into motion; the ship began to descend, sails furling as the sea anchor splashed into the waves.

Allyndra knew it would hold the *Wind Dancer* steady against the wind. She returned below to change out of her heavy Warraquim gown. In the narrow passage, she nearly collided with a young woman carrying several neatly folded garments—crew attire suited for climbing the rigging.

"Mother, these aren't exactly what you wanted," the woman said with a sheepish grin, "we tend to wear our dresses a bit shorter—but they'll be better than that heavy thing."

"That's fine. I'll find something suitable."

Allyndra took the clothes from her.

"Please fold and carefully store this gown. I'll leave it on the bed—it has sentimental value."

The crewwoman studied the garment curiously.

"It looks like standard House wear, Mother. What's special about it?"

Her expression was open and sincere.

"It's the last thing I wore when I was with the Mother of my House," Allyndra said, managing to keep her voice steady. "And I fear I'll never see her again before she passes into the arms of the gods."

"Ah! If it please, I'll have the dress cleaned, folded, and protected until I can return it," the woman offered.

"Thank you…" Allyndra hesitated, realizing she didn't know her name.

"Oh—my name's Wy'thelia, Mother."

"Wy'thelia," Allyndra said gently, her tone turning serious, "might I ask one last favor of you?"

"Of course!"

"If this vessel returns without me," Allyndra continued, "take this garment and present it to whoever serves as Mother at Warraquim. Tell her that Allyndra illm Warraquim, Mother Named, did her best."

Wy'thelia blinked several times as the weight of the words sank in. She dropped into a deep curtsy.

"Please forgive me, Mother Named of House Warraquim! I didn't realize such a high personage was aboard!"

Allyndra reached out, helping her rise, and shook her head.

"Only Captain Hila'ar—and now you—know. I ask that this secret remain between us. This task was given to me by the old Mother herself."

Wy'thelia looked pale, clearly overwhelmed. Allyndra suspected she had never expected to meet someone of such rank—much less be gently lifted and spoken to kindly by one.

"Yes, Mother!" Wy'thelia said, almost breathless.

"Thank you, Wy'thelia. Now, I must prepare for the flight."

Wy'thelia departed, moving as though she herself might take to the air at any moment.

Allyndra found a garment that was loose but serviceable.

It's baggy, she thought, *but this crew has more muscle than I do. Water dancing has toned me differently.*

Once more, she returned to the prow, noting that the *Wind Dancer* now floated about two persons' height above the waves. *There are things in the seas that can be dangerous. Hila'ar is wisely cautious.*

"Ah, looks good on you," the captain called with a grin. "Sure you don't want to join the skyship crew?"

She chuckled, and Allyndra laughed softly in response. Then Hila'ar's expression turned serious.

"How long should we hold position?"

"Two days," Allyndra replied. "If I haven't returned by then, I likely never will. If you sense any danger, sail away."

She stepped up onto the railing.

"Yes, Mother," Hila'ar said. "The weather should hold, if I judge it right. I'll wait a day, then sail around the island once and hold again. If you're not sighted by the second day—then by Ring Rise that night—I'll set course back to Warraquim as fast as the *Wind Dancer* can fly. May the gods be with you."

She lifted a hand in farewell as Allyndra leapt from the railing, dropping briefly before her wings caught the air. Allyndra waved back once, then angled her flight toward the distant shore.

As she neared the beach, Allyndra saw that the vegetation had been flattened by the object's passage. Beneath the broken branches, a metallic gleam shone through—brighter now, almost blinding as the light of the Twins struck it. Crossing over the sand, she gained a clearer view of the scene. Whatever the thing was, it was massive—and heavy, judging by the torn earth and crushed foliage.

Hovering slowly, she studied its outline.

This isn't natural, she realized. *The edges are too defined, too deliberate. Some sections must have broken off as it landed.*

She climbed higher, scanning the scattered fragments before turning her attention to the bulk of what was clearly some sort of ship. Then she froze. Near the wreckage, a figure stood—humanoid in shape—holding a dark, stick-like object.

A sharp, invisible force whizzed past her ear, followed by a thunderous crack. Another report split the air—and searing pain exploded in her abdomen. She looked down to see red blooming across the fabric of her borrowed dress.

Gasping, Allyndra veered sharply, but another invisible strike cut the air beside her. Breath failed her; the taste of blood filled her mouth. Far off, the *Wind Dancer* was only a tiny dot against the horizon. She knew she would never make it.

Her wings faltered. She dropped, landing hard on the sand. The pain burned through her as she lay staring up at the bright sky.

"May the gods bless and protect you, Captain Hila'ar," she whispered. "Flee… please. Gather the Houses."

Her voice faltered, and she smiled faintly.

"Gerrin, my love… I come to join you. We'll dance with the Twins."

Then the world went dark.

Chapter 2

THE RELIANCE

STEPHEN & ALLYNDRA

"**J**esus Christ on a donkey, Conner!" Jane, the chief scientist, was shouting at the captain while Stephen focused on his alien patient. "We end up on this world—the first intelligent species humanity's ever encountered—and you go and *shoot* one of them. What in God's name were you thinking?"

Oh, here it comes, Conner. You've gone and riled Jane's West Texan hackles again. Thank God I'm in here and not out there.

Stephen could hear Conner and Jane perfectly well through the glass of the isolation bay, even without the comms in his suit.

Is the ventilation even working right? This thing smells like melted plastic and rubber, and I'm sweating like a pig.

He shifted the overhead lights aside and glanced at the monitor mounted on the wall.

Why am I even bothering? I've got no clue what normal blood pressure or heart rate is for her species. Hell, she's got three hearts—if I read those scans right.

He tried to focus on his patient instead of the shouting just a few feet away.

Please don't die on me. I've already lost too many.

"Shut it, Jane," Conner shot back. "She got a good look at the ship and was taking off to warn—well, whatever that boat floating out there belongs to. We don't know what these people are, what they have, or how dangerous they might be."

He turned toward her, hands on his hips.

"There are only four of us awake right now. The rest are still in deep sleep. We've already lost a lot, but I've got several hundred souls to protect."

"And you think you're protecting them by *shooting* the locals?" Jane snapped. "Lord have mercy, no, I ain't shutting up for your stupidity. Just what we needed—the ship goes off course, and now you're out here *hurting* the natives. Of all the damn idiotic moves. Well, Doc, what's the prognosis?"

The comm was open, but Jane was loud enough that she didn't need it. Her voice cut through the glass like a buzzsaw, and Stephen winced at the noise.

God, I hate these isolation suits. Can't feel a thing through them. Not much I can do anyway—just bandage the wound and hope.

"She's going to live," he said aloud.

I think. Sound confident, Doc—that's what they drilled into you in med school.

"The bullet went clean through. Doesn't look like it hit anything vital."

He rapped a gloved finger against his helmet.

"But I feel claustrophobic in this thing. Not sure the air supply's even working right."

"You can take it off," Jane said.

"What? What about pathogens or whatever?" Conner interjected.

"You've got less chance of catching something in here than getting bovine encephalitis," she said dryly.

"So we're good?"

"Yes," Jane replied flatly.

Stephen sighed in relief.

The Captain will listen to her before he ever listens to me. It's her field of expertise, anyway.

He started pulling off the hood and suit while Jane continued.

"Yes. Come on, Conner— even for Big Blue, they didn't have time to check the full environment. But like I said, viruses and microbes here would've evolved with entirely different receptors to bind to. Our cellular makeup would be nothing like what they've encountered. I'm not giving you a full dissertation on the subject. You should've asked first."

Stephen grabbed a clean towel and wiped the sweat from his forehead.

"Good thing they put sickbay in the most secure section. Even so, half the systems aren't working properly. How's the rest of the ship holding up?"

Conner shook his head.

"Pretty busted up. I'm not sure how things are gonna go. This ship was supposed to be our base once we reached Big Blue, but now? This place is home sweet home. We're not going anywhere. Guess I should be glad we don't have to worry much about catching some weird disease."

He gestured toward the figure on the table.

"She gonna be all right for a while? *She,* right? We need to start getting people up, pronto. That other ship out there hasn't made a move, but who knows what'll happen when she doesn't come back. I need some of the marines on their feet and ready."

"She'll be fine, I think," Stephen replied. "And yes—if I'm interpreting the form and readings correctly, *her.* Alien physiology or not, it's fascinating. They've developed a humanoid structure—wings and eyes aside, dress her up differently and she could almost pass for human."

"Convergent evolution," Jane said. "Like mice and rats—different species, but similar body plans. How long do you think she'll be out?"

"Unknown. I didn't dare give her anything. No idea what's compatible with her system."

"Leave her," Conner ordered. "I need you working on getting others up. Lock the room down."

He jerked a thumb toward the door.

"Not sure that's a good idea," Stephen said.

"I'll keep an eye on the monitors, Doc," Jane interjected. "If anything changes, I'll let you know. That work for you, Captain?" Her tone made it clear she wasn't taking no for an answer.

"Yeah, that'll work. I don't need her dying on us."

Jane shot him a look.

"Should've thought of that before you *shot* her."

Stephen glanced down at the woman on the surgical table.

All I could do was patch her up. First contact—and we go and shoot her. Great start, humanity.

He turned toward the airlock to stow his helmet and suit.

"Guess there's no need for decontamination, then."

Jane ignored the comment.

"She restrained?"

"Yes. I don't need her waking up and reopening the wound."

Conner's brow furrowed.

"I'm going topside to see what that flying ship's doing. When you've got some marines operational, send them out. I want a perimeter—just in case."

"Will do," Stephen said. "Jane, if anything changes with my patient, you yell loud and clear."

"Sure thing. Now go—I've got plenty to do, but this stays top priority. No telling how long before her people come looking for her."

Yeah—and once they find out we hurt one of them, that'll go over really well.

"Okay, I'm off."

***

"Hey, Doc! You'd best get up here. The monitor's going crazy—beeping and making all kinds of noise," Jane's voice crackled through his comm.

"Be right there."

Stephen finished settling one of the newly awakened marines. "Stay put for at least thirty minutes."

"Will do, Doc. So... we made it?"

"Not exactly. We're somewhere other than Big Blue."

"Where?"

"I haven't a clue but we're not alone here. Whatever this place is, there's a sentient species out there."

Alien to us. Hell, we're the aliens here, not them.

"What? Are we under attack?"

"No. There's been... an incident. I'll explain later. For now, just rest and hydrate. Thirty minutes, minimum."

"I'll grab my gear, Doc."

"Absolutely not!" Stephen snapped. "You've been under for thirty years. Push yourself too fast and you'll end up with a stroke or a heart attack. We're fine for now."

I hope.

He made sure the man had water, did a quick vitals check, then hurried toward sickbay to check on his other patient. The corridor lights flickered as he reached the elevator leading up to the medical deck.

We're going to lose a lot more if the power keeps failing.

He knew one side of the ship had taken heavier damage than the other. *And the bad side is where Sandra's pod is.* He didn't want to think about what might have happened to his wife.

***

Stephen glanced at the monitor.

"Yeah, she's awake. Get Conner in here."

Jane called for the captain while Stephen moved to his patient's side. He reached out and gently touched her arm.

"Miss, it's all right—you're safe. I'm Dr. Stephen Banks."

***

Allyndra felt someone touching and rocking her. She couldn't understand what they were saying. The pain in her abdomen was still there—sharp, deep, and unrelenting. Fear took hold, and she wondered if she could still fly; the instinct rose naturally within her. She forced her eyes open and saw three figures—people, perhaps, though only somewhat shaped like them. Their eyes were mostly white, which struck her as strange. The one leaning over her appeared to be male, though she couldn't tell if he was fertile. He had the height of a fertile male but the heavier build of an infertile. The other figure was shaped differently—broader in some ways, narrower in others—and Allyndra guessed it might be female, though she couldn't be sure.

The room around her was unlike anything she had ever seen. The walls and ceiling were stark white, lined with strange devices that blinked with lights and emitted faint sounds. Above her hung some kind of glass-covered fixture with a steady glow. The space felt small and suffocating—too enclosed. Panic surged through her chest.

She tensed and tried to leap up, to run—but she couldn't move. She thrashed, struggling for several moments as the woman and the man tried to hold her down. A flash of motion caught her eye: a shiny black strap looped around her wrist. She turned her head and saw her other wrist and both legs restrained in the same way.

She cried out, the sound raw and hoarse—then fell back as pain tore through her abdomen. *That was a mistake,* she realized. *It still hurts to breathe.*

***

"'A wia 'oe? He aha kā hanna mā 'ane'i? 'O wau mahuhahikia, kapa 'ia 'o Allyndra illm Warraquim!"

"Whoa there, honey," Jane said, raising her hands in a calming gesture.

She glanced at Stephen with a shrug.

"Well, she speaks."

"That she does," Stephen replied. "Whew—what a mouthful."

Jane turned back to Allyndra and patted her chest.

"Jane," she said slowly, repeating it several times before gesturing toward Stephen.

"Stephen."

She repeated both names again, speaking gently and clearly.

***

Allyndra watched them carefully and realized they were giving names. She took several slow breaths to calm herself, trying to ignore the pain.

"Allyndra illm Warraquim," she said.

The woman—Jane—wrinkled her brow, bringing her hands apart and then together as if trying to simplify something.

"Ah..."

Allyndra drew in a deeper breath and forced herself to focus. *I think they want something shorter.*

"Ah... llllyyn... drr... ahhh."

Though her wrists were still bound—and though it was impolite—she lifted a finger, pointing first at the woman, then at the man.

"Jane. Stephen."

She was certain she had the names right.

There's no music to their names. They're flat... like a calm sea.

***

"That was perfect," Jane said, glancing at Stephen. "Remarkable."

"She has a respiratory system similar to a bird's," Stephen replied. "And her vocal tract's not far off, either. They could make excellent mimics—but I think she's doing more than that."

He shrugged.

"They're clearly intelligent—just look at the clothing, and that ship out there."

"I'm getting a computer," Jane said. "Let's see just how intelligent they are."

***

The one called Jane brought something over—a flat pane of glass set into a frame of shiny black material. She tapped it, and images appeared.

The first was of a plant of some kind, followed by several similar pictures as Jane said, "Tree."

Then Jane released one of Allyndra's hands from its restraint and gently took it. Allyndra's first instinct was to pull away, but curiosity overcame fear. She allowed the woman to guide her finger to the glass surface. When she touched it, new images appeared. Beneath each was a line of strange symbols, and a mechanical voice spoke a word.

A teaching device! Allyndra thought, eyes widening. *Oh, I wish I had something like this to study the old language.*

***

Conner stepped into the doorway and watched for a moment before snorting.

"Well, all right—get her started on the language. Doc, you've got a lot of people to wake up. I'm heading back to keep an eye on that boat out there. Jane, work with our guest for a bit, then I'll need you to help the doc."

He turned and left.

Jane shot him a brief look before sitting down on the edge of the bed. She programmed a simple alphabet lesson into the device and began working with the alien woman.

***

The one called Jane guided her gently, exchanging words as they went. It reminded Allyndra of learning the old language, except now the symbols matched pictures, making everything much easier to grasp.

They worked for several hours, and Allyndra soon learned how to bring up new words on her own. Focusing her mind, she began swiping faster and faster, absorbing the lessons at a remarkable pace.

Jane touched her shoulder—a gesture Allyndra didn't appreciate.

"Whew! Slow down there, honey!"

"Slow... my task," Allyndra managed to say.

"What was that?"

"My task."

She was confident she had the word right.

"Work. Task. Learn."

Jane tilted her head, brow furrowing.

"You mean your people sent you here to learn about us?"

Allyndra didn't understand every word, but she caught enough to recognize the question's intent.

"Yes," she said, nodding.

Jane's eyebrows rose. Then she bit her lip thoughtfully.

"So that means yes."

She nodded again, then shook her head.

"And this means no?"

Allyndra concentrated, searching for the right response in her still-limited vocabulary.

"Correct."

Jane nearly fell off the bed.

"That's incredible—high-speed learning."

Allyndra pointed to herself.

"A'ksu."

"Ahh-skew? I thought it was Ahh-lyn-drah?"

"No. Name—Allyndra. I A'ksu," she corrected. "I can... fast learn."

Over the intercom, Stephen's voice echoed, "I need some help down here."

Allyndra flinched at the disembodied voice. *How does Stephen do that?*

"It's fine, honey," Jane said, giving her a reassuring pat. "Nothing to be scared of. You keep working on this computer a bit more. I have to go."

Allyndra wanted to laugh as Jane made two of her fingers walk like little legs.

They think I'm not that intelligent. They're treating me like a child. I'll show them what an A'ksu can really do.

"All right, coming," Jane said, standing up.

She started toward the door.

"We'll be back in a few hours."

Allyndra watched her leave—and noticed that the woman had left one of her arms unrestrained. Smiling, she slipped it free, then easily released the other arm and her legs. She didn't try to run. Instead, she tested the door and found it locked.

Rolling her shoulders, she returned to the strange machine, eager to see what more she could learn. Focusing her mind in the way only she could, she reengaged with the device, absorbing everything it showed her. In time—she wasn't sure how long, having no sight of the Twins—she had a far better grasp of the language and was moving beyond basic vocabulary.

When the door slid open at last, Stephen and Jane stepped inside, clearly startled to find her sitting calmly on the edge of the bed. If she read their expressions right, they hadn't expected that. Jane frowned, nudging aside several empty cups that had accumulated on the floor.

Allyndra gave them her full attention.

"I see we have a great deal to discuss."

The two exchanged glances. Stephen's voice carried open astonishment.

"You learned to say all that already?"

Allyndra touched her chest.

"As I told Jane, I'm A'ksu. It means I have a talent for learning quickly."

It's only a partial truth.

Jane approached slowly.

"And all your people can do this—or just you?"

"We all learn," Allyndra explained, "but some of us learn much faster than others. That's what the term means."

Again, not the whole truth—but they don't need to know the rest.

"It's why my House—my Guild, I think is your word—sent me. We're the Guild of Knowledge Keepers. I came because I'm A'ksu. We didn't know what this thing was."

She gestured in a small circle with her hand.

"We didn't know it contained... people."

The two exchanged another glance before Stephen pulled up a stool and Jane took a chair.

"You're right," Stephen said. "There's a lot to discuss. But first, let me check that wound of yours. I want to be sure everything's healing properly—you were thrashing around pretty hard earlier."

"I was frightened," Allyndra admitted.

Jane crossed her arms.

"You had every right to be. I'd have reacted the same way if our positions were reversed."

Allyndra tensed as Stephen stepped closer. He hesitated, sensing her discomfort. She was uneasy with a male—*and a fertile one at that*—touching her without invitation. *Humans,* as they called themselves, had only two sexes, not three. *Their ways are different. I must endure this to learn. Twins, forgive me.*

She gave a small nod, and Stephen carefully opened the odd garment they had dressed her in. He examined the bandage, then peeled it back gently.

"Good," he said. "The bleeding's stopped. The bullet nicked the edge of one of your air sacs—or at least, that's what I think they are."

"Sort of like birds, Stephen," Jane observed. "You mentioned that before. Makes sense if they're built for flight."

Allyndra reflected briefly on the word *birds.* She had seen images of them on the learning device. They flew, yes—but differently than she did. Their limbs were shaped for it.

"Well," Stephen said, reapplying the dressing and fastening the garment closed, "hopefully you won't have a big scar."

"Scar?" Allyndra repeated, unfamiliar with the term.

She made a mental note to look it up later—if she could access the machine called a computer again.

"It's where an injury heals," Stephen explained, pushing up his right sleeve to reveal a thin white line along his forearm. "The damaged skin fills in, but the new tissue looks and feels a little different from the original."

Allyndra looked at the mark on his arm, puzzling over the words.

"An injury?"

She lifted her left hand and wiggled her fingers.

"Like losing fingers? Would that be such an injury?"

He seemed surprised—if she was interpreting his body language correctly.

"Losing fingers would be far more serious," Stephen said. "Much worse than an injury that just leaves a scar."

Allyndra tried to piece together his meaning.

"Yes, it is. These took over a year to grow back."

She flexed her fingers again.

Stephen appeared stunned—at least, that's how she read his expression.

"You lost a finger?"

"These here," she said simply. "It was an accident."

"May I?" Stephen asked—and didn't wait for an answer.

He took her hand, turning it over as he examined her fingers closely.

He didn't wait for permission.
The thought struck hard.
I must endure being touched by an uninvited male—not my husband, not a partner in a mating dance, nor one of the Iresemia House. Twins, grant me patience.
Allyndra clenched her teeth but did not pull away.
"Jane, this is remarkable," Stephen said. "There's no sign of any damage."
Jane rose to take a look herself, exhaling in astonishment as she had Allyndra move her fingers again.
"They must be able to regenerate—and damn well, too."
"You're going to have her picking up bad habits," Stephen warned lightly. "Watch your language."
Jane shrugged, then glanced at the empty cups scattered nearby, concern flickering across her face.
"What have you been drinking, dear? I'm not sure everything here is… compatible. It might harm you."
"I wonder how she even got to those," Stephen said, nudging a couple of cups with his foot.
"Sorry," Jane admitted. "I think I forgot to put the restraint back on."
"Good thing everything's locked up except the refrigerator," he said, turning back to Allyndra. "So, what did you have?"
Allyndra looked up at Jane.
"What appeared to be water, and something called apple juice. It tasted fine, though it could be sweeter. I'll admit, I'm hungry. Before flying here, I only had a single mug of Blood Flower juice. I thought I would return to the *Wind Dancer.*"
"Blood Flower juice?" Jane repeated, frowning slightly.
"It's from a plant we cultivate for its nectar."
"*Wind Dancer?*" Stephen asked, picking up the thread.
"Yes—it's the name of the skyship that brought me here."
"Skyship?"
"It's that vessel waiting for me offshore," Allyndra explained.
"Stephen," Jane said, glancing at him, "we'd better make sure we feed her. She's still recovering."

"You're right, Jane."

"I'll need to run some tests," Jane continued, "but if the apple juice were harmful, you'd probably know it by now. I'll get started on that so we can provide a proper meal. Ship's stores are limited, but I'll determine what's safe for you."

She stood and turned back.

"Is this Blood Flower juice your only source of nourishment? Do you understand what I'm asking?"

"A little," Allyndra said. "And to answer your question—we live on juices of various kinds, some soft fruits… and blood."

Jane blinked rapidly—almost comically, Allyndra thought, for one of her kind. She seemed confused.

"Bl—blood?" Jane stammered.

"It's our protein source," Allyndra replied matter-of-factly.

Stephen chuckled and nodded.

"Come over here, Jane. Let me pull up her scans—I was wondering the same thing myself. Her digestive system's pretty simple."

He brought several images up on the monitors behind the bed, pointing out various details as Jane joined him.

"There's something I'd call a crop, then a first stomach, a second stomach, and finally a relatively short intestinal tract compared to ours. Based on what she just told us, I'd guess the juices she mentioned are absorbed in the first stomach, with any excess stored in the crop.

"When it comes to blood, I'd say it enters the first stomach, and—similar to some hematophages on Earth—a membrane is probably secreted to filter out pathogens. Then the blood moves to this second chamber here."

He pointed.

"Notice how extensive the direct circulation is to the kidneys—here and here. The body just squeezes the liquid out. The rest passes into the intestines. Blood is a high-energy source and doesn't require much digestion. Weight is the enemy of flight, after all. Easy peasy."

Jane still looked a little pale—or so it seemed to Allyndra, though she was still learning to read human expressions.

Stephen laughed softly at Jane's expression.

"Come on, Jane, it makes perfect physiological sense. I can give her some plasma or synthetic substitute, assuming she can tolerate it. The last thing we want is to starve her after shooting her."

Jane swallowed hard.

"As you say, Doc. I'll get started."

She gathered several glass tubes filled with dark fluid and headed off.

"Sorry about her attitude, Allyndra," Stephen said with a warm smile. "We have old stories about creatures that survived on blood. I'll tell you about them sometime. Maybe you can share some of yours when your language improves."

He still hasn't said my name quite right. Allyndra folded her hands, thoughtful. *I still have much to learn myself. I need many more hours… I wish I knew how much time has passed. Captain Hila'ar was going to hold for two days.*

"Yes," she said simply, piecing together both the words and the nuances of their body language.

She was beginning to notice how similar humans were to her own kind in expression and movement.

Sweeping her gaze around the room, she asked, "What is this place—and why have we never seen you before?"

"Ah," Stephen said, "this is a spaceship. A colony vessel, actually. Did you understand that?"

Allyndra tried what she hoped was a negative gesture, and he seemed to understand.

Good—then I'm making the correct assumptions. I caught some of what he said, but I'll look up the words when I can.

"From the stars," Stephen said, pointing upward. "Does that make sense?"

"Yes," she answered, though she didn't truly grasp the concept.

The stars were lights in the sky—but she was fairly certain these beings were not gods either.

"Ah, good." Stephen smiled. "Well, we got here by accident. Do you comprehend?"

"Another place—a world somewhat like this one, if I understand correctly?"

He nodded, and she was growing more confident in her interpretation of human gestures.

"Very good," he said. "Another world, like this one. Our ship can't leave—we're stranded here. So, we'll need to be neighbors. Friends."

That is going to cause problems. Allyndra frowned. *I need to learn how these people act—their history, their ways. How much time do I have?*

"May I use the machine—the computer—again?" she asked. "I must improve my language and understanding."

I know the basics. I need more.

Stephen smiled, showing his teeth.

"Of course. But you'll have to stay here, all right? It's for your protection."

The teeth are strange... like those of a plant-eater. A quicklick, perhaps.

She set the observation aside and tilted her head in agreement.

"Good," Stephen said, patting her leg.

They touch a lot, she noted. *I'll need to study their customs further. But there's a question I must ask.*

"Can you see well?" she asked suddenly.

"What?" His eyebrows rose. "Of course I can. Why?"

Allyndra pointed first to her eyes, then to his.

"Your eyes are flat. They have no sparkle. Only the old ones begin to look that way. And you have wrinkles. Is your time upon you?"

Stephen blinked, taken aback, and tilted his head.

"What do you mean, 'time is upon you'?"

"Are you close to death?"

Stephen stared at her for a moment, speechless.

Allyndra made a note of his movement.

"Wrinkles mean death?" Stephen asked, his brows drawing together.

Surprise? Or thought? she wondered. *If I'm reading his body language correctly.*

He hadn't answered her first question—only responded with one of his own. Allyndra sighed. It no longer hurt as much to breathe; her body was healing.

"When a person develops wrinkles in the skin—the sags, the dullness of the eyes—it means their time has come upon them," she explained. "They have only a short time of life left."

She was suddenly reminded of Mother O'lathe.

Mother, I'm trying. I hope you haven't gone to the gods yet.

"You mean you don't age?" Stephen straightened abruptly in his chair.

"We do," Allyndra said, "but we don't show age—inside or out—until the very end. Then it comes upon us all at once."

Stephen seemed deep in thought again. He rocked slightly in his chair.

"It must be those regenerative powers your bodies have. We're not built the same way. Our process is slower—we age gradually."

He tapped a few notes into his pad.

"I'll record this, if you don't mind, Allyndra. When you arrived, I examined your eyes. They're about the same size as ours, but they have facets—compound structures—and the center seems modified into an acute fovea, a point for detailed focus. I'd guess it helps with flight. I can see why you think our eyes are dull. Yours sparkle—they look like faceted sapphires. Beautiful, really."

He stopped, then chuckled self-consciously.

"Lord, I'm talking way above your current understanding. Sorry."

I suppose I should learn how these people are made, Allyndra thought. *It isn't a high priority... but perhaps it should be. So much to study. Mother O'lathe, you've tasked me with more than I can bear. Still, I must try. What I learn here could mean everything to our people. Twins preserve me.*

She gave a small nod. She hadn't understood most of what he said, but she committed the words to memory so she could later ask the computer for their meanings.

While she was recalling them, Jane's voice came from the ceiling speaker.

"Okay, Doc—chemistry looks similar enough. It should be safe to give her... something."

Ah, they must have some way of speaking to each other from a distance. Fascinating. *I've read that some of the larger skyships use speaking tubes to carry commands from the helm to other decks. I wonder how far their device works. I'll have to look that up.*

"Thanks, Jane," Stephen replied.

"Doc, that ship out there—Conner says it's gone. Disappeared before the sun—suns—came up. We're guessing it took off to tell others their guest didn't return. Conner wants to know how she's doing with the language. We'll need her soon if they—or anyone else—come back. So far, we haven't exactly made a great first impression. Shuttles are all banged up, and most of the crew's still asleep. If we get attacked, we can't hold out."

They're afraid of us hurting them? Allyndra thought. *We haven't done that to one another in ages. I must learn more.*

"She's learning much faster than I expected," Stephen said, "and healing just as quickly."

Conner's voice replaced Jane's over the intercom.

"Good to hear, Doc. We're still assessing the impact damage. Lost a few shuttles completely, and the rest are in bad shape. If we're lucky, we might get two operational in a few days. Whatever it takes, Doc—but we need extra hands getting people up and moving so we can start repairs."

"All right, Captain," Stephen replied, exhaling slowly.

Allyndra listened carefully, filing away every word she recognized. She understood some of what was said—but not all.

These people are in trouble. They fear that hurting me may bring consequences. They're right to worry. She nearly laughed but held it in. *They've wounded the Mother Named of the most powerful House in the world. I'd be concerned, too. Still, I must assess their true capabilities. They're frightened—and frightened creatures can be very dangerous. I must proceed with caution.*

Stephen stood, crossed to a panel in the wall, and pressed a few buttons. It slid open, revealing several clear bags filled with dark fluid.

"Here, Allyndra."

He's getting better with the name.

"These are emergency stores of synthetic blood," he explained. "I'll get you a cup."

He moved to another section, retrieved an odd metal instrument that opened and closed, and used it to snip the ends off the bags.

"You can drink straight from the bag or pour it into a cup— whichever you prefer. I've got to go, but I'll be back in a bit. The captain—the man who was here earlier—is eager for you to keep learning, so do your... Ahkskew thing."

He put the tool away, rose, and left. The door slid shut behind him with a soft click.

A'ksu, she corrected silently. *Very well. I'll apply myself to the utmost—but first, I need energy.*

Allyndra didn't bother testing the door since she assumed it was locked. Besides, there was still much to learn. She examined the bag in her hand. The fluid inside appeared almost black. Dipping a finger into it, she tasted it—and nearly spat it out. It had no sweetness, only a metallic tang.

She eyed the bag warily. Still, hunger gnawed at her, and she needed strength. Closing her eyes, she lifted it and drank, grimacing as the bitter fluid hit her tongue.

I need to find some of that apple juice to wash this taste away.

There were a few containers left where she'd found them earlier. The juice wasn't particularly sweet, but it was far better than the blood substitute. The mild sweetness revived her, and she soon felt her strength returning.

Settling back onto the bed, she picked up the computer device and began again—typing in the words she had memorized, focusing her mind as it reengaged. She was deep in study when the two humans returned.

"Any progress, Allyndra?" Stephen asked as he came in and took a seat.

"Indeed. I've learned quite a bit more," she replied. "You were correct—you were headed toward a place called *Big Blue* from your home planet. I read the engineer's report before his accident, when your ship entered this system. He speculated that there was an imbalance in the warp field that shifted the vessel's course. If I've understood the concept correctly, it involves a small bubble of space-time existing separately from the rest of the universe. Your artificial intelligence detected the change and redirected the ship here, to the closest potentially habitable world. Do I have that right?"

That, humans, is what one with the full, ancient talent of being A'ksu can do.

Jane braced herself against the wall, her face going pale. Stephen stared at Allyndra, eyes wide. For a moment, neither of them spoke.

In a hoarse voice, Jane managed, "Goddamn, Stephen—she picked all that up in twelve hours! She sounds like she knows more than most of the engineers. Shit, we better not tell Conner she knows all that—he'd probably shoot her again and make it fatal this time."

Stephen frowned.

"Allyndra, just how much have you learned?"

"I know the basics of your science and engineering," she said. "I couldn't duplicate your systems, not with the technology on hand, but I understand the principles. I've also learned something of your history—and that your people are sometimes violent."

Allyndra began reciting a list of wars that had taken place on Earth until Stephen held up a hand.

"Good Lord, no—what you've learned is impressive enough. I mean, how's your understanding of the language?"

"Which one?" Allyndra gave a small shrug. "Your people have several. I determined that the one called *English* is the most common, so I concentrated on that. I didn't study what you call *Middle* or *Old English*, except for a few words. They're similar to our ancient tongue and are no longer used."

Jane was wheezing heavily.

"Fuck—fuck," she gasped.

Stephen quickly grabbed a small device and handed it to her. Jane took it and inhaled, the tool making a soft puffing sound. Her breathing remained ragged, but she managed to shake her head.

"English, engineering, science—and who knows what else? She's got a mind like a fuckin' sponge!"

Allyndra sat up straight and pointed to herself.

"No, I'm A'ksu. I told you—it's a trait a few of us have. It's why I was sent here to investigate."

The old talent has served me well. Mother, you were right to send me. I must get this information back to you and the Council so we can decide what to do. But how do I get away from these people?

Jane was still wheezing but managed to point at her.

"Well, missy, you'd better not let the captain know you know so much. Stick to English, speak it badly, and keep quiet about everything else. I mean it."

Almost as if he'd been listening, Conner's voice came over the speaker in the ceiling.

"So, how's our guest doing? I think we'd better get some answers before we send her back. That floating ship showed up again. It's just sitting out there, hovering—and it's making me nervous. We don't need any more of them showing up."

Ah, it's been more than a day. Hila'ar said she would hold for one day, then circle the island. I hope it isn't close to Ring Rise, or I'll be stuck here.

Stephen answered, since Jane was still catching her breath from the asthma attack.

"She's doing fine, Captain. Just… don't get too technical, and we should be all right."

Allyndra recognized the lie.

I'll play the fool, as the one called Jane suggested. I'll keep what I've learned to myself—it seems they're uneasy with what an A'ksu can do.

Stephen walked over to a wall panel, pressed a button, and retrieved her flight dress. It had been cleaned, the hole neatly patched. He laid it on the bed.

"Time to get dressed—and please, no technical talk. All right?"

"Very well."

Allyndra stood and began to undo the garment they had given her.

Stephen coughed and immediately turned away. Allyndra blinked, surprised.

They're shy about the body? Touching is acceptable, but seeing another is forbidden. It's the opposite for us.

She rolled her shoulders slightly in puzzlement. Jane watched for a moment or two before quickly averting her eyes.

Allyndra slipped into her own dress and tied the straps behind her neck. The familiar weight of the fabric restored a sense of dignity. Once more, she felt like a Mother Named of the House—someone of standing and purpose—instead of a specimen. Even if the dress was ill-fitting, made for a skyship crew, it grounded her.

"I'm ready," she said, her tone carrying a touch of authority.

Stephen turned and nodded. Jane pushed off from the wall, her breathing steadier now.

"Fuck," she muttered. "I'd kill to have a body like that."

"Stop the swearing, Jane."

Jane didn't reply. Stephen gestured toward the door.

"Excellent, Allyndra. Shall we?"

Allyndra didn't move.

"In my culture, it is customary for a male to bow, for a lower-ranked female to curtsy, and for both to use the term *Mother*."

She demonstrated with a graceful curtsy.

Jane laughed.

"Good God, I'd fall flat on my face if I tried that!"

Stephen regarded her seriously.

"This is their world, Jane. We'll have to learn to adapt. God knows if they ever turned against us, we wouldn't stand a chance in our current state."

He bowed deeply toward Allyndra.

Jane sighed, then imitated him clumsily—it looked awkward to Allyndra's eye, but the effort was noted.

Stephen added respectfully, "Mother."

Jane didn't echo the title, but it was enough. Allyndra smiled and inclined her head.

"Then lead on, Mothers."

They're afraid, she realized. *That's both good and bad. Desperate, frightened beings strike out—but they can also be reasoned with.*

Jane chuckled and gave Stephen a light punch on the shoulder. He shot her a sour look but said nothing. Together, they stepped through the door and down a short corridor to where Conner and another woman were waiting.

A wide window let in a pale wash of daylight, though the view beyond was mostly obscured by broken branches and tangled foliage.

The Wind Dancer is still out there, Allyndra thought. *And it's still daylight—there might still be time. After what I've learned, Hila'ar should have run the moment I didn't return.* Her jaw tightened. *Be ready to sail, Captain. If I can escape, we'll flee as fast as the ship can carry us.*

She silently prayed that the gods would carry her thoughts to Captain Hila'ar.

We must prepare—the Houses must be called together. These people are dangerous.

As Allyndra stepped into the room, she forced a smile—it seemed to be something these humans did often.

I wonder if I should bare my teeth as they do. Perhaps not. If what I've read is true, my fangs might unsettle them. No—I must remain calm and find a way out of here. Hold fast, Captain. If all goes well, I'll return before Ring Rise.

Chapter 3

THE RELIANCE

ALLYNDRA

Allyndra followed them down a short corridor. There was little to see—just metal everywhere, exposed struts, and blank white walls. The narrowness of the passage made her uneasy, forcing her to take several deep breaths to calm herself. There was no room to spread her wings here.

"Here we are, Allyndra," Stephen said, pressing a button on the wall.

A door slid open with a soft hiss. The room beyond was filled with instruments and displays, much like the medical area—panels covered in blinking lights, most of them red.

Her attention, however, was drawn to the man inside. He had been in the medical area earlier. He appeared older than Stephen—if she judged age correctly among these beings. His hair was black streaked with white at the temples, and wrinkles framed his eyes and mouth. The woman beside him had hair the color of pale gold—rare among Allyndra's people. She was thinner than Jane and had blue eyes that, unlike those of her own kind, did not sparkle. Allyndra guessed she was younger than the scientist. Both sat in chairs facing away from a large window that let in a dull wash of daylight.

Stephen gestured toward her.

"This is Allyndra. She's some sort of highly placed figure on her world—and a kind of scholar. Allyndra, this is Captain Conner and Shelia, his second-in-command."

He indicated first the man, then the woman.

They refer to the male first and the female second, Allyndra noted. *And they use their hands to point. Not something we do, but I must remember—they are not us. Keep smiling and act as though all is well.*

Stephen had nearly gotten her name right this time. Allyndra dipped her head politely to each in turn.

"Mothers," she said in greeting.

The two exchanged puzzled glances before looking back to Stephen and Jane.

"I believe they use the term as an honorific," Stephen explained before Allyndra could speak. "From what I can tell, females on her world seem to hold higher status. Possibly a matrilineal society. Am I right, Allyndra?"

I can speak for myself.

Allyndra reminded herself to remain diplomatic.

"Yes. Only a female may serve as the ultimate Mother within the Great Houses."

If I understand the term correctly, we would be considered matriarchal—but that isn't worth correcting. Stephen cautioned me not to reveal how much I've learned.

"Remarkable," Shelia said, leaning forward with interest. "You've picked up the language so quickly. Aside from a bit more melody in your speech and some trilled vowels, your English is remarkably good."

"I'm A'ksu," Allyndra replied, allowing a trace of pride to color her voice.

Stephen interjected, "It's a term her people use for those unusually gifted in learning."

Allyndra managed not to clench her teeth.

Do all males in this society insist on speaking for others?

"That is interesting. Well, good enough," Conner said, leaning back in his chair. "So, lady—"

"*Mother* or *Allyndra* would be preferable," she interrupted sharply.

"Okay, Allyndra," Conner said, his jaw tightening. "As you probably know, we're not from here. We came from—"

"Earth," she finished for him.

How do you like being interrupted? She silently scolded herself. *No, stop it. I must focus on finding a way to leave.*

Conner's expression hardened, irritation flashing in his eyes. He glanced at Jane and Stephen for support.

"Allyndra knows," Stephen said quickly. "We're a colony ship that went off course and ended up here—permanently. We discussed it with her earlier."

"Well then, Allyndra," Conner said, sitting forward again, "I suppose that makes us neighbors."

"You say *neighbors*," Allyndra countered, "but are we to be friendly ones? I would say that injuring me was not a gesture of welcome."

Conner frowned, his tone shifting to defensive.

"I do apologize. But look at it from my perspective. We crash here with a damaged ship and hundreds of vulnerable people, and then we discover another intelligent species already on the planet. We had no idea what you were capable of—or what your intentions were. I'll admit, when I saw you and that flying ship of yours, I overreacted."

He exhaled, his voice dropping slightly.

"Speaking of that ship, we've tried to hail it, but it just sits there and doesn't respond."

Allyndra wasn't certain how much time had passed, but she had a fair idea.

"By tonight, when the rings appear in the sky. The ship has orders to leave, presuming I'm dead. It won't respond to anyone but me."

"I see." Conner leaned back slightly. "Well, I'm not sure I'll let you just fly off. It's... interesting that your kind can do that, by the way. So tell me—how do I know you won't come back with a fleet of those ships?"

"What makes you think that if I *don't* return, such a plan might not already be in motion?" Allyndra countered evenly.

"While I've no wish to die," she continued," I came here knowing that might be the outcome. The ship will do what it must—warn the rest of the Houses. Wouldn't it be wiser to show good faith and let me return? It would be a gesture of goodwill, even though you injured me."

I can't trust any of them, she thought. *Their history shows they are still a violent people, though fewer in number than we are. They have great technology, but that's not everything. I'll smile, observe, and play the diplomat—for now. Soon enough, we'll learn their true intentions.*

Her thoughts drifted briefly.

I wonder how Alekelia fares with her mission. The Mothers must be gathering. We'll need a swift decision once I return.

"Still," she said aloud, softening her tone, "I understand, Captain."

She used their term deliberately.

"You were like a mother protecting her young, uncertain of what danger something unfamiliar might bring. That's reasonable."

She gestured toward the distant view.

"Anyway, the vessel you saw is a *skyship*. It's what we use to transport people and goods between the islands."

She turned her gaze toward their massive craft.

"I imagine it must seem primitive compared to this. So—allow me to return. Perhaps one of these two can accompany me. It would let you learn more about us and our world while we learn about you."

Conner tapped a finger thoughtfully on the arm of his chair.

"You make a good point. Yeah... I was trying to protect my people, not knowing what kind of threat we were facing. It's not a bad idea—to start learning from each other."

Shelia shrugged.

"It would give us time to assess the damage and wake more of the crew, at least."

Allyndra had no intention of revealing that her people had abandoned warfare long ago.

"Like you, Captain, as long as we feel safe, we have no reason to disturb others. My House—think of it as a kind of guild—is the most powerful of all the Houses here. House Warraquim is the House of Knowledge. They sent me to learn. None of the others would act without first consulting Warraquim. So, let us learn from each other and see how we might become true friends and neighbors."

Shelia nodded.

"She makes sense, Conner. They might not be on our level technologically, but they could easily overwhelm us with numbers. And really, why fight at all if we can come to a mutual understanding? We need time to get settled, but learning to coexist should be a priority."

Interesting, Allyndra thought. *I wonder how long it takes them to become "situated." I never studied that part of their behavior.*

Conner leaned back, considering.

"All right. Sounds like a deal... Allyndra."

He extended his hand. She looked at it, puzzled, and after a moment, he awkwardly lowered it again.

"We're trying to get a couple of shuttles operational," he went on. "It might take some time before we can get you back to your... House."

"Then allow me to return to the skyship and have it come in," Allyndra suggested. "Whoever you assign can come with me."

"And how do I know they won't end up as hostages—or that you won't simply fly off?"

"You don't," Allyndra admitted calmly. "But we don't tend to be so suspicious of motives, Captain. Somewhere, one of us has to take the first step toward trust."

Though given what I've read of their history, she thought, *perhaps it's wiser if we never trust them fully.*

Conner rubbed his chin.

"Very well. Whoever I send will stay in contact through a communicator. If I don't get a check-in within a reasonable amount of time—say, a day—we'll assume you've gone hostile. Fair enough?"

Allyndra knew she had little room to bargain.

"Understood."

Conner seemed satisfied and turned to Stephen and Jane.

"I really need both of you, but Jane, I need you a bit more here. We've got a couple of other medics up now, so I can spare you, Doc. You'll be our ambassador to these people for a while. Try not to mess it up, all right?"

Stephen nodded.

"Yes, Captain. Thank you. I mean that."

He exhaled, glancing toward the window.

"I've got to admit—the walls have felt like they've been closing in for the last several years we've been traveling."

He looked back to Jane.

"You said the chemistry's similar enough, or should I bring my own food supply?"

"Stick to simple things," Jane advised, studying Allyndra as she spoke. "You should be fine. I'd say more, but you know the rule—everything in moderation until we see how it affects you. We don't have any reliable data on the flora or fauna yet. If you get sick, call immediately."

"Will do."

Conner looked up from his chair.

"So, you're saying we might actually be able to eat some of the local food?"

Jane shrugged.

"Possibly. I ran a quick compatibility test—it looks like the biochemistry here is close enough. We'll need to go through things one by one, but for now, I'm giving a tentative thumbs-up."

Conner nodded, visibly pleased.

"Good. Very good. That'll take some strain off the food banks while we get our systems running again."

He straightened and gave Jane a sharp look.

"That's your task, Jane—top priority. Get to it. And you, Doc," he gestured to Stephen, "try to make nice."

Finally, his attention returned to Allyndra.

"All right, good neighbor. I'm authorizing your departure—and you can take the Doc here with you."

I'm concerned that this captain of Stephen's already calls this island theirs. To her, it did not bode well. *It reminds me of what I've read in their histories—humans are very territorial. We can plan as we must, but I worry whether Mother O'lathe will be up to the task, her age being upon her. In truth, she may already have passed into the arms of the gods. Then it will fall to me to guide not only my House but all the Houses. Twins preserve me— I feel as though I'm flying through a storm. One wrong move, and disaster could follow.*

She made a small curtsy.

"Thank you, Captain."

"Good enough, Doc," Conner replied. "Have a pleasant flight. I'll let the guards know that thing out there is cleared to approach and that it's non-hostile."

He made a dismissive gesture toward them both.

"Doc, you'll have to show her the way off the ship."

Turning to his controls, he pressed a few buttons and issued the command not to engage the approaching skyship.

Allyndra noted, not without irritation, that despite her showing the proper honorifics, the captain seemed to have already forgotten—or simply didn't care.

Another thing to tell the Mothers, she thought.

Stephen touched her gently on the arm and indicated the direction they had come from. She didn't bother with another curtsy; it was clear such niceties were lost on this man.

At least Stephen tries, she mused. *Perhaps all is not lost. Captain Hila'ar had been much the same until she learned I was the Mother Named. Maybe this Captain Conner is simply preoccupied. Something to consider.*

She followed Stephen down the corridor. They passed the medical section where she had been kept, then continued about twenty strides farther. Stephen leaned forward and pressed a button on the wall. The surface slid open, revealing a small enclosed chamber—just tall enough for him, and wide enough for the two of them to stand side by side.

Allyndra quickly memorized every motion he made.

"After you, Allyndra," Stephen said with a faint smile. "Or should I say... Mother?"

Her opinion of him rose slightly.

She stepped into the chamber, glancing around as she replied, "Allyndra is fine for now. 'Mother' can wait until we reach the ship—and later, I'll teach you the proper words. I'll explain that you're unfamiliar with our customs so no one will take offense."

He seemed pleased by that and stepped in after her, pressing a series of buttons. The door slid shut, and Allyndra's hearts began to pound. Her breathing quickened as the floor shifted beneath her. Panic flooded her chest as the small room began to move.

What is this? I'm a child of the open sky!

"Whoa—stop! It's fine, Allyndra. Just breathe. It's only an elevator. You're safe."

The sensation changed. The floor pressed upward beneath her feet, and within moments, the door opened again to reveal a vast, cavernous space filled with machines and a handful of humans working.

Allyndra hurried past Stephen into the open area, spreading her wings fully. She hovered for a moment, forcing herself to breathe and suppressing the panic that had seized her. Several of the humans stopped to stare, pointing and murmuring among themselves. She ignored them. Beyond the machinery, she could see a glimpse of open sky.

It won't help to flee now. I must stay calm. My task has only just begun.

"Allyndra," Stephen said gently, "I should have realized—being confined in a moving space like that must have been... uncomfortable, to say the least."

She landed gracefully and took several long, steadying breaths.

"Yes, you're correct. We don't do well in tight places—it disturbs the mind."

Stephen waited patiently while she regained her composure.

At last, she closed her eyes, inhaled once more, and opened them again before saying, "I'm ready."

They walked together toward the open end of the ship in silence. A small vehicle rested there on skids, its surface smooth and its windows gleaming. A man stood beside it, bent over some mechanical component. As he noticed them, he straightened and gave a curt nod.

"Crewman Wright, Doc. Captain said you were taking a short trip with the native girl he brought aboard."

He gave Allyndra a slow once-over, appraising her as though she were a piece of produce at market.

"Looks human enough," he said with a smirk. "Kind of cute—but could use a bit more curve."

Stephen opened his mouth to respond, but Allyndra spoke first.

"Yes, I'm the 'native girl,' as you call me," she said evenly. "I'll admit I know little about your customs, but the tone and choice of words sound... dismissive. I hope I'm mistaken—but then again, I'm only a *native girl*."

Color rose in the man's face.

"Sorry, ma'am. No disrespect meant. I just—"

Stephen cut in, his expression sour.

"Didn't realize the locals here could learn fast, did you? She's picked up most of our language in just over a day."

The man blinked, visibly chastened.

"Interesting. Again, ma'am—sorry."

Allyndra inclined her head slightly but dismissed the apology.

It will take time to adjust to how their males speak and act. Another thing to warn the Mothers about before we allow too much contact—or there will be problems.

She drew a steadying breath and turned to Stephen.

"Well, with your permission, I'll see about bringing the skyship in. Hopefully, there won't be any more target practice?"

Stephen gave a brief wave.

"Captain's orders—no one's to fire."

She didn't answer. Instead, she took several quick steps and leapt into the air, her wings catching the wind. The movement filled her chest with relief—the freedom of open sky banishing the last of her tension. She hovered briefly to warm her flight muscles, then angled toward the *Wind Dancer*.

As she neared, she saw Captain Hila'ar and several crew members gathered at the prow, watching her approach. Allyndra lifted a hand in greeting and landed moments later.

"Something to drink, please," she managed, her throat dry.

The captain thrust a large mug into her hands—sweetened Blood Flower juice. Allyndra murmured her thanks, savoring the taste as the rich sweetness washed away the memory of the sterile fare aboard the human vessel.

"Mother, is all well? I was worried when you didn't return."

"Another time, Captain," Allyndra said. "Right now, I need you to take the *Wind Dancer* to shore. We have a passenger to bring aboard."

"A passenger? Who?"

"The sooner we're away from here, the better—for all of us. I promise I'll explain later, Captain. I know I'm asking a lot, but I need your trust. I must report back to the Mothers with everything I've learned."

Captain Hila'ar nodded once, then turned and shouted to the crew.

"You heard the Mother! Move! Move!"

The deck came alive with activity. Within minutes, the *Wind Dancer* angled toward the shore, maintaining altitude until the waters grew shallow, then dipping lower toward the sand. Allyndra stood at the prow, the wind tugging at her hair and dress. Hila'ar joined her, squinting toward the human ship in the distance.

"By the Twins, what is that thing?" Hila'ar breathed. "I've never seen anything like it. Where did it come from?"

Allyndra smiled faintly and lifted her chin toward the sky.

"It's a ship—from far beyond our world. From the stars, Captain. And it carries a people of its own."

"Are they to be trusted? Are they dangerous?"

"I'm still trying to determine that," Allyndra admitted. "But pride aside, I want you to make the *Wind Dancer* seem... clumsy. Don't let them see what a skyship can really do in skilled hands."

Hila'ar studied her for a moment, a wry smile curving her lips.

"Are you sure you're a scholar and not a gambler? You play your hands close and bluff your opponents before striking. Remind me never to play against you."

Allyndra laughed, joined a heartbeat later by Hila'ar. The captain then strode toward the helm to take control of the ship.

A few minutes later, as the *Wind Dancer* crossed toward the shore, Allyndra had to grip the railing for balance. The vessel dipped and swayed, the deck rocking beneath her feet while Hila'ar's sharp commands echoed across the ship. The small sails that had been raised were quickly furled, and the land anchors dropped, biting into the churned ground left by the starship's landing. The *Wind Dancer* slowed to a halt, and the crew tossed a rope ladder over the side.

Allyndra chose the easier way—she leapt from the prow, wings unfurling, and glided down toward where Stephen and another man stood, staring up in disbelief at the wooden flying ship.

"I'm sorry, Stephen," she called, hovering a few feet above the ground. "The ladder is for you—since you can't fly."

Stephen shaded his eyes, gazing up at the ship.

"Impressive, Allyndra. The vessel, I mean. I'd love to study its design, but I suppose this isn't the time."

He stepped toward the ladder, which swayed gently with the ship's motion, then began climbing. Several of the crew leaned over the rail, watching the strange male ascend. Allyndra hovered nearby to make sure he didn't slip—and to gauge her crew's reaction. She needn't have worried. When Stephen reached the deck, several hands reached out to help him over the railing.

She landed lightly beside him.

"Best be on our way, Captain Hila'ar—but make it look as clumsy as you can."

Hila'ar said nothing, only gave her a conspiratorial wink before shouting new orders and returning to the controls. Allyndra turned to Stephen, who was being steadied by one of the infertile males and a broad-shouldered female crew member as the ship lifted.

"I suppose I'll need to get my sea legs—or air legs?" Stephen quipped, half-smiling.

Allyndra shook her head lightly.

"I'm not sure I understand that expression. You should hold on to the mast or the railing rope if you want to remain on deck. Otherwise, we can find you a cabin."

"And miss something like this? This ship is incredible, Allyndra! Sorry—Mother."

"Either is fine," she replied. "The captain and crew can't understand your language, but if anything arises, I'll intervene. You are a guest of House Warraquim."

Allyndra steadied herself as the vessel pitched upward, noting how Hila'ar deliberately kept the *Wind Dancer's* movements awkward and uneven.

"Whoa!" Stephen stumbled and lurched backward, arms flailing.

Allyndra caught him easily, her wings flaring to steady them both. She hadn't been this close to him before. He carried a strong, musky scent—different, yet oddly pleasant—reminding her faintly of the males from the Iresmia Houses.

"Thanks!" Stephen said, regaining his balance. "I didn't expect it to lift like that! Guess I'll have to pay closer attention."

His eyes swept across the crew and the helm.

"Tell me about this ship—please, Mother?"

Allyndra smiled, pleased by his effort to show respect.

"You're welcome. This is one of the smaller skyships, only about eighty of your feet long. Bags within the hull contain a gas that provides lift."

Stephen drew in a deep breath.

"God, fresh air. It's been far too long."

Allyndra chuckled softly.

A wide smile crossed his face.

"I love your laugh. I think that's what it was—it has a beautiful, musical sound."

"It may be due to differences in our vocal structures," she said. "If you don't mind, I'll drop the pretense. I've learned far more than I let your captain believe."

"I understand," Stephen said. "Look, I'm amazed by what you've accomplished. I realize we weren't supposed to end up here. The captain—well, he's military."

He hesitated, brow furrowing.

"Do you have a military? Do you understand that word?"

"Yes, I understand both the word and the concept," Allyndra replied evenly.

She chose not to elaborate, aware this human would carry any information back to *his* Mother.

"Come—you asked about the skyship."

She extended a hand, though she hoped he wouldn't take it. He was far less steady on his feet than the other males aboard. *I'd rather he not fall overboard.*

Stephen grasped her hand anyway.

"It's wind-powered?"

"Yes. Not unlike the ships your people once used long ago—except ours sail the skies, not the seas. You had something similar once, called a... zeppelin."

Stephen chuckled.

"You're good—but you're having a little trouble with the Z sound."

He repeated the word slowly a few times while Allyndra listened intently. She tried to mimic him; the shape felt strange in her mouth. Her own language had no such sound.

"Not bad," Stephen said, smiling. "So this skyship—it surprises me you don't use regular ships, the kind that sail directly on the oceans. From what we saw coming in, this planet's nearly ninety percent water."

"We fly naturally," she explained. "It's our nature to look to the skies rather than the sea. Besides, the oceans are full of large predators, and while storms in the clouds are bad enough, one can often fly around them. On the surface, one must endure them."

"Interesting." Stephen looked around the deck. "I see a few of the big fellows without wings. Are they like us—another sex? Do they have, uh, a human-like male morphology?"

Allyndra noted how he compared everything to his own species and tucked the observation away.

"Yes. They are infertile males. There are others, closer to your size, who are fertile. No male, except in very rare cases, is born with wings."

"Why?" he asked, curious.

They moved slowly across the deck toward the central controls. Allyndra paused, glancing at Hila'ar. Though she knew the captain wouldn't understand, she continued for Stephen's sake.

"They don't bear young," she said simply.

Stephen looked puzzled—at least, that's how she interpreted his expression.

"We lay our young in certain places within the seas," Allyndra explained. "One must fly to reach them—hence, only females have wings. They would be wasted on males. However, it's been speculated that we all once possessed them, but the trait was..." She searched for the word. "Suppressed. Forgotten?"

"Evolutionarily selected out," Stephen supplied.

"Yes, that's the phrase. You're correct. I need to study more—if your Mother will allow it."

"Not sure that's going to happen," he said, a touch apologetically. "Sorry. So, you're egg-layers?"

"The eggs develop internally," she clarified. "Then the hatched... nymphs, I believe you would call them, are released into the sea. However, you said you were interested in the ship, not reproduction."

Stephen laughed lightly.

"Actually, both—but in due course. I'm a medical officer—a healer, you might say."

"We have a small Guild that serves a similar role," Allyndra said. "It's not quite the same, though, since little goes wrong with us. We have no diseases—or the ailments your kind seems to suffer from, such as Jane's asthma, if I understood the diagnosis and your medical terms correctly."

"Correct," Stephen said, impressed. "Say, how much did you learn?"

"I know your ship is a colony vessel," she replied, "carrying eight hundred souls—five hundred and fifty remaining after the damage you sustained entering the debris field around the fourth planet. As for the extent of my learning—" she gave a modest smile "—I could probably pass one of your medical exams, though theory isn't the same as experience. I focused mainly on language, biology, and history. There was a vast amount I didn't have time to study."

Stephen shook his head, half in disbelief.

"I'd be very worried if all your people were like you, Allyndra—uh, I mean, Mother."

"We all learn—some faster than others—but the trait of the A'ksu is something else entirely," Allyndra said quietly. "We don't exalt it."

She turned her gaze forward. They were flying high now, and she could see a storm churning over the sea below. The *Wind Dancer* was climbing as far as she dared, but even Allyndra judged they would soon be brushing the clouds.

"We'd best show you how the ship steers before we reach that storm," she said.

They walked the rest of the way to the helm. Allyndra dipped her head respectfully.

"Captain, if I may—may I show our honored visitor how to sail? You know I'm a water dancer. Let me guide the ship for a short while."

Hila'ar frowned, then nodded.

"Very well. I'll stand alongside, though."

"Thank you."

Allyndra stepped into the place the captain had vacated and gestured for Stephen to join her.

"Now then," she said, "it's quite simple. The control stand—or helm—sits here at the center of the deck. Move it left, and the ship turns that way. Pull it back to climb, push forward to descend. Here—come, get a feel for it."

Stephen took her spot and gripped the handles of the yoke-like control. He moved it gently—first up and down, then side to side—and the *Wind Dancer* responded with a slight lurch.

Allyndra caught Hila'ar's disapproving look as the ship rocked.

"Easy," the captain said. "You must learn how she feels—how she reacts, what she likes."

Allyndra translated for Stephen, smiling faintly.

"Sorry," he said, steadying the controls. "I'm not sure how it all works yet."

"Let me guide you—and teach you," Allyndra said to Stephen. "Take your shoes off. I will handle the helm."

He looked puzzled but did as she asked.

She motioned for him to take his place again. As he did, she stepped behind him, pressing lightly against his back and reaching around to place her hands over his.

I don't like this, she thought, *but I must set aside my feelings—for diplomacy's sake.*

His scent reached her again, faint but intoxicating, and she forced herself to focus.

Captain Hila'ar continued to scowl but held her tongue.

"Now," Allyndra said softly, "feel the ship through your feet— the way she moves, the wind on your face, the moisture in the air. Notice how the right side feels slightly warmer?"

Stephen took a few moments, then nodded.

"Yes."

"There," she murmured. "You must become one with the wind—and with all the world around you. Open your senses and let nature speak. Feel the electricity as we climb—less to the left, which means the storm is weaker in that direction."

She placed her hands gently on his and guided the controls, so the ship's prow shifted with graceful precision.

"That's the path of least resistance. To fight nature is a losing battle. Work with her, and she'll reward you. This is what it means to be a navigator of a skyship."

Stephen's face broke into a wide smile.

"Fantastic! Yes, I can feel it—the ship, the wind. She makes different sounds as she moves, and the way you're steering—it's smoother, quieter. This is incredible, Allyndra!"

Allyndra stepped back from the helm.

"Thank you, Captain Hila'ar, for allowing this honored guest to guide the ship for a time."

Hila'ar made the briefest of dips in acknowledgment.

"Yes, Mother. I couldn't understand the words, but watching and listening as you taught—ah, I wish it were so with many. I'll keep my eyes open for recruits among those who've learned to water dance."

She glanced at Stephen, waiting for him to step aside.

Allyndra touched his arm lightly and motioned for him to move back. He did so, then turned to face Hila'ar and bowed.

"Mother," he said.

Allyndra translated, and Hila'ar blinked in surprise before giving a small bend of her knees in return.

"For an odd one, he seems respectful enough," she murmured.

"We're all going to have to learn from one another," Allyndra said. "They cannot leave this world, and we cannot match their technology."

Hila'ar resumed her place at the controls.

"I don't envy you, Mother Named of Warraquim. You have treacherous currents ahead to navigate."

"Indeed," Allyndra replied.

She looked toward the darkening clouds on the horizon.

"As with our path now, I fear a storm lies ahead—one we cannot avoid. We'll have to pass through it and hope for only minor damage."

Hila'ar nodded.

"A storm indeed. As you say, let's hope it won't be too severe."

"Well," Allyndra said softly, "tomorrow is a new day. Perhaps the gods will bless us with fair weather—in the skies and in our dealings with these newcomers."

Hila'ar kept the *Wind Dancer* steady and gave a small smile.

"May the Twins bless us all. I trust you to guide us through, Mother. From what I've seen, I'd sail with you anywhere."

She winked.

"Water dancer."

"Thank you, Captain," Allyndra said, returning the smile.

I only hope your trust is not misplaced.

Chapter 4

House La'Gave

Alekelia & Lei'ilian'a

Alekelia drew in a slow breath through her nose, savoring the layered notes of *kihapai*, underpinned by *molihua*. She was certain there was *puakenikeni* or *kupalo*—perhaps both—adding that subtle, intoxicating overtone. The strong fingers of the man massaging her back were expert, finding every knot along the base of her wings.

Well, she thought with a faint smile, *he was one of my lovers last night.*

Peach-colored silk curtains billowed gently as a tropical breeze drifted through the latticework near the ceiling. Warm, humid air carried the mingled perfumes, intensifying them.

I could live out my days in an Iresemia House, she mused. *It's been far too long since my last visit.*

The previous evening had been devoted to the pleasures of the body—her way of indulging herself before returning home.

I wonder what is happening there now.

"Is something troubling the lady?" came the deep, gentle voice of the infertile male working her shoulders. "You're still tense. I thought Tellith and I had eased that last night."

He chuckled softly.

"The distraction was pleasant," Alekelia admitted, "but there are worries I can't seem to set aside."

"What burdens you, Mother? You know anything spoken within these walls remains between us."

Alekelia shifted as he lifted his hands. Propping herself up on one elbow, she turned onto her side.

By the gods, he is magnificent.

Her gaze traced his tall, well-muscled, naked form. He sat on the bed beside her and stroked her long black hair, the strands gleaming with red-metallic highlights.

"The Mother of my House," Alekelia said quietly. "Her time has come upon her. Soon, she'll be dancing with the gods."

"Ah. I'm sorry to hear that. May the Twins bless her passing."

"That isn't what troubles me, though."

"Oh?"

"No. She named me Voice."

He raised an eyebrow.

"A very prestigious position."

"Yes, but it is not the Mother's place. That is what I truly desire. I've no wish to marry or take a matron's flight, but I do enjoy the pleasures of the body—and the little bites."

He laughed softly.

"And so your visit to an Iresemia House—where you may have all the pleasure and none of the burdens." He traced a finger over a faint love bite. "Of course, a Mother of a House wouldn't usually be found in such a place."

Alekelia made a face.

"There is no rule against it."

"As you say," he replied. "I've never had the honor of pleasuring a Mother of a House. Travelers like yourself, crew from the skyships—and, of course, those who've just earned their wings—yes. But never one of your rank."

Alekelia smiled at that.

"Yes, I remember my first visit, just after I got my wings. Almost all of us do."

"Almost all?" He arched an eyebrow. "I've never known a lady who hadn't."

"Allyndra," Alekelia said, her tone cooling.

"Who is that?"

Her expression darkened.

"Someone I grew up with. We competed at everything, all our lives—and she always came out first. Everything seemed to come easily for her."

Alekelia flopped back onto the bed, staring at the ceiling.

"The Mother always favored her. Even if she was probably A'ksu."

"A'ksu? I thought they'd long ceased to exist."

"No, the trait appears from time to time." She waved a hand dismissively. "Anyway, I doubt she's ever visited a place like this. When she got her wings, she flew as though she were already on a matron's flight."

Alekelia chuckled at the memory.

"What's so funny?"

"She woke up delirious in a Blood Farmer's field." Alekelia shivered slightly as his fingers traced a lazy path across her abdomen. "I suppose her flight didn't go quite as planned."

"So this Allyndra—might she become Mother? Is she unmarried?"

Alekelia's breath caught as his touch deepened.

"Widowed. No children returned from the sea. But she's A'ksu—and no A'ksu has ever been made Mother of a House. They're detested, feared even."

"Then I see nothing standing in your way," he murmured. "When you become Mother, send for me. What happens in a Mother's private chambers remains there. And I," he smiled faintly, "am nothing if not discreet."

Alekelia laughed softly, looping her arms around his neck before giving him a playful bite.

"The Voice wishes to have some more fun?" he teased. "Then Jorath will make certain you leave this place... very well satisfied."

***

Lei'ilian'a accepted the message from the weary flyer.

The poor woman looked utterly spent but managed to gasp out, "For the Voice of Warraquim, from the Mother of that House. I was told it's of the highest importance, Mother."

"Thank you."

Lei'ilian'a gestured to several women wearing the livery of House La'Gave.

"See that she's refreshed and given rest. Tend to her well. I'll take this to the Voice of Warraquim myself. Which ship is she on?"

"I heard she's aboard the *Water Dancer*, under Captain Killian."

"Thank you. Which berth?"

Neither woman knew exactly where the *Water Dancer* was moored among the docks of the House of Skyships.

Wonderful. Well, once I'm there, someone should know.

Lei'ilian'a left the main house, heading toward the busy docks, the heat of the Twins oppressive beneath her heavy House dress. The air smelled of tar, oil, and salt. All along the docks, skyships were loading and unloading both cargo and passengers. The sides of the vessels hinged downward near the hulls, forming wide ramps that allowed access to the decks, gas bags, and inner mechanisms for repair.

Swarms of broad-shouldered infertile males hauled crates to and fro, while officers shouted orders above the din. Spotting a woman who appeared to be a captain overseeing a crew, Lei'ilian'a approached.

68

"Captain, do you know which ship is the *Water Dancer*? I have an urgent message to deliver to one of her passengers."

"The *Water Dancer*?" The woman nodded toward the far end of the dock. "Aye, she's that smaller ship down there. I just hope she's tied up tight."

"Oh? Why is that?"

The captain pointed westward.

"A storm's rolling in—and it looks like a bad one. That's why everyone's in such a rush. If we can't lift soon, none of us will be going anywhere. We'll have to ride it out here."

Lei'ilian'a followed her gaze. On the horizon, stretching as far as she could see, rose towering banks of black, roiling clouds.

That does look bad.

"Thank you, Captain."

"Twins bless."

"And to you—and fair winds," Lei'ilian'a called back, waving as she hurried toward the indicated vessel, lifting the hem of her dress to keep it from dragging.

Once that storm arrives, whatever's in this message won't matter until it's passed.

The ship she sought was moored at the very end of the La'Gave docks. She spotted the captain barking orders while handlers hauled crates on wheeled carts toward the gangway.

"Captain Killian!" Lei'ilian'a shouted over the din.

The woman turned, puzzled, until she caught sight of the sigil on Lei'ilian'a's dress. She dropped into a quick, awkward curtsy.

"Administrator! What brings you here? Is something wrong with the cargo we're taking on?"

"No, Captain," Lei'ilian'a replied, slightly out of breath. "I'm looking for one of your passengers. I have an urgent message delivered by flyer."

"I've only one passenger—the Voice of Warraquim. But, Administrator, she's not aboard."

"What?"

Killian gestured back the way Lei'ilian'a had come.

"She took herself off to the Iresemia House as soon as we docked last night. Said after all her travels the past few days, she wanted a proper massage and a bath." The captain laughed. "Though I imagine the kind of massage she had in mind wasn't entirely professional. She's a beauty, that one—with those green eyes. I wouldn't mind giving her a few love bites myself."

"Captain!" Lei'ilian'a's tone was sharp.

"Oh, get over it, Administrator," Killian said, waving off the rebuke.

"Voyages can be long, and the Iresemia Houses are only at the major ports. Anyway, that's the last I saw of her. If she plans to leave today, she'd best get back soon. If we don't lift within the hour, that storm will be right on top of us."

"I saw it. Hold as long as you can, just in case."

"Yes, Administrator."

Killian turned and bellowed to her crew, "Storm coming! Let's get this ship loaded and ready to sail immediately!"

The handlers sprang into even more frantic motion.

Lei'ilian'a turned and began retracing her steps, gathering her skirts and, abandoning all pretense of dignity, trotted back the way she had come.

***

"I need to speak with the Voice of Warraquim—now!"

"The Mother is otherwise engaged. You may wait, if you wish."

Lei'ilian'a drew in a sharp breath, struggling to steady her temper.

"I am a Chief Administrator of House La'Gave! I must speak with her immediately!"

"As I said—"

"I heard you, *male*. Now you will hear me."

Lei'ilian'a swept past him, despite his being twice her size, and strode toward the central chamber of the house. Like all Iresemia Houses, it was circular, with private rooms radiating outward from the central hall. She halted there and raised her voice.

"Alekelia of Warraquim! An urgent message has come by flyer!"

***

Alekelia heard her name being shouted and pushed Jorath off her, rising from the bed while snatching a nearby towel to wrap around herself.

Though we are not exactly body-shy, there is still etiquette. What could be so important?

The voice continued to call her name, and Alekelia caught mention of a message delivered by flyer. She knew what that meant—a relay of swift couriers, each flying until exhaustion before passing the message to another. Skyships could move quickly, but they had to stop at ports. This, then, must be urgent.

Has Allyndra returned? Or... perhaps it's Mother O'lathe. She may have passed.

She pulled the door open.

"What is it?"

"Alekelia, Voice of Warraquim?" The speaker was a tall woman with blond hair streaked in green and bright amber eyes, dressed in a house gown bearing the sigil of La'Gave.

"Yes."

The woman reached into her pouch, withdrew a folded paper, and handed it over.

Alekelia awkwardly unfolded it with one hand while keeping hold of the towel with the other. Her eyes raced across the text.

I am Gellia of House Me'olia. I have examined Mother O'lathe, and she is about to pass into the arms of the gods. May the Twins bless her journey. Allyndra, who was named Mother, has not returned and is long overdue. Mother O'lathe feared this and named you as second. She urges you to return in all haste.

I've been named—and Allyndra hasn't returned.

Alekelia pressed the letter to her chest.

"Is it ill news, Voice of Warraquim?"

"Yes and no," Alekelia said evenly. "The Mother of my House has passed. She has named me the new Mother of Warraquim."

Lei'ilian'a blinked, then dropped into a deep curtsy. Behind Alekelia, Jorath sank to one knee.

Alekelia smiled at their deference. *Soon, they will all bow to me.*

"I must wash and dress before I return."

Lei'ilian'a straightened.

"If you wish to leave today, there's no time. A major storm is approaching. In an hour at most, all skyships will be grounded. I've had the *Water Dancer* hold for you, but if you delay much longer, you'll have to wait until it passes."

Alekelia stamped her foot.

"Then we'll fly through the storm if we must! Tell the captain to dump the cargo and make the ship as light and fast as possible. I shall be there within the half-hour."

"Dump the cargo?"

"Did you not hear me? Yes! By the authority Warraquim holds over all Houses, go and prepare the ship."

Lei'ilian'a dipped her head, turned, and left, shaking it as she went.

Alekelia faced Jorath.

"Get the shower running and lay out my outfit."

"Yes, Mother."

He vanished into the adjoining room, and moments later she heard the water begin to flow.

Alekelia glanced at the message once more and let out a sharp, triumphant laugh.

"Lost to the sea, Allyndra! Gone to dance with your husband and your lost children! Good!"

Then another thought struck her—the letter said *overdue*, not *lost*. There was no confirmation of the *Wind Dancer's* fate.

"I must make haste," she muttered, "and ensure I assert my authority first."

She turned and began to ready herself.

***

Alekelia hurried toward the *Water Dancer*, her long, flowing dress whipping to one side in the rising wind. The storm loomed closer by the moment. As she passed, she noticed the remaining skyships—those unable to depart—battening down for safety. Ahead, she spotted the La'Gave administrator speaking with a broad-shouldered woman whose hair was cropped so short it was little more than fuzz. The latter's scowl was deep enough to carve lines into stone. Around them, crates and bags lay stacked haphazardly on the dock, while handlers milled about looking confused.

"You finally made it. The storm's almost on top of us," the short-haired woman snapped.

"Yes, Captain, very good," Alekelia replied coolly. "Shall we be away? I must make haste to Warraquim."

Without waiting for a response, she swept past both women and climbed aboard the skyship.

Captain Killian turned to Lei'ilian'a with an exasperated huff. "We could've been airborne half an hour ago."

"Understood, Captain. You'll be properly compensated," Lei'ilian'a said, glancing up as a few fat drops of rain splattered on the dock. "Best get the ship aloft before it breaks."

"Aye, Administrator. With the cargo offloaded and the wind at our backs, we should reach Warraquim by late afternoon—if the gods are kind."

"Fair winds," Lei'ilian'a said dryly. "Though perhaps not so fair today."

"Gods preserve us, Administrator, if *that's* going to be the new Mother of Warraquim," Killian muttered under her breath.

"Indeed," Lei'ilian'a murmured. "Best to you, Captain."

"And to you."

Killian turned toward her crew and bellowed, "Get us up! Turn her! Hurry!"

The lines were already cast, sails unfurled, and within moments the *Water Dancer* lifted from the dock, rising into the turbulent sky.

Lei'ilian'a waved once before turning back. The rain came down in earnest, drenching her as she ran for shelter. She reached the main house just as the storm broke in full, wind and water lashing at the walls.

"A storm to start your reign, Mother of Warraquim," she whispered. "Not a good omen from the gods—but may they bless you all the same to make the right decisions."

Chapter 5

THE WIND DANCER

ALLYNDRA & STEPHEN

Allyndra woke to a sharp knocking on her cabin door.

"Mother Named, we must talk!"

She resisted the urge to groan, *I barely got any rest on the human ship.*

"Pardon, Mother Named of Warraquim," Hila'ar called again.

Now what? Her tone sounds serious. *Something with the human, perhaps?*

Allyndra sighed, slipped from the bed, and opened the door.

"Yes, Captain? Is there a problem?"

Hila'ar stood grim-faced in the passageway.

"Aye. The storm's strengthened. The *Dancer* can't climb high enough, and the winds are worsening. We've already shredded a sail, and one of the masts has cracked. We'll have to pull back and wait for it to pass. There's a small island just beyond the storm's edge—we can anchor there and make repairs. Mother Named, I tried, but the *Dancer* can't push through. We'll be delayed reaching your House."

Allyndra nodded.

"It's unfortunate, but whatever you think best. The gods decree as they must. My need or vanity isn't so great as to risk the ship or crew. I wouldn't have anyone injured or lost for the sake of haste. How long to the island?"

Hila'ar's posture eased, as though she had been braced for an argument.

"Blessings upon you, Mother. I'll set the course immediately. Again, you prove your worth—you think first of those under your care. It will take five hours to reach the island and perhaps three more to brace the mast."

"A brace?"

"We've no spare mast. The brace will keep it from breaking outright, but it means we can't carry full sail—too much strain, and it'll snap."

"Ah. I see. Then we arrive when we arrive."

"I've sent our strongest flyer ahead to your House to let them know we're delayed."

"Thank you, Captain. At least the Mother of my House will know we are safe. I presume she'll await us there?"

"Yes."

Hila'ar turned to go but paused after a few steps, glancing back with a faint smile.

"The journey may be halted, but I must say—you've given me a fine reward."

"Oh?" Allyndra tilted her head. "How so?"

She couldn't recall giving Hila'ar anything.

"Many in the crew bet me that the Mother Named of Warraquim would insist on flying straight through the storm, no matter the damage," Hila'ar said with a laugh. "I told them you were a water dancer, that you knew the ways of wind and wave, and you'd understand. They didn't believe me, of course. Several asked how anyone from your House could know more than a few lines from a book. Well, I'll have a bit more jingle in my purse the next good port we reach." She winked. "Excuse me, Mother Named—"

"Allyndra, please. Formality when needed; friendship until then."

Hila'ar nodded and glanced around the small cabin.

"You say you're A'ksu, and I don't doubt your word. But you don't act like the tales say. It's said the A'ksu never thought about consequences—you do. You seem to look ahead, to weigh what's best. I'm starting to question things I've believed my whole life."

She smiled wryly.

"Well then, water dancer, prove my wager was right. We'll be here for the better part of the day."

Allyndra smiled.

"Very well. I'll show you I haven't forgotten the dance."

"I haven't seen one performed in ages," Hila'ar said, her eyes brightening. "I'd love to watch you. You've the form for it—lithe, strong. Not one who spends her time behind a desk. When you guided that odd male through the sky-sailing, I could tell you knew the ways of air and sea alike. If you prove me right, that's a bit more for me—and a bit less for them."

She chuckled.

"Ah, I hope not too much. They work far too hard," Allyndra said lightly.

Then, her tone softened.

"Speaking of the human male—has he roused yet?"

"Yes. He's asked many questions. We tried to communicate with gestures, but it's slow going—and you told me not to say much to him yet. He's up on deck now with a cup of hot tea, if you wish to join him. Shall I have something brought for you? Tea, or perhaps Blood Flower juice?"

"The latter, Captain. I nearly starved on the humans' ship. Their blood lacks taste."

Hila'ar's eyes went wide.

"You *mated* with one?"

"No," Allyndra said calmly. "They keep stores. They don't heal as we do, so they must preserve blood and other fluids for emergencies. I took my sustenance from there."

"They can *keep* such things?" Hila'ar shook her head in astonishment. "That would've saved some of my crew in the past. Perhaps we can learn how to do the same. I've lost excellent sailors to blood loss before."

She pointed upward.

"Just like last night—sometimes a mast snaps or a line shifts, and something pierces the body."

"Ah! Yes, perhaps we can learn from one another. That's my hope."

"I don't envy your task," Hila'ar said, smiling faintly. "As I told you, you've a hard course ahead—uncharted waters and tricky currents. Go on up. I'll have Blood Flower juice brought to you."

Allyndra climbed to the deck and noted the *Wind Dancer* was steering toward a small atoll. The pale blue-green lagoon shimmered in the morning light, calm and shallow enough to keep out the larger sea predators.

A perfect place to anchor—and perhaps to water dance.

She moved toward the prow, where the human, Stephen, stood holding a mug in both hands.

"It appears you've found your balance," she said.

He turned and smiled.

"For now. It's calm enough, but I wouldn't want to try my luck in rough weather. I see we've changed direction—heading for that atoll, are we?"

"Yes."

Allyndra pointed to a mast with its sails missing.

"The storm damaged one of the masts and several sails last night. The captain thought it best to let the storm pass while the crew makes repairs. I'm afraid our journey will be slower than expected."

"That's fine," Stephen said. "It gives me more time to enjoy being outside again. I checked in with Conner—everything's steady on that front. He thinks they'll have one of the shuttles running in a week or so."

He tapped his mug absently.

"The tea's good, but I'll need something with more flavor after a while. The captain offered something else, but it was *very* sugary."

"*Wa'a puak kohi?*" Allyndra asked.

Stephen shrugged.

"Something like that. Unlike you, I don't pick up languages easily. I'll have to work at it."

"I'll begin teaching others your English," Allyndra said with a small smile. "*Wa'a puak kohi* means Blood Flower juice. It's made from a plant we cultivate—and no, you don't need to worry. The name comes from the color, not the content."

"Ah! I'd almost forgotten that," Stephen said. "Something I'd like to explore further—but not now. Right now, I'm just enjoying being outside with real air."

He looked out across the waves.

"Twenty years, Allyndra. For twenty years, all I saw were metal walls. Twenty! I'm not sure how that compares to your years. I'll have to ask Jane, but it's a long time for us."

"Nearly a quarter of your lifespan," Allyndra replied thoughtfully. "From what I could reference, our year is slightly longer than yours."

"Damn, Allyndra, just how much did you *pick up*?"

"Whatever journey my mind took me on," she said lightly. "There's still much I don't know. I found some of your tales, but I had no time to study them."

"Oh! Well, perhaps that's something I can help with. I presume your world has tales of its own?"

"Indeed, we do."

"Then could you tell me one—to pass the time?"

That pierces the heart. Mother O'lathe had loved the old tales, as did my husband. And now I'm being asked to tell them again.

The *Wind Dancer* drifted into the lagoon and dropped anchor.

I can tell him a tale—and dance.

She thought for a moment, choosing a story that might interest him, and finally settled on one.

"A moment, then."

Allyndra crossed to the center of the deck, where Hila'ar and several crew members stood. After a few quiet words, one of them hurried off and soon returned with what she had requested. Allyndra thanked them, then made her way back to the prow, holding the object delicately in her hands.

"This," she said, "is one of the most precious commodities on my world."

She handed over a small, iridescent scarf. Stephen set down his mug and accepted it carefully.

"What's this? So light! It feels a bit like what we call silk. Look at that—rainbows running down the length of it. I've never seen anything like this."

"We call it something similar," Allyndra said. "*Trellium silk* would be the closest translation in your language. A special kind of spider makes it—small, delicate creatures that spin only a little and live for a short time. A scarf like that is rare. The Mother of my House owns a full dress made from it. I can't even imagine the fortune it must have cost."

"So why this?" Stephen asked, turning the scarf over in his hands. "I thought you were going to tell me a story."

"I will," she replied. "The story of how Trellium silk came to be."

She paused.

"Wait a moment."

Allyndra took back the precious scarf and spoke again with the crew. Hila'ar called out orders, and soon the sailors gathered at the front of the ship beside Stephen, curiosity shining in their eyes.

"Let me do this properly," Allyndra said.

She slipped off her shoes, ran lightly across the deck, and leapt into the air. Hovering above the waves, she found her rhythm. *The balance of wind and wave.* Slowly, she descended until her bare feet just brushed the surface of the warm water.

Closing her eyes, she felt the breeze against her skin, the soft motion of the sea around her toes. Subtly, she adjusted the pitch of her wings, flashing iridescent light under the twin suns. She began to sway—moving with the air, with the water—until she became part of them both. Then, lifting her voice, she began to sing.

Her arms moved as gracefully as her voice rose, telling the story as much through motion as through song. Every so often she would dip her foot into the sea and flick water into the air, scattering droplets that shimmered like silk in the sunlight.

First, she sang in the human tongue, then in her own.

"There was once a poor woman who lived in a humble village. She and her neighbors wove cloth to sell, each helping the other to survive. One cold day, as the poor woman worked, her hands ached from the chill. She set aside her weaving to rest—and looked up. In the corner of her home, a small spider spun its web.

"'Ah, little one,' she said, 'we both labor so hard for so little reward.'

"And so she began to care for the spider, catching small insects when the web stayed empty, for she knew well what it meant to go hungry.

"One day, as the woman paused in her weaving, she noticed her tiny companion had spun a small silk sac. She knew at once what it was—an egg sac.

"'Oh, little one,' she murmured, 'I can hardly keep us both fed. How shall I ever care for so many of your children?'"

"Suddenly, a flash of brilliant light filled the cottage. Startled, the old woman turned to see a figure of surpassing beauty standing before her. In that instant, she knew she was in the presence of a goddess. Trembling, she fell to her knees on the rough stone floor, though the pain bit deep.

"The goddess reached out, took the old woman's hands, and gently lifted her to her feet. Then she led her to the window and pointed toward a great rainbow spanning the horizon.

"'You, who have worked so hard with so little,' the goddess said, her voice like music, 'and who thought of the needs of even the smallest creatures—you have been seen.'

"She beckoned toward the rainbow, and to the old woman's wonder, it seemed to bend and drift closer until it touched the humble cottage. The goddess turned and pressed a portion of its shimmering light toward the spider's egg sac.

"'When these hatch,' she said, 'raise them well. When they spin their silk, weave it. People will come from far and wide when they see what you have made. They will pay any price. Share, as you always have, with your neighbors, and none of you shall ever be poor or hungry again.'

"'Then the goddess vanished, leaving the scent of sunlight and rain in her wake.

"The woman did as she was bidden. Though it was hard work, she tended to the tiny hatchlings and cared for them until they grew. When they began to spin their silk, she gathered it and wove a small piece of cloth.

"It was unlike anything she had ever seen—threads that shimmered with living color, as if the rainbow itself had been captured in each strand. She showed it to her neighbors and told them what had happened. She shared her spiders with them, and they raised their own. Before long, a wealthy traveler saw the cloth and offered a great sum for it. Others came after, bringing gifts and trade from distant lands.

"Just as the goddess had promised, none of them were ever poor again. Yet the woman and her neighbors never took more than they needed, and they always shared with one another—lest the goddess take back the gift she had given."

As the final words left her lips, Allyndra spun gracefully in the air, her wings scattering droplets of water that caught the sunlight in fleeting arcs of color. She came to rest in a poised stillness, standing lightly upon the water as the waves lapped gently at her feet.

***

Stephen watched, utterly captivated by the dance. *It's almost like a cross between ballet and hula,* he thought. *There's a formality to it—but the hands, the movement... they flow like water itself.*

He was startled when the captain and several crew members began to clap—a rhythm not unlike a human's applause—before each made a curtsy or a deep bow. Taking the cue, Stephen followed suit as Allyndra dipped gracefully in response, her motion still echoing the rhythm of the waves beneath her.

She flew lightly back to the ship's prow, where Captain Hila'ar stepped forward and handed her a large mug.

"I've seen water dancing before, Mother Named of Warraquim," Hila'ar said, still catching her breath, "but you have a style and grace I've never beheld. If you weren't of Warraquim, I'd have sworn you belonged to the House of Artisans."

Allyndra accepted the praise with a slight bow, offering warm acknowledgment to the rest of the crew before Hila'ar shooed them back to their duties.

Stephen waited respectfully until Allyndra had drained the mug of juice before speaking.

"That was incredible," he said softly. "I've never seen anything like it. It's almost like our ballet—but the story..."

He hesitated, emotion thickening his voice.

"It nearly made me cry. It was beautiful, Allyndra. From what I've seen so far, there's so much beauty here."

"There *was* more at one time," she said quietly.

"Oh? At one time?"

She didn't answer immediately.

Stephen worried he'd said something wrong, but after a long pause, Allyndra drew a slow breath.

"A long time ago," she began, "there were many more A'ksu like me. The closest word in your language would be *dangerous*. It's said that the A'ksu of that age learned too much, too quickly. They couldn't see the consequences of their knowledge—or their actions. We made... mistakes."

Stephen nodded.

"That's true for us as well. I think every intelligent species must stumble as it grows. Some never recover."

He looked toward the open sky, shading his eyes.

"Sometimes I wonder how many others there were—who didn't survive their own mistakes. You're the first intelligent species we've ever discovered. And the irony is, we may never even get to tell the rest of humanity, *'We're not alone.'*"

"Why?" Allyndra asked. "What makes you fear being alone?"

"Don't your people ever look up at the sky," he said, "and wonder if someone else is out there? Like a longing to go beyond your own world?"

Allyndra gave a small, rolling shrug, her wings rustling softly.

"Why? Our world is enough for us. Why would we wish to intrude upon another—especially one where we might not be wanted?"

What? Stephen blinked. *They don't have any curiosity about other worlds?*

"To explore," he said, "and to find new places!"

"I read some of your history, Stephen—*humanity's* history, if I'm using the word correctly."

Her tone was thoughtful, not accusatory.

"From what I've learned, your kind is never content. There must always be something new to discover—some land to conquer, some wonder to claim. Yet in reaching for everything, it seems you've destroyed much of what you already had. You never found peace... or rather, not peace exactly, but balance. Yes— balance. I still have a few difficulties with your concepts."

Stephen exhaled, half-smiling.

"Interesting. I suppose because—other than a few differences, like your eyes or the wings on your women—you seem so human. I made the mistake of assuming you'd think like us."

"We must both be careful with assumptions," she said gently.

"I agree, Allyndra. That's what I'm hoping for—that we can learn from each other. Our differences, our shared desires."

He paused, then added with sincerity, "I loved the story you told—and the way you told it. The crew did too."

"I'm glad you enjoyed it."

"I did," he said warmly. "And I want to learn more. I'll need your help, though—to learn enough of your language so you don't have to keep translating everything for me."

He glanced down at the calm turquoise water beneath them, thinking, *I thought I was beginning to understand things here. But I'm going to have to tread carefully.*

Captain Hila'ar returned, her expression brisk but proud.

"Mast repaired. We ready sail, Mother—honored guest."

The words came out haltingly but clear—in English.

Stephen blinked in surprise.

"Where did you learn that?"

"From the Mother," Hila'ar replied, gesturing toward Allyndra. "I not so good as she. I not..."

She hesitated, then glanced at Allyndra, who gave a small nod of permission. Hila'ar lowered her voice.

"A'ksu."

Stephen realized, with sudden clarity, that although Allyndra had said the trait was rare and diluted, it must still linger in many of her people.

"How long?"

Both women tilted their heads slightly in identical gestures of curiosity.

"How long did it take for the captain to learn?" he clarified.

"Captain Hila'ar came to me last night," Allyndra said. "We shared a pleasant meal and spent several hours together. I taught her the basics of your language. She doesn't have the command that I do."

Stephen shook his head in disbelief.

"Amazing—absolutely amazing."

His gaze moved between the two alien women. *I'd better warn Conner,* he thought. *If they all learn this quickly and ever gained full access to our files—our science, our engineering—what might they become?* He pushed the thought aside.

Hila'ar made a rolling shrug and pointed toward the railing.

"Something hold on to. We ascend quick."

She turned and shouted commands to her crew in her native tongue.

Allyndra plucked lightly at a rope running along the rail.

"Unless you wish to learn to fly, I suggest you do as the captain advised."

As the skyship lifted, Stephen barely managed to grab the rope in time. The prow tilted sharply upward, and the wind whipped through his hair as the vessel climbed into the bright sky. He clung tightly until, after several long minutes, the ship leveled off and steadied.

He exhaled, grinning despite himself.

"I still can't get over this," he said. "This—this is freedom, Allyndra. At least to me."

The woman shaded her eyes.

"I'm concerned the delay may be too long. Captain Hila'ar makes good speed, but if I had to guess, we won't reach House Warraquim until tomorrow."

"That's a problem?"

"I'm not sure how much longer the Mother of my guild has," Allyndra said quietly. "She was in very poor health when I left."

"Oh—I'm sorry, Allyndra."

Stephen meant it. Though he knew little about how her people viewed life or death, he assumed they cared for one another much as humans did.

Am I just projecting human emotions onto them? he wondered. *So many things feel familiar—and yet alien at the same time.*

He knew he would have to move carefully, learning as he went.

What troubles me most is their lack of curiosity. From everything I've seen that ship of hers wasn't sent to explore, but to make sure we weren't a threat.

His thoughts were interrupted when Allyndra spoke again.

"It happens to us all. We all pass into the arms of the gods."

She turned her luminous eyes toward him.

"I feel sorrow for your kind, Stephen. To suffer ill health for so much of your lives must be difficult. For us, it lasts a year at most before the end. I think that's better."

Stephen noticed the faint frown on her face, the shadow of concern.

Maybe we do share some things after all.

"Knowing how your people age—or rather, that you hardly age at all—I think I agree with you," he said with a wry smile.

A thought struck him, and he chuckled softly.

"You find something amusing about age and death?" she asked, brow furrowing slightly. "Am I interpreting that correctly?"

"No, no," he said quickly. "Forgive me, Allyndra. It just reminded me of a story from my world."

"I would like to hear it," Allyndra said. "I've told you one from my world, and there's still a long journey ahead."

Stephen gave her a small, playful salute.

"As you wish, Mother."

She inclined her head with a faint smile.

Good, he thought, *I'm starting to get the cultural nuances right.*

He launched into his story—the tale of *The Portrait of Dorian Gray.*

When he finished, he added, "To me, you're like that story—full of life until the very end, when age catches up to you all at once."

Allyndra was silent for several long moments.

Then she said, "I can see the parallels to us. However, we don't seek ways to… dissipate—yes, that's the correct word—our bodies."

"Yes, you've got it right," Stephen said. "Still, don't your people ever overindulge in food or drink?"

A thought occurred to him.

"Do you drink alcohol—or anything like it?"

Allyndra studied him intently before replying.

"Why would we do something like that? We eat and drink because it sustains life. To take more than what is needed—to the point of harm—would be… illogical."

Christ, Stephen thought. *These people really are different. No vices?*

"Because," he said carefully, "people can become addicted to something. Do you know that word from your reading?"

"I remember it," she said. "But I didn't study deeply beyond basic biology. I was more focused on learning about you—your people, your society, your history, and, of course, your language. Perhaps I should have stayed longer and studied more."

If Conner knew how much she's already learned, Stephen thought grimly, *he'd have shot her on sight. She knows more about the light engine that got us here than most of the engineers—and he'd probably have me dissect her to see how she works.*

He changed direction.

"Is there anything your people use—something that alters the mind, changes how you feel, or creates a craving that's hard to resist?"

Allyndra's brow furrowed as she considered.

"Yes. There is one thing. We don't become… addicted, if I understand the concept correctly, but it can alter mood and emotion."

Stephen leaned forward with interest.

"Ah! And what might that be?"

She turned her head toward the direction the ship was sailing, sunlight catching her eyes. For an instant, they flashed like two perfectly cut sapphires.

Damn, Stephen thought, *they really are.*

"Our bite," she said simply.

Stephen blinked. The tone was flat, almost clinical.

"Your bite?"

Then it hit him. *Right—she said they're hematophages!*

"Indeed," Allyndra replied after a long pause.

Stephen was about to ask again when she continued.

"There are substances in our bite that prevent the blood from coagulating, as well as others that dull pain. But there are also compounds that induce... euphoria."

"Interesting," he said, leaning forward slightly. "That sounds like a logical evolutionary development. So, tell me more—what about your bite?"

"It's said that in times of famine, males would give their blood to ensure the next generation survived. Beyond physical pleasure, the little bites bring a certain... bliss of the mind."

She hesitated, searching for the words.

"I'm not sure I can describe it properly."

Stephen's mind raced. *Fascinating. I wonder...*

"Do you think it might work on me?"

Allyndra turned sharply toward him.

"Why would I wish to mate with you? We don't do that outside of marriage with a fertile male—and you said yourself that you are one."

Stephen nearly laughed out loud. *Oh, I walked straight into that one.*

"No—no, I'm sorry! That's not what I meant!" He raised both hands quickly. "I only wondered if a small bite might produce any reaction in me. Purely out of scientific curiosity—to compare our neurophysiology. Do you understand what I mean?"

"I understand the concept," she said.

Allyndra drew a deep breath, the sound close to a human sigh but not quite the same. Stephen couldn't tell if he was reading too much into her expression.

"Very well," she said at last. "For curiosity's sake—but not in front of the crew. I'll tell the captain we've chosen to share an evening meal together."

Stephen bowed slightly. The small courtesies of her people seemed to carry weight.

"Thank you, Mother."

***

Stephen walked down the corridor, past the rows of gas bags that kept the ship aloft, toward Allyndra's quarters. His mind was still turning over what he'd learned—and what he hadn't.

Their society clearly has structure and hierarchy, he thought. *Every rule seems to fit together to keep the whole system balanced. How long did it take us to build something even close to that? And even now, ours barely holds together.*

From their earlier conversations, he'd gathered that these people—*the Allidians*—didn't have the same competitive drive as humans. Or at least, not with each other.

I'd love to explore that more, he mused. *If she's willing to talk about her culture, maybe I can learn how it all works.* Then another thought tempered his curiosity. *I have to be careful. I talked her into something that clearly goes against her customs, even if she understood what I meant. Best not to push too far.*

He reached her door and knocked softly. There was barely a pause before it slid open. Allyndra stood there—not in the formal, high-collared gown she'd worn earlier, but in a white flight dress that tied at the neck and fell just above her knees.

That's the same style she was wearing when Conner shot her, Stephen realized.

The light behind her outlined her form. Though he'd already examined her after the injury, this was different. He noticed the delicate curves of her body—the small, firm breasts, the subtle swell of her hips. Her build was more slender than most human women's, but unmistakably feminine. The faint blue highlights in her dark hair echoed the blue facets of her eyes, giving her an almost ethereal beauty.

His pulse quickened. His breath did too.

Settle down, man, he warned himself. *She's stunning—but this isn't that kind of visit. Still, we're going to have trouble with some of the crew if she walks around like that.*

"Come in," she said, stepping aside. "I thought a crew flight dress would be more appropriate—less formal than my House robes. I hope you don't mind."

Stephen shook his head, forcing himself to focus.

"No, not at all."

Not really. It makes you look sexy as hell.

"There's food for you—melons and other fruit. They may not be quite what you're used to, but there's little on this ship that matches your kind's diet. I did read enough to know that much," Allyndra said. "We don't have meat or grains as you do. Once we're back at Warraquim, I can arrange something more substantial. There are various fish, if you can tolerate those."

Stephen stepped further into the cabin. A single place had been set at the small table. He glanced over the selection of fruit while Allyndra closed the door and waited quietly.

"I appreciate this," he said, "but I'm not that hungry right now."

He gave a crooked smile.

"So... what do I do? Bare my neck?"

"We're not like the creatures from your mythology," Allyndra replied dryly.

She tilted her chin toward the bed.

"Sit there, please. If something goes wrong, you'll be less likely to hurt yourself."

"Thank you."

He sat down. The bed was a little more ornate than his own quarters but still simple enough.

"I appreciate that you're worried about that. Let me apologize again for not showing you the same consideration."

"If you end up with bruises on your neck," she said, "your captain will be suspicious—and we can't afford that right now."

Damn, she's right.

If he showed up with bite marks or bruises, Conner would lose his mind—and probably send in the Marines as soon as a shuttle was functional.

Allyndra sat beside him and gently took his arm. She reached to the table, picked up a soft cloth, and dipped it into a clear liquid that looked like water. With careful, practiced motions, she swabbed the inside of his wrist.

Then, without warning, she bent her head.

Stephen couldn't see what she was doing—her hair fell forward in a curtain of blue-black silk. There was a brief, sharp prick, like two needles piercing his skin. Almost immediately, the pain vanished.

All right... that must've been the bite, he thought. *And whatever's in her saliva—it's fast. Some kind of natural anesthetic...*

Suddenly, a surge of the most intense, erotic sensation he had ever felt flooded through him.

"Oh—oh!" was all he managed before the feeling overwhelmed him completely.

He fell back, the world spinning—and then everything went black.

***

Stephen squinted as sunlight streamed through the porthole. Sitting up made his head swim, and then memory hit—those incredible, intoxicating sensations.

Oh, hell. Allyndra had said the bite would be euphoric, but that was the understatement of the year. *Erotic as hell was more like it. If that ever gets out, we're going to have problems—big ones. I'll have to warn Conner about that little detail.*

He blinked again, trying to clear the haze from his mind. The tray of fruit had been replaced with fresh ones, but Allyndra was nowhere in sight. Hunger crept up on him, and he glanced at his wrist. Four small punctures, barely inflamed.

Good—no infection, nothing red. I survived the experiment. And what an experiment it was.

He tried standing, but the room spun, forcing him back down onto the bed.

Damn it. How much did she take? Or is this just an aftereffect of whatever's in that bite?

He grabbed a piece of fruit—something that tasted like a peach—and took a bite.

Maybe I just haven't eaten in hours.

"Well," he muttered aloud between bites, "I asked for an experience, and I sure got one."

He leaned back with a sigh.

Still... I can't help wondering what actually being with one of them would be like.

He shook his head hard.

Stop it. You're supposed to be a diplomat. There'll be enough trouble without that kind of thinking.

Chapter 6

HOUSE WARRAQUIM

O'LATHE & ALEKELIA

I can't even lift my arms anymore.

O'lathe endured the quiet indignity of her attendants helping her dress.

Oh, Allyndra... what has happened to you?

It had been almost a week since she had sent her on her way.

How long to sail there, to see what's become of things, and return?

She had glanced in the mirror that morning and shuddered at the reflection. Where smooth skin had been only a year ago, now it hung loose and wrinkled over fragile bones. Her skull showed starkly beneath the thinning flesh, and her once-bright amber eyes had dulled to a faded yellow.

O'lathe closed her eyes.

It isn't fair, she thought. *To remain as one was for decades, and then to age in the space of days.*

"Please help me to the balcony," she said aloud. "I want to feel the Twins on my face—perhaps for the last time."

"Yes, Mother."

Three attendants all but carried her to the stone balcony and settled her carefully onto the couch, arranging the cushions around her frail frame.

"Is there anything else?" one asked softly.

O'lathe didn't answer immediately. Every joint, every beat of her hearts, brought pain.

Finally, she murmured, "Yes. Send a flyer with a message for Alekelia. She should be at or near La'Gave by now. She was scheduled to return within a few days. Then you may leave."

"Of course, Mother."

One attendant hurried off to fetch pen and paper; and another went to find a messenger.

I fear I can't last much longer, O'lathe thought. *Though it pains me, Allyndra, I've sent for Alekelia to return in haste. The House needs a Mother, even if she is not my choice.*

O'lathe relaxed once the message had been sent and her attendants had withdrawn, the soft warmth of the Twins' light falling across her face.

***

This morning was much like the last two since O'lathe had sent her message to Alekelia. The younger woman had arrived the day before the storm. Now, once again, O'lathe lay in the sunshine, shivering despite the warmth.

She was interrupted when one of the senior healers from House Mil'ola entered to examine her, listening to her chest with a delicate instrument. The healer straightened and shook her head sympathetically.

"I'm sorry, Mother of House Warraquim. Your hearts are beginning to fail. They can no longer move enough blood through your body—hence why you're always cold. I can only recommend rest, and perhaps warm water bags beneath you to ease the chill."

O'lathe nodded faintly and thanked her. Both women had avoided speaking the truth aloud: time had finally caught up with her. She turned her thoughts not to her own mortality—she would soon join the long line of Mothers before her—but to the troubling news that had reached her. There was still no word of the *Wind Dancer* or of her named Mother, Allyndra. The mystery of the stone from the heavens remained unsolved.

The healer stepped back just as Alekelia entered, concern written across her face.

"Mother, it grieves me to see you so. I know this pains you, but a new Mother must be named. A terrible storm struck yesterday, and we believe Allyndra and the *Wind Dancer* were lost. It came from the direction of the island she went to."

O'lathe's voice was weak but steady.

"And what is it you wish, Alekelia? That you be named Mother of the House? You are—if Allyndra does not return. You left in haste, but I made Allyndra the Mother Named."

Alekelia did not hesitate.

"How long are we to wait, Mother? Until you have flown to the gods? A week? A year? We cannot remain leaderless. You must accept that Allyndra and the *Dancer* are gone."

"Enough," O'lathe's tone was sharp despite her frailty.

She knew Alekelia was right—the House needed a Mother—but unease stirred in her chest. The declaration naming Alekelia as successor had already been recorded before witnesses, should Allyndra fail to return. Yet O'lathe could not shake her worry.

Impulsive, she thought, shivering even in the heat of High Summer. *She doesn't think things through. She complained that Allyndra bore the A'ksu trait, but perhaps she inherited a trace of it herself. We've always said the A'ksu could not foresee the consequences of their actions. I wonder now if that story was ever entirely true. Allyndra—when she focuses—always tries to look ahead, to weigh the outcomes. There is no doubt she bears the old gift.*

A sudden, sharp pain flared in O'lathe's chest, forcing her to grimace.

As much as I hate this, she's right. It must be done—for the good of all.

"Very well, Alekelia," she whispered. "Who is here to witness?"

"The guards, Mother. I dismissed the others—they were suffering from the heat."

O'lathe frowned faintly.

Unusual, she thought. *But then, I don't imagine I'll need much attending for much longer.*

"They shall have to do," she said at last. "Bring them here."

Alekelia went to fetch the two large infertile males, who entered and bowed deeply.

"Mother," they said almost in unison.

"You will bear witness to this," O'lathe said, her voice thin but steady. "I name Alekelia the Mother of House Warraquim."

She glanced toward the younger woman and caught the faintly smug expression on her face.

"However," O'lathe continued, "if Allyndra returns, she remains the true Mother of this House. You will testify to this before the scribes."

I won't let that decision be erased, no matter what Alekelia desires.

The two guards exchanged a brief glance before bowing again.

"Yes, Mother."

"Now, bring me something cool to drink," O'lathe said. "Alekelia, see to this last task for me while they give their testimony."

"Yes, Mother."

Alekelia turned away with a lightness in her step that did not escape O'lathe's notice.

O'lathe beckoned to the two guards once more.

"And you—go now. You've heard my words, and you know they must be recorded. There is no more work for you here."

They bowed again, but one hesitated, stepping forward and dropping to one knee. The other followed suit.

"Mother," he said softly, "it has been an honor to serve you. May the Twins bless you, and may the gods receive you with open arms."

Tears shone on both their faces. The sight made O'lathe's failing hearts ache even more.

"Thank you," she whispered. "You have served well. Now go—quickly. I do not trust Alekelia."

The two guards rose and departed without another word. As they left, they passed a fertile male entering with a stack of papers.

"What is it?" he asked, puzzled to see them leaving their post.

"The Mother has declared Alekelia illm Warraquim to be the new Mother," one replied.

"I thought she had named Allyndra?"

"Alekelia will serve only so long as Allyndra does not return. We must bear witness to that and have it recorded."

The male nodded gravely.

"Then come. I'll take down your testimony at once."

Meanwhile, O'lathe's thoughts drifted, tumbling briefly through memories and worries before settling into peace. She closed her eyes and turned her face toward the warmth of the Twins, feeling their full light upon her frail skin.

"I shall dance with you soon," she whispered, as the sky blazed with their glory.

***

Alekelia returned carrying the chilled Blood Flower juice. As she entered, she noticed one of O'lathe's arms hanging limply over the edge of the couch.

"Mother?" she called softly.

There was no response. Setting the jug and cups on the nearby table, Alekelia bent to check on her. After a brief moment, she straightened, expression unreadable.

She poured herself a cup of the sweet crimson liquid, lifted it in a small gesture of acknowledgment, and murmured, "Rest with the gods, old Mother."

Then she drank deeply.

I am the new Mother now.

Still, the thought followed swiftly—*there are things I must see to at once.*

***

Alekelia sat in the quarters reserved for the Mother of the House. There was much to do, and she wanted everything in order should Allyndra return. It had been several days since Allyndra had departed to investigate the strange occurrence, and no skyship had reported seeing the *Wind Dancer.*

I have no idea if she's dead or alive—and it makes no difference now. I am the Mother of the House.

At least they had time, without interruption, to send O'lathe's ashes to the sky, so she could take one final flight. The words of the ceremony still echoed in Alekelia's mind. She had never expected to speak them herself, much less for her own predecessor.

"Lords and Ladies of Light and Darkness, you raised us up from the earth so we could touch the sky. From earth we came, to the sky we go, and then return to earth. Accept my thanks for the gift of flight, and grant that this one flies to thee."

She knew Allyndra would take the loss hard—and harder still that Alekelia had taken the place O'lathe had intended for her. The dying Mother had asked her to step aside if Allyndra returned, but that no longer seemed wise.

There are so few who know what O'lathe said. A delirious old woman and the word of two infertile males against mine—no one will believe them. I'll see that the record is destroyed. Then it's only my word that remains. Ah, but wait... there was another male, the one who recorded their sworn statement. I'll deal with him as well.

Alekelia's thoughts were interrupted when she caught sight of a flyer approaching at high speed. Before the servants could even announce her, the exhausted messenger landed directly on the balcony, panting heavily.

"Mother," she gasped, "the *Wind Dancer* has been sighted! One of the crew flew ahead—Allyndra is returning... with an odd male she brought from the stone that fell from the sky."

An odd male from the stone? Alekelia frowned. *Whatever that means, I'll handle it later. First, I'll make certain my position is secure. Then I'll send Allyndra to the archives where she belongs. She'll probably love it—she always did have a fondness for those dusty old books, even the ones too decayed to read.*

"Thank you, daughter. Go, refresh yourself and rest."

As Alekelia turned, she noticed a fertile male standing nearby. She recognized him—the same one who had been with the two guards and had recorded their testimony for the old Mother.

"You there. What's your name?"

She motioned him forward with an imperious wave.

He bowed.

"Li'hue, Mother."

"Very good, Li'hue."

Her voice softened slightly, though her eyes did not.

"How would you like to become the Voice of Warraquim?"

"Me?" He blinked in astonishment. "How could that be?"

"I was named Mother by O'lathe herself."

"I was there with the guards," Li'hue said cautiously. "She named you as a successor only if Allyndra did not return. From what the flyer said, that's no longer the case."

Alekelia's composure cracked and she stamped a foot in fury.

"O'lathe named me with the last of her breaths!"

Li'hue quickly lowered his gaze, startled by her vehemence.

"Mother, I recorded the guards' statements."

"Has that record been delivered to the archives yet?"

"No, Mother. I was planning to do it later today. The passing of the old Mother and her cremation this morning have caused much disarray."

"Then, Li'hue, is it?" Alekelia's tone turned silken, though her eyes were sharp as glass. "Bring it to me. I will see it delivered myself—as my final duty to the old Mother."

"Why, Mother?"

Alekelia trembled with controlled anger.

"You question the Mother of the House?" Her voice dropped to a dangerous calm. "Do you wish to be remembered as the only male ever denied the honor of becoming a Voice? Or will you obey?"

Li'hue paled, bowing deeply.

"Yes, Mother. As you command. It will be my honor to serve."

Alekelia settled back into her seat and smiled.

"Then, Voice, you and I shall make a fine pair. Now, as soon as the *Wind Dancer* lands, have Allyndra brought to me."

Li'hue bowed.

"Yes, Mother."

He turned and departed.

Alekelia drew a deep breath and unfurled her wings, a slow, deliberate stretch of triumph.

At last, the gods smile upon me.

Chapter 7

HOUSE WARRAQUIM

ALLYNDRA & STEPHEN

Stephen climbed the stairs to the deck.

"Wow. I'm still feeling the effects of that bite. I wonder what the long-term effects would be, although I'm not sure I want to find out."

Sunlight flooded his vision as he stepped out, the sea breeze sweeping across his face with a crisp freshness that banished the last haze from his mind. The air was warm, the twin suns nearly at their zenith. As he took in his surroundings, he spotted the captain, a crew member whose hair was cropped so short it was little more than fuzz, and Allyndra standing together at the prow. The ship was approaching the same gleaming white, ten-story spiral structure he had glimpsed during the *Reliance*'s crash landing. Allyndra was once again wearing her formal House dress.

We must be at House Warraquim, he thought. *She said we'd arrive the next day.*

Still feeling slightly unsteady, Stephen caught hold of a rope to steady himself. He didn't want to interrupt the three women, but when the captain turned, spoke briefly to Allyndra, and the latter nodded before beckoning him forward, he made his way to the prow. He inclined his head respectfully as he passed the captain and the crewwoman.

"Good morning, Stephen. May the Twins bless," the captain said as she stepped aside.

"Thank you," he replied, hesitating a moment before adding, "Captain. The same to you."

She gave no reply, already shouting instructions to the crew working the white sails.

Stephen shrugged, hoping he hadn't made a cultural misstep, and continued to where Allyndra stood.

"Good morning."

"Ah, I wish it were."

Stephen noticed the faint streaks of wetness on her cheeks. "Something's wrong?"

"Yes." Her voice trembled slightly. "That crew member who flew off after we left the island—she was waiting here for the *Dancer*. She brought news that Mother O'lathe has gone to the arms of the gods."

"The arms of the gods?" Stephen frowned. "I don't quite understand."

Allyndra closed her eyes and shook her head gently.

"What you would call... having passed, if I'm using the term correctly."

"Oh—oh, I'm so sorry, Allyndra."

He reached out instinctively, but she flinched away.

Right. No touching unless invited. He let his hand fall, awkwardly. *I hate to ask, but... now what?*

"I was to be the Mother of the House," she continued quietly, "but Ari'alia tells me that Alekelia is now the Mother."

"I see."

I don't, he admitted inwardly. *But if something's disrupted the succession, that's bound to cause trouble.*

"Do you think everything will be all right? I know this isn't exactly good timing."

"No. It isn't." She drew a shuddering breath. "I need to learn what's happened and go from there."

She quickly brushed her fingers across her eyes, wiping the tears away.

They cry just like we do, Stephen thought. *Alien, and yet not so alien. Humanity's first contact with another intelligent species, and we find they share the same emotions. And we can't tell anyone. Not for decades.*

Allyndra inhaled deeply and steadied herself.

"I take it nothing's amiss with you—that you simply had a good sleep?"

"Good sleep," Stephen said with a rueful grin. "Pretty much passed out."

And the dreams... yeah, those were something else.

"Were you affected?"

"No," she said, a faint smile tugging at her lips. "Though I'll admit, you taste somewhat bitter. Perhaps not enough sugar in your blood."

She chuckled softly.

"I told the crew you'd had trouble with part of the meal. Please keep what happened between us. It's enough that they know I'm A'ksu. If they also learned I performed the *Honik'a Kohi*—the Blood Kiss—on a stranger, an alien no less, it would do my reputation no favors."

Stephen took that in. She had mentioned that such things weren't done outside of marriage, and he was beginning to realize that, in a society as stratified as hers, that act might carry real stigma.

"It's our secret," he said quietly.

Then, eager to steer the conversation away from the memory of those vivid, erotic dreams, he added, "That's your House, then?"

"Yes. I will present you to the Mother." Allyndra turned her head slightly, her tone softening.

"If I seem less talkative today, it's because I'm tired. I had little rest on board your ship, and after you passed out on the bed, I couldn't remain there. I stayed on deck for the rest of the night. And now, this sad news this morning..."

She paused, exhaling slowly.

"I'm sorry, Stephen. There are limits to my endurance."

Yeah, she's been through a lot. He lifted a hand, wanting to offer comfort, but stopped himself and let it fall. *I wish I could do more. Words just aren't enough.*

"I didn't know what might happen," he said. "And again—for what it's worth—I'm sorry about the Mother of your House. I should probably inform my captain that there's been a... change in leadership."

"In time, please," Allyndra replied. "First, I must impress upon Alekelia how precarious our situation is—if what has transpired is true."

Stephen nodded silently, acknowledging her need for caution.

The *Wind Dancer* began to bank, its sails catching the sunlight. Allyndra tapped the railing.

"We'll be landing soon. It would be best if you held onto a rope—it'll be much like when we left the island. A fairly sharp descent."

Stephen followed her advice, securing his grip.

Moments later, the ship dipped sharply, the prow plunging toward the ocean before leveling out. He braced himself as the vessel completed its sweeping turn, revealing what looked like docks extending into the water.

He could see why they were built that way. The suns cast long golden light over the shore, and behind the towering spiral structure, steep hills rose abruptly, their sheer sides gleaming white in the afternoon heat.

Just like where we landed, Stephen thought. *Volcanic islands—steep-sided, with arable land at a premium.* He could already picture the possibilities. *We could reshape some of it for them, level a few areas easily once the machinery's up and running.*

Then another thought struck him.

They could have done that themselves, even by hand—but they haven't. Maybe they don't want to. He exhaled softly. *Damn it, there I go again—imposing human logic on a different culture. No... not different. We're the aliens here. They're the natives.*

The skyship descended until it nearly skimmed the ocean, gliding low over gentle waves toward the long wooden docks and wide, sandy shore. The landing was smooth, almost graceful. Several female crew members took to the air, wings beating steadily as they carried ropes down to the dock. With practiced efficiency, they looped the lines around pilings, and winches aboard the ship tightened them, drawing the vessel snugly alongside the pier.

"Come on," Allyndra said. "If there's one thing I envy, it's your ability to communicate so easily between places. We can only send word through flyers—it's not nearly as quick."

Stephen chuckled.

"Well, that might be one thing we could share. Though honestly, from what I've seen so far, it doesn't look like you need much from us."

Allyndra tilted her head in acknowledgment, a gesture that might have been a smile in her culture and then started down the deck toward the hold and cabins. Stephen followed, noticing how one side of the skyship had been lowered to form a wide gangplank.

He stepped off onto the dock and paused to glance back at the ship.

Primitive by human standards, he mused, *but still an incredible piece of engineering. A flying wooden vessel, shaped by instinct and need rather than technology. Of course—they're a species that flies. Why sail the sea when you can sail the air?* He smiled faintly. *All right, Stephen—looks like you're going to write the first field notes on an intelligent alien species.*

The walk toward the great structure wasn't far, but as the twin suns slipped past their zenith, the heat and humidity surged. Sweat dampened the collar of his jumpsuit, and he began to long for the ship's shade.

As they neared the entrance, Stephen got his first close look at the infertile males. Several stood nearby wearing only loincloths, each one tall—at least a head and a half taller than him—and powerfully built.

Workers, he guessed. *They're made for it. There's something almost eusocial here—like ants or bees—but not entirely. Fascinating.*

The entrance loomed ahead as they approached the massive mahogany-colored doors carved with intricate designs. They stood open, a dark contrast to the white, tapering walls of the spiral tower. Allyndra stopped just inside, and Stephen followed, blinking as his eyes adjusted to the filtered light.

The interior was breathtaking—a vast circular hall surrounded by curtained rooms, the whitewashed walls covered with delicate carvings and artwork. A winding walkway spiraled upward around the inner wall, following the building's conical rise, leading his eyes to a crystalline dome at the top where sunlight poured in, scattering rainbows across the smooth stone.

As he took it in, two women approached, their movements graceful and deliberate. Both dropped into a curtsy, their heads bowed low in respect.

***

"Mother," said the woman on the right, bowing slightly. "Welcome. We had word of your coming, and the sighting of the *Wind Dancer* brought us hope. It has also been noted that this being arrived with you. The Mother will attend to you here."

Allyndra dipped her head in return.

"Stephen, we may enter further. If I perceive correctly, you are warm."

"Thank you," he said, wiping his brow. "I'm still not used to the humidity—and this uniform doesn't help."

"Come."

Allyndra led him deeper into the building, the two women following.

"It will be cooler farther in, though the Mother has asked that we wait here. Shall I request chilled water or juice to be brought?"

He shook his head.

"No, that's all right. It's warm outside, but this isn't too bad. I'm guessing the building's designed to let air flow through and cool naturally?"

"That's correct," Allyndra said. "However, I believe we are more physiologically adapted to the warmth and humidity than you are." She paused, then added with quiet pride, "Welcome to the Guild House of Warraquim—the keepers of knowledge."

"Thank you."

"You are an honored guest here."

Stephen turned slowly, taking in the vast open space.

"So, I'm guessing there are quarters here—but how do you keep your knowledge preserved?"

"Yes," she replied. "On the upper levels, where you see the doors, are the living quarters. The next levels above hold classrooms and study areas. The town outside exists mainly to support the House. As for our knowledge—it's written on paper, as yours is, and stored in the archives beneath us. The air there is cooler and drier to preserve the pages."

"We used to do the same," Stephen said. "I—"

He stopped short as movement drew his attention.

At the far end of the hall, where the ramp met the floor, a woman in a richly embroidered robe appeared, attended by several women, a fertile male, and four of the towering infertile males.

Allyndra leaned close and whispered, "The Mother. Don't point with your hands—it's considered impolite."

Then the regal woman spoke.

"Allyndra, we thought you lost!" Alekelia's smile was faint, but her eyes gleamed with something unreadable.

"Alekelia," Allyndra replied evenly.

The smile vanished.

"It's *Mother* now, Allyndra. Mother O'lathe now dances with the Twins."

Allyndra's brows drew together.

"Was I not to be the Mother of the House? There is a record of Mother O'lathe naming me as Mother Named."

Alekelia straightened, her posture imperious.

"Only if you returned. When you did not, Mother O'lathe—at the very end—named *me*. The new Voice was present to witness it. Isn't that correct, Voice?"

The fertile male glanced nervously between them before giving a quick, uncertain bow of his head.

Something's going on between these two. Stephen watched silently. *I don't fully understand it, but diplomacy—not argument—is what's needed right now.*

Allyndra inclined her head.

"It is as it is. The Twins bless, Mother."

She made a deep curtsy, and with a subtle gesture of her fingers, Stephen followed her lead, bowing low.

"Mother," he said carefully—one of the few words he had learned in their language.

Allyndra waited, still bent slightly at the waist, until Alekelia's expression softened enough for her to wave a delicate hand.

"And what is *this thing*?" she asked, the last word curling with disdain as she turned her gaze on Stephen.

"Stephen is a male of a people called *humans*—that is what they name themselves," Allyndra said calmly. "They come from a place very far away—a completely different star."

Alekelia's eyes narrowed.

"And why are they here?"

"Their vessel suffered a malfunction," Allyndra explained. "It drifted off course and came to rest here. From what I understand, it's beyond their ability to repair. They are stranded. The vessel that fell from the heavens a week ago—the one you saw—that was theirs."

Alekelia frowned.

"How many?"

"A few hundred. Their vessel is stranded on a small island to the west."

"And why have you taken so long to report back?" Her words carried a sharp edge.

"The humans accidentally injured me," Allyndra said evenly. "However, they cared for me and allowed me to learn much about them. On our return, the *Wind Dancer* was caught in a storm, and a mast was damaged."

"I see."

Alekelia began to circle Stephen, examining him with open curiosity.

"They look similar enough, but the eyes are strange—no sparkle. Are they truly intelligent?"

Did you not hear a word I said? Allyndra thought but kept her tone calm.

"Yes, Mother. There are more differences, of course. I can prepare a full report if you wish."

"Another book to gather dust in the archives?" Alekelia scoffed. "Unnecessary. I suspect we'll learn all we need once another ship goes there."

"Most likely, Mother," Allyndra replied carefully, "they will come here instead. Their ships are much faster than ours. Their technology is far beyond what we possess. I would urge caution—"

Alekelia stamped her foot.

"Enough, Allyndra! I don't care to discuss this now. There is much unsettled in the House since O'lathe's passing."

"Matters within the House are nothing compared to this," Allyndra pressed. "Their presence here could change the balance of the entire world!"

"I said enough!" Alekelia snapped. "I do not wish to hear more."

Allyndra clenched her jaw before replying, "As you wish, Mother."

O'lathe would have asked a hundred questions by now. Alekelia's indifference could cost us dearly.

She hesitated, then added, "Perhaps hearing what they are capable of, and what may come, in his own words might convince you—or the Council."

"The Council? Whatever for?"

"They will soon make themselves known to the world," Allyndra said. "The other Houses would not look kindly upon the new Mother of Warraquim for withholding such knowledge."

Alekelia's gaze hardened.

After a moment, she said, "Very well, daughter."

The word *daughter* came out almost dismissive.

"I place this creature in your care. Teach it some of our language, and in return, teach others of ours its tongue."

She waved a hand impatiently.

"Go refresh yourself. The attendants will take you to your new quarters. Since we presumed you lost, your old room has been reassigned."

"Yes, Mother."

Oh, Mother O'lathe, how I wish you had stayed longer.

Alekelia seemed satisfied.

"For now, you will teach as I have directed," she said, turning away. "And you are not to be found water dancing or in the archives until I give express permission."

"As you wish. Then, please, show us to our new rooms."

The attendants bowed.

"Yes, Mother—this way, please."

As they followed, Allyndra leaned close to Stephen and whispered in English, "You must learn our language quickly. You must make Alekelia understand that though your numbers are few, your power is not."

"Problems?" he murmured.

"Yes," she said softly. "I'll explain later. For now, learn as much as you can."

***

Allyndra had spent nearly a week teaching a handful of others English while attempting to teach Stephen her own language. He quickly realized he was the slowest learner among them. Even the skyship captain had managed to pick up the rudiments of English within hours, while after several days, Stephen still struggled with even the most basic elements of the Allidian tongue.

There was more to their lessons, of course. Stephen peppered Allyndra with questions about her culture, but she often replied only in general terms, reminding him that Mother Alekelia had officially instructed her to teach language—nothing more. Still, the two had found a way around that restriction. Each afternoon, during the customary rest period when the heat grew heavy and work slowed, they took long walks together. Stephen had noticed that, as in many warm-climate societies on Earth, it was common here to seek shade and quiet during the sultry afternoons.

Now, seated on a beach of velvety black sand shaded by lush green foliage and flowers that released a faint, sweet fragrance, they could talk freely without fear of violating Alekelia's orders.

Stephen watched her as she sat with her knees drawn up, gazing at the blue-green waves that rolled gently toward the shore. There was a quiet longing in her eyes.

She's been forbidden to water dance.

"I'm sorry, Allyndra," he said softly. "That the Mother of your House no longer allows you to water dance. I can see you miss it."

"Indeed," she replied, her voice low. "But perhaps I did too much before. It was always a way to forget the pain."

"Oh?" Stephen frowned slightly. "Pain? I thought your people healed completely—and remarkably fast."

"Not the body," she said, "the mind."

Of course, Stephen thought. *They're highly intelligent—why wouldn't they suffer emotional pain as well?* He couldn't help thinking of Alekelia and the cold hardness he'd seen in her eyes.

"I'd be interested in listening," he said gently. "It's part of my calling—to listen. But if it's too painful, I'll understand."

Allyndra studied him for a moment, then turned back to the ocean.

"I was married once," she said quietly.

There was a long pause, and Stephen began to think she wouldn't say any more. He was about to speak when she finally began.

"My husband, Gerrin, was from House Hi'ilar—the artisans. He was a painter of some renown, known for his delicate pigment work in water."

"Watercolors," Stephen said softly. "We have something similar."

She gave a small nod of acknowledgment.

"It was near this very place," she continued, "that he painted the portrait you've seen on my wall. He finished it the night of my first—and only—matron flight."

"Matron flight?"

"We bear our young in the ocean," she explained, "where they spend a year developing before they return to us."

"Fascinating. Sorry—I didn't mean to interrupt."

Allyndra smiled faintly.

"I remember sitting there while he painted. I was irritable, heavy with the fruit of our love. He laughed at me and said, 'Come, smile, my love! See—the Lock and Key are aligned. Tomorrow, the Twins will be kissing.' I remember looking up at that bright white point of light. I teased him: 'The Twins kissing brings change, not fortune!'"

Stephen leaned forward.

"The Twins kissing—what do you mean by that?"

"Once every few hundred years, the Lock and the Key align," she said. "Then the Twins—the two suns—can kiss."

"Ah," Stephen said, intrigued. "It must be the two massive planets we passed earlier. When they align, the stars exchange plasma. That must be quite a sight."

He smiled.

"Would you tell me the story? I'd love to hear it. I recorded the tale of the Trellium silk, remember?"

Allyndra gave a graceful shrug.

"Very well. It's only a child's tale, but this is how it goes.

"'Long ago, there were two lovers. Their love was so deep and true that even the gods grew jealous. To punish them, the gods placed the lovers in the sky, where they could see each other but never touch. Yet their love did not fade—it grew stronger and brighter until, with a burst of light, they outshone even the gods themselves. The Queen of Night saw what had been done and pitied them. Though she could not undo the curse, she softened it. She decreed that when the Lock and Key aligned, the lovers—the Twins—would be allowed to kiss once more. And she refashioned the moon into the rings, so all would remember that the gods must never again sunder true love.'"

Stephen smiled gently.

"That's a lovely tale."

He hesitated before adding, "You said you *were* married once—and mentioned your matron flight. What happened?"

Allyndra's eyes closed tightly, pain etching her features.

"When I left for my matron flight, Gerrin had to take a skyship to paint a portrait for another Guild House. As I returned from the sea, exhausted, the Twins were rising—and they were kissing."

Her voice wavered.

"When I reached the House—" she nodded toward the great spiral structure on the promontory "—Mother O'lathe herself was waiting for me. She took me into her arms and told me that the skyship Gerrin was on had been struck by lightning and set ablaze. If only he'd had wings of his own."

What a way to die, Stephen thought. *Burn or fall.*

He wanted to reach out, to hold her, but he had learned these people did not welcome touch unless invited.

We've both lost those we loved. The ache stirred something he had kept buried—he hadn't truly grieved for Sandra. *What's wrong with me?*

"A year later," Allyndra continued, "I returned to gather our K'tareth from the sea, but none ever came. I stayed long past hope."

Her voice trembled as she said, "It was Mother O'lathe again who comforted me—who dried my tears and mourned with me when my children were lost to the sea."

Stephen saw tears streaming down her cheeks. He said nothing.

"I devoted myself then to the oldest parts of the archives," she said softly, "to the fragments of knowledge from the age of the A'ksu—and to water dancing. Mother O'lathe thought naming me Mother of the House would make me rejoin the world. Now, I suppose I needn't bother. I imagine Alekelia will be content if I disappear into the dust and the old books forever."

I can't stand it anymore, Stephen thought. *We both need comfort.*

He reached out and pulled her close. She resisted for a moment, then finally yielded, her body trembling against his.

"Thank you for telling me, Allyndra," he murmured. "I'm so sorry about your husband—and your children. I don't have any children either. I had a wife once, but the pod she was in failed. We'd hoped to start a new life together on Big Blue."

Allyndra reached for his hand, her touch light but sincere.

"May the Twins bless her," she said softly. "And when the time comes, may you be reunited to dance together as the Twins do."

Her words surprised Stephen, but he could feel the truth in them.

"Thank you," he said quietly. "And, if I'm not overstepping— may you dance again with your husband as well."

Stephen's curiosity stirred again.

"Allyndra, I'm still amazed at how quickly you learn things. We've never recorded anything like it among humans. A few people show exceptional abilities, but usually at the expense of other skills. What was the word you used for it—Ak'su?"

"A'ksu," she corrected gently. "The stop is on the *A*."

She released his hand and gave a faint smile.

"You're improving."

"Ah! I still struggle with those glottal stops," he said with a chuckle. "You mentioned it applies to those who learn quickly. I remember you told me what it meant, but I've forgotten. It also sounds a little different from the rest of your language."

She regarded him thoughtfully.

"It is. It's from the old tongue—something like your ancient English. It's no longer spoken and nearly forgotten. Only fragments survive that a few of us still use. The literal translation of *A'ksu* is 'dangerous.'"

"Dangerous?" Stephen frowned. "But why? I'd think it would be a gift. Even Captain Hila'ar learned a little English in just a few hours."

Allyndra turned her gaze toward the sea. Her voice dropped, soft and distant.

"The ability to learn quickly is only part of it. The trait also includes the capacity to make intuitive leaps—to connect ideas that others can't. It's said that, long ago, our people bred for that ability. But there was a flaw. Those who had it couldn't foresee the consequences of their actions. Some believed the trait should be encouraged, that progress was worth any risk. Others feared it would destroy us. Eventually, we turned on one another. The wars that followed nearly ended our world."

Stephen listened silently as she continued.

"When the fighting ended, a few survivors realized that no one should ever hold all the knowledge—or power—alone. They built our society anew, binding it together so that every group depended on the others. That's how the Great Houses were formed, each with its own purpose to keep the balance."

She gestured toward the bright water of the bay.

"We also learned that we had outgrown what our world could sustain. We protected the *K'tareth* in the sea, allowing nature to choose how many would return. Now the ocean takes what it takes, even when it breaks our hearts."

She murmured a phrase, her tone reverent.

"Oa k'ano o kala honua."

Then, turning back to him, she translated softly, "The way of the world."

Remarkable! These people—unlike us—recognized that their society was overpopulating and depleting its resources, and instead of pushing further, they simply chose to stop and change. We built technology to escape our own world. I wonder if Carl Sagan was right—that once a civilization gains the power to destroy itself, it inevitably does. This is the first time we've ever seen proof either way.

Allyndra stood, brushing the sand from her legs and wings. Stephen rose more slowly.

"I'd like to know more," he said.

The woman turned her faceted eyes toward him.

"*Ha'iela mākouua i uā mea i hale i mea o mālamia o i ke wā e liki mai anamai,*" she said sharply, then turned and walked away.

Stephen watched her go and shook his head.

I guess I crossed some kind of line. Diplomacy isn't exactly my field. He sighed. *She didn't even bother to translate.*

He waited a few minutes, not wanting it to look as though he were chasing after her, then brushed the black sand from his clothing. The suns were sinking toward the west, and it was nearly time for the evening language sessions.

Maybe one of the others can tell me what she said.

He also needed to contact Conner. The last message from the ship had mentioned serious problems. *I wasn't sure how much longer I could stay. The only thing keeping me here is that the shuttle's still not operational.*

Stephen hurried back to his quarters to wash and change. He'd learned quickly that cleanliness was highly valued among the Allidians. They didn't perspire; instead, they panted lightly when overheated.

With respiration that efficient—more like Terran birds than mammals—it makes sense. Not wanting to offend, he made a point of showering often.

The Allidians had running water—hot and cold, or at least *warm*. The Twins' heat was harnessed to warm water piped from nearby streams using gravity, a system surprisingly similar to the ancient Roman aqueducts. He'd learned just enough about it to admire the simplicity.

Having shaved that morning, he only needed to wash up. His uniform hung in the small closet, but he chose the light shirt and trousers he'd been given—woven from a breathable fabric much like linen. Once dressed, Stephen moved quickly.

Punctuality, he'd discovered, was another thing the Allidians prized highly. Any tardiness or mistake could earn a verbal reprimand. Stephen hadn't seen any corporal punishment, though Allyndra had told him it existed—rarely.

She had explained, *"The world can be harsh enough. Why should we add to its cruelty? Shame within the House is punishment enough."*

So ostracism works as social control, Stephen mused. *Likely another byproduct of their stratified society. I'll need to talk to the anthropologists—if we have any left on board.*

He finished getting ready with a few minutes to spare and was straightening his shirt before the mirror when a knock sounded at the door.

Turning, he said in his best Allidian, "Please enter."

The door opened to reveal another student—Rel'iya. Stephen smiled. He liked her; she was curious and talkative, and her questions made the long lessons less tedious.

"Are you ready?" she asked.

"Yes. Is it class time already?"

"Soon," she said, stepping inside. "I thought I'd stop by first. I'd like to learn more—to write a paper on your kind eventually."

"Of course."

Stephen watched as she sat on the edge of the bed. Among the Allidian women he had met, Rel'iya was more physically endowed than either Allyndra or Alekelia. Her hair, black like most of her people's, gleamed with metallic green streaks, and her eyes were a bright amber—a color he'd noticed was quite common here.

She had once explained that their breasts functioned much like human mammary glands but also played a critical biological role. The milk produced after childbirth contained hormones that determined the fate of their offspring—the *K'tareth*. Those chemical cues, combined with the mother's status within the House, decided whether a child became female, a fertile male, or an infertile male.

Maybe that's why a reprimand works so effectively, Stephen thought. *It doesn't just affect one's standing—it could shape the next generation.*

He had also learned that while female offspring were highly valued, they were often lost during what Rel'iya had called a *matron flight*. During this ritual, mothers flew to designated areas over the sea to bear their children. A sudden storm could exhaust them, rough waters could drown them, or an ocean predator might strike. Many never returned.

Stephen had once asked why they didn't use the skyships instead, given the dangers.

Rel'iya's reply had been simple. It was to *keep the balance.*

That phrase—*the balance*—seemed to guide everything in Allidian society. Stephen made a mental note. *Conner and the others need to understand just how deeply that belief runs if we're ever going to communicate effectively with them.*

Stephen felt comfortable enough with Rel'iya to ask about the phrase Allyndra had spoken earlier.

"Earlier today, Mother Allyndra said something to me. I still can't understand your language as well as I'd like, and I was hoping you could help."

Rel'iya laughed—a light, melodic sound, though not as musical as Allyndra's.

She's not a trained singer like Allyndra, Stephen thought.

"Of course," she said. "Do you remember any of it?"

Stephen frowned, trying to recall.

"Only part of it. Something like *Ha'iela mā...* I think."

Rel'iya looked surprised but recited smoothly, "*Ha'iela mākouua i uā mea i hale i mea o mālamia o i ke wā e liki mai anamai?*"

What a mouthful!

"Yes, that sounds right."

Rel'iya shook her head.

"That's the old language. It isn't spoken anymore. Only Allyndra probably knows more than that single phrase."

"You seem to know it," he said.

"We were all taught that phrase and its meaning as children," she explained. "It's the only part of the old tongue that any of us still learn."

"You said you know what it means?"

"Yes. It translates to, *'We put away the past in order to preserve the future.'* It comes from the time of the A'ksu."

Stephen nodded slowly.

So Allyndra was telling me to stop digging into their past—to let it rest.

"Remarkable," he said aloud. "Your people changed so completely after that time. I wonder what might have happened if we had done the same."

Rel'iya tilted her head, her amber eyes steady.

"Then you would not be here," she said softly. "You would have had no need to intrude where others live—or to interfere with how a world finds its own balance. Your presence here already disturbs ours."

There it is again—the idea that balance must always be maintained. Allyndra, despite losing her husband and children, had accepted that the world sometimes demands something in return. *It's not a one-way street; you can't just take and take without giving back.*

He thought further. *That must also explain why Allyndra wasn't curious about other worlds. Each one should be left alone to evolve in its own way. The cultural team back home would have a field day with this.*

"It wasn't our intention, Rel'iya," Stephen said aloud. "We're here by accident. But there's no way for us to leave."

And even if we could, he thought grimly, *how long before word spread and others came? That could still happen.*

"That's what the Mother says," Rel'iya replied. "I suppose we'll have to find a new balance."

She repeated the phrase Allyndra had once used.

"It's the way of the world."

"I hope so. We could offer you new technology—make life easier," Stephen suggested.

"Perhaps," she said thoughtfully. "But to find balance here, you may have to do as we once did—put away your past. Forget what you were, embrace what you must become, and find a new future."

She pointed with her chin toward the doorway.

"Our break is over. Time to learn more language."

Stephen stood and offered her his hand. Once she was up, he bowed slightly.

"Thank you, Mother, for enlightening me."

Rel'iya smiled and dipped her head.

"You're learning. Very good," she said in her own tongue.

Stephen responded in kind.

"Thank you."

They returned to the classroom and took their seats as another long session began.

But Stephen's mind wasn't on the lesson.

Will we ever be able to let go of so much—to fit in here?

Allyndra had been right. Humanity's history didn't offer much hope for that.

I need to report what I've learned to Conner—and find out what's happening with the ship.

***

After hours in the classroom, Allyndra finally called an end to the session. Exhausted, Stephen returned to his assigned quarters and pulled out the comm device. It looked vaguely like an old walkie-talkie, though with far greater range.

Conner's voice crackled through almost immediately.

"Hey, Doc. You're just about past check-in time."

"Sorry, Captain. They've been taskmasters with the language lessons."

"Hope you're getting something out of it. Anyway, it's been a shit show here. I've thought about pulling you back, but without a shuttle running, you've been stuck where you are. That's about to change."

"You've got a shuttle up?"

"Yeah, finally. We'll be sending it over in the morning. We're getting all kinds of warnings about a potential meltdown in one of the sub-light engine reactors. I need everyone up here in case it blows. That brings up another problem—we might have to start evacuating people off this island. Maybe even from where you are."

"They've got a Council that would need to approve that," Stephen said.

"Well, tell them to get it together. If we have to abandon this place, I need a plan."

"It'll take time. Their ships aren't fast, and neither are the flyers—the women who travel between islands."

There was a long pause before Conner replied.

"You've got no more than a week. Maybe less."

"Yes, Captain."

"Good. See you tomorrow."

"Night, Captain."

The comm clicked off, leaving Stephen staring at the dark screen.

"Crap," he muttered. "I'd better find Allyndra."

***

Stephen stood with Allyndra and Alekelia, along with several attendants, waiting for the shuttle. He had already told Allyndra that he was being recalled—that the situation back at the human ship was becoming desperate. He wasn't sure what she had said to Alekelia to bring her here, but he was grateful for her presence.

A sudden sonic boom rattled the ground and the nearby structure, causing the attendants to gasp and look around in alarm.

"Earthquake?" Alekelia asked sharply.

Before Stephen could answer, a shadow swept across them. He looked up and chuckled.

Switching to English—since he didn't trust his command of the Allidian language—he said, "No, one of our ships."

The shuttle descended through the humid air. By human standards, it wasn't large, but it was roughly the size of the *Wind Dancer* that had brought him here—about fifty feet long, sleek and gray against the double suns.

The Allidians watched, wide-eyed, as it dropped vertically and settled gently before the House.

All except Allyndra—she only smiled faintly.

Stephen caught her leaning toward Alekelia and saying quietly, "You see, Mother? Things will now change. We must prepare for a new world."

Alekelia gave only a small nod, her gaze still fixed on the shuttle.

"Fair winds, Stephen," Allyndra said in English, her accent soft but clear. "I think you've managed to shake the Mother here out of her complacency."

"Thank you, Allyndra. It's been a pleasure learning from you. I hope all goes well—until we meet again."

Allyndra lifted a hand in farewell as Stephen stepped aboard the shuttle. The craft rose, engines humming, and the ground fell away beneath him.

I hope so too, Allyndra thought, watching the vessel climb into the bright sky. *Why do I feel, as Mother O'lathe once did, that everything now balances on the edge of a blade? A tilt one way or the other—and it could all come apart.*

Chapter 8

House Warraquim

Allyndra

Allyndra hurried to the hastily convened Council meeting. The two of them had drafted letters and sent them by fliers to as many Houses as could be reached. Not all would arrive before Stephen and the rest of his shipmates. As she descended the spiral ramp toward the tables set for the gathering, she smiled at the extra carvings, tapestries, and the like hung for the occasion.

Alekelia is trying to make an impression—on both the Council and the humans.

At the hall, the Mothers were already gathered. The tables had been rearranged into sections. One half a semicircle with the Mothers seated along its curve, the other half left empty, awaiting the human contingent. Allyndra stepped into the slight hollow of the semicircle and dipped a deep curtsy. She had never seen so many Mothers assembled—not even at a High Summer matchmaking dance.

This is almost a full Council meeting. I see all the major Houses, but some are missing.

When she straightened, her attention fixed on the Mother of her House.

Alekelia tilted her head.

"Thank you, daughter, for being here and for your information. We must use what little time we have to answer questions rather than worry over formalities."

Thank the Twins—she's acting more like a Mother should. The shuttle landing has finally impressed on her the enormity of the situation.

"Yes, Mother. Mothers, by your leave, I've sent as much background as I could as you arrived, but I will attempt to inform you to the best of my ability."

Mother He'a of the Lakalla—the weavers—wasted no time.

"Allyndra," she said—she did not use *daughter*, as Allyndra belonged to the House of Warraquim, not her own. "You have been to the place—or ship—of the strangers, as you called it. According to your letter, you said their world has died, and thus they have fled in search of a new home, and now they are here. Further, you state that they have a history of violence. Is that true? Elaborate as much as you can on what you learned."

"Yes, Mother illm Lakalla, these people are indeed accustomed to violence," Allyndra began. "From what I could gather before I was cut off, they have a long history of harming one another. They fled because their world became poisoned and unlivable, and so they sought a new home. Their arrival here was not intentional—their destination was elsewhere. A malfunction in their means of propulsion, and then a type of machine that can think, to some extent, directed them to the nearest habitable world. The ship was damaged during its arrival and landing. The human Stephen has told me that many of their systems are failing, and they are in trouble."

The Mother of Lakalla waved a dismissive hand.

"Yes, yes, but what of them now? That was their past. What of the present?"

"From what I could tell, they made mistakes they could not recover from. I think they've learned from them, but I am not certain they truly understand how to live in balance with a world."

"And we would have to teach them a new one."

The Mother made a face.

"You said, Allyndra, before you were cut off?" Mother He'a pressed.

"Yes, Mother He'a."

Allyndra inclined her head. She had already addressed the House once. There was no need to repeat it.

"Their 'computer'—a marvelous device that holds vast knowledge, which can be accessed almost at will—shared much information once I learned some of their language. But later, when I tried to inquire further, I was told that access was restricted. I couldn't learn more."

"So these strangers did not want you to see everything," Mother He'a said sharply. "They are hiding things from us! You see, Mothers? They cannot be trusted. They destroyed their own House and now seek to move into ours!"

"Mother He'a," said Mother Ti'iha evenly, "while that is concerning, perhaps they have learned. If I understand correctly, they've come a long way, and we have given them no benefit of the doubt. Besides, let me ask Allyndra—"

She turned toward her.

"You say they possess technologies far beyond ours. Does that extend to weapons as well?"

Allyndra nodded.

"Yes, Mother illm La'Gave. A device I had never seen before injured me—from a distance. I do not know exactly what they have in their restricted areas, but it is clear their capabilities are formidable. The very fact that they could cross such vast distances, from one star to another, is a marvel. From what I learned, they have devoted much of their history to developing weapons."

"I see. Then, Allyndra, give us your assessment after being with them," Mother He'a said, absently tapping her finger on the wooden table, the sound like a soft drumbeat.

"Yes, Mother He'a. These strangers at first hurt me accidentally, but they realized their mistake and took care of me."

A murmur rose among the Mothers, but curiously, it was Mother He'a who clapped her hands for silence.

"Stop. Let's hear the rest of the story. Continue, Allyndra."

Allyndra couldn't help noticing Alekelia's face twist momentarily in anger—this was *her* House, not He'a's.

"They had just landed, with many of their people injured. Their captain—a mother, much like our own skyship captains—wasn't sure what I was or whether I posed a threat. I took it as a mother protecting her young."

That seemed to calm the rest somewhat.

He'a once again drew the Council's attention, then paused before turning back to Alekelia. The latter appeared satisfied at being acknowledged and gestured for Allyndra to continue.

"They treated me well, though they are curious about us. They find us fascinating, yet some of our traits are repulsive to them. For instance, the drinking of blood is, from what I can tell, a strong cultural taboo.

"As for what has happened to them—yes, they have made grave mistakes. Have they learned from them?" Allyndra gave a rolling shrug that set her wings rustling. "I believe many have, but they are also desperate. From what I understand, their ship is so badly damaged that it cannot travel farther—it's useless to them now.

"That they possess power should be clear. An armed and desperate creature, backed into a corner, will fight with everything it has to survive. Can we share this world with them? I don't know how much balance the world can bear. And I'm not sure what we can do if we say no—and they say yes."

"So, we should seek as much compromise as possible, Allyndra?" Mother Ti'iha asked, concern evident in her tone.

"That's not for me to decide, Mother Ti'iha."

Allyndra made a small bend of her knees in respect.

"Of course not! That isn't my point!" Ti'iha snapped. "You've indicated they are desperate—and desperate creatures do rash things! How many of them are there?"

"That is perhaps one thing they did wrong."

Allyndra took a breath before continuing.

"While I could no longer access certain records, the area of the ship I was in—a medical section where they studied me and allowed me to learn a little about them—gave me access to other data. Approximately five hundred and fifty are still alive on board."

There was a sharp intake of breath among the Mothers, but Allyndra held up a hand. She needed to finish, even if it seemed rude.

"Almost all of them, however, are asleep. I don't fully understand it, but they are in some kind of induced, profound sleep—where the body is minimally active yet preserved."

"Almost like being caught in a snowstorm in the high peaks," Alekelia offered. "Except that death does not quite come, if I understand correctly."

"You are correct, Mother."

Allyndra gave a brief nod.

"I would imagine you would know," Alekelia continued, "having once been found delirious in a blood-flower farmer's field long ago."

He'a banged the table sharply to regain attention.

"We've no time for such things!"

She pointed—an almost unheard-of gesture—at Allyndra.

"How long would it take to wake them?"

"They had already begun the process," Allyndra replied. "I would say a few hours, and then a few days more for them to fully recover."

"Then the full complement could soon be awake. This isn't good news."

Ti'iha turned her head toward Alekelia.

"What are we to do, then, Mother of Warraquim?"

Alekelia blinked in confusion before finally saying, "Let's see what happens."

"What happens? That isn't a plan, I'd say!" Ti'iha retorted.

Then, breaking decorum, she turned to Allyndra.

"And you—what do you think?"

Allyndra was taken aback.

To address her directly, bypassing the Mother of her House, was an insult. Still, as Alekelia began to speak, Ti'iha waved her down and appealed to the rest of the Council, insisting that Allyndra had more firsthand experience than the Mother of Warraquim. After a brief murmur of agreement, Alekelia's jaw tightened, anger plain on her face—but she gestured for Allyndra to speak.

Allyndra drew a deep breath.

No doubt I'll get an earful from Alekelia after this session— but it isn't my fault.

"I hope they have learned from their past," she began. "There are regions Pa'hole has newly created that might sustain them— though not all. They are on a small island now, which I believe we should allow them to keep. But we must emphasize that this world must remain in balance. Its resources are limited.

"While they have not said it outright, I sense that some of them do not think much of how well I've learned their ways. I know their ship is gravely damaged, and they rely on it for survival, which means they cannot leave. They are short on resources—making them dangerous.

"So, I believe we must listen to their words carefully when they arrive. Weigh what they say. Appear cooperative. The problem is that they possess things we do not—advanced weapons, flying machines they call *shuttles*, and more. If they choose to act with force, there will be little we can do but bend to their will—for the moment."

Ti'iha interrupted.

"You say *for the moment?*"

"Yes, Mother. While they have a House's worth of people, we could possibly overwhelm them with sheer numbers. As I've said, they seem to have learned, but from what I know of their history, there will probably be factions. Like us, some of them will think differently from others. Some may be willing to cooperate; others will not. I urge great caution, but we cannot resist as we are."

Allyndra's voice took on a sterner tone.

"It will be difficult. We must begin to observe, plan, and prepare. We should be conciliatory in our words, but I urge the Houses to devise ways to resist if the time comes and to determine when the strangers are most vulnerable."

She closed her eyes briefly.

"Perhaps even see whether, from the time of our conflicts, there is anything that could help us. We should prepare for conflict again, even if it means death."

Alekelia sprang to her feet and struck the table with the flat of her hand.

"The words of an A'ksu—go into conflict once more. And how would that go, daughter?"

Her tone dripped like heavy blood-flower juice.

"You can read only a little. How long did it take you to piece anything together? Dusty, forgotten records! And now you speak of death and destruction! That you are A'ksu should be obvious to this Council—those are the words of one of those detested beings!"

She wrinkled her nose in disgust.

A brief discussion followed about what Allyndra had said and the Mother of her House's response. Ti'iha turned to Allyndra again.

"And what if they appear reasonable but are later found to be liars?"

"As I have said, there are roughly five hundred and fifty of them," Allyndra answered. "From my study, it takes them many of our years to reproduce a functioning being. We outnumber them several times over. They sustain injury and do not heal as we do. They possess technologies that compensate for their smaller numbers, though. Still, I stand by my recommendation: we bend at first, then find when and where they are most vulnerable. We may become desperate and be forced to resort to old ways—or invent new ones."

Allyndra stared directly at Alekelia.

"I am A'ksu, and yes, Mother, I foresee things we might have to do, even if they are repugnant to us."

"You mean to kill others once more?" Ti'iha asked quietly.

"Yes—to kill, if need be. It's not what I would hope for, though we might even consider turning to House Wussuru and seeing if they have anything."

Again there was a sharp intake of breath, followed by murmured discussion. Wussuru was a small House—if one could even call it that. The name came from an old word meaning *those who refused*—those who had rejected the new ways.

Ti'iha spoke again.

"You mean to see if they know of anything we might use—as the House that Refused."

Before Allyndra could answer, Alekelia half-rose and shook her head sharply.

"Allyndra!" Her tone was cutting. "You will not speak of weapons, fighting, or conflict in anyone's presence again, you miserable A'ksu. We'll see what these people have to say and do. As for you—when this session is finished, you will confine yourself to those dusty archives you love so well. It was useful having an A'ksu learn about these strangers, but this has gone too far!"

"Yes, Mother." Allyndra infused her reply with humility.

Alekelia sat back down, clearly annoyed.

To Allyndra, it seemed not entirely because of her words, but because several of the Mothers had listened to *her* more closely than to Alekelia—as though Allyndra, not Alekelia, were the Mother of House Warraquim.

I'll be more than happy to return to the old archives, she thought. *I want to understand that ancient past I'm so often accused of belonging to.*

"Very good," Alekelia said briskly. "The strangers will arrive soon. Let's take a short break before we endure another round of listening. I, for one, am thirsty—and this outfit does nothing to keep me cool."

She stood, and the rest of the Mothers rose with her, drifting toward the refreshment tables.

While Allyndra remained by the Council tables, Mother Ti'iha approached with two cups of blood-flower juice, one in each hand, and offered one to her.

"You'll need the energy to translate."

"Thank you, Mother Ti'iha."

Allyndra accepted the cup and took a sip after Ti'iha did. The chilled blood-flower juice was wonderfully refreshing, the sweetness lingering on her tongue. It was among the best she'd ever tasted.

Ti'iha took another sip of her drink.

"Did you mean what you said?"

"In what way, Mother Ti'iha?" Allyndra asked carefully.

She knew she shouldn't discuss anything said during Council without her Mother's permission.

"That we may have to resort to conflict again," Ti'iha said flatly, her tone severe.

"Yes, M—" Allyndra began.

"We are speaking as two people," Ti'iha interrupted softly. "Forget all those titles."

She made a small gesture and glanced around; the others were still occupied in conversation.

"Yes," Allyndra said quietly. "I meant it."

Ti'iha nodded, satisfied that they would not be overheard. She was silent for a moment, lost in thought.

"Allyndra, if things do not go well, I suggest you go to the Wussuru order. I know you are not of my House, and I have no right to command you, but something feels wrong."

Her gaze drifted toward Alekelia.

"I do not trust that your Mother will guide us properly. Why she was chosen as Mother over you, I cannot fathom. I knew O'lathe well, and that decision does not sound like one she would have made."

She gestured vaguely, her expression grim.

"From what you've said, your counsel shows greater wisdom. We must play the game but prepare for the worst. As for Wussuru—take this as advice from one who has a sense for when things are amiss."

Mother O'lathe would have said much the same, Allyndra thought. *She could always tell when something was right—or when it wasn't. The wisdom to see through false words and hidden motives.*

"House Wussuru?" Allyndra asked aloud. "I know I mentioned that odd, almost religious order. From what I understand, they make clothing and trade a little, but I'm not sure they have anything more than we do—perhaps even less. It's been so long since those old conflicts."

She couldn't help but wonder why Ti'iha had brought them up.

"Yes, but go there," Ti'iha urged. "You said it yourself—they might possess something even Warraquim has forgotten. They are, after all, the ones who refused."

Ti'iha laid a hand gently on Allyndra's arm.

"It's only advice because..." She hesitated, her eyes flicking again toward Alekelia. "I don't think Alekelia knows what to do. She's new to being a Mother, and I'm not sure she ever will fit the role. As you know, Warraquim holds great influence—but I wonder..."

Her voice trailed off as Alekelia turned and began moving toward them, her expression sour and suspicious.

Wonder what?

"Mother?" Allyndra began, wanting to know more about Ti'iha's cryptic remark—but she saw Alekelia approaching, suspicion etched on her face.

Ti'iha leaned close and whispered, "We never spoke to each other except on matters of obedience. Is that clear?"

Alekelia reached them.

"What are you two talking about?"

Her question was sharp, her eyes darting between them.

"Mother Ti'iha reminded me that I must watch what I say and how I say it—that I was being dishonorable to my House," Allyndra replied smoothly. "She is, of course, quite correct, Mother."

She dipped into a respectful curtsy to both women.

Alekelia studied them for a long moment, then exhaled through her nose.

"Thank you, Mother Ti'iha, but I shall deal with my daughters in my own House."

"Yes, Mother of Warraquim. I've overstepped," Ti'iha said evenly. "However, I cannot stand unruly daughters."

She gave Allyndra a deliberately stern look before moving off to take her seat at the table.

Alekelia watched her go, then gestured toward the cup in Allyndra's hand.

"Finish that—and then get yourself ready."

A sudden, echoing *boom* sounded from outside. Alekelia turned toward the door of the House.

"They've arrived," she said, her voice as cold as mountain snow. "They'll be here shortly."

A few minutes later, Stephen entered, now back in uniform. He mimicked the gestures of the other male who served as the Voice and even managed a few words in their language. After a brief exchange between them, the rest of the Earthers followed, and Stephen took his place among them.

Alekelia took a moment to introduce the members of the Council, and the one Allyndra knew as Conner did the same with his contingent.

Without much delay, Alekelia asked directly, "So, what is the purpose of your visit here? Allyndra has told us that you come from far away, seeking a new home. Why have you decided on this one when it is already occupied?"

The implication—*why not move on?*—was unmistakable in her tone. Allyndra winced inwardly as the Mothers exchanged puzzled glances.

Alekelia, that is not the way to start this. Didn't you listen? Can't you see?

Conner seemed taken aback by the bluntness of the question. Two of the men with him immediately grew alert, their hands sliding down to rest on the instruments at their sides.

Stephen shook his head slightly.

"See, Captain? I told you—they learn fast. I'm guessing Allyndra briefed them on what she learned aboard the *Reliance*. Minds like sponges."

Conner shot him a sharp look, then turned his gaze to Allyndra.

"Maybe I should've made sure to mount you as a trophy on the wall."

He gave a half-shrug before refocusing on Alekelia.

"All right then. If we're going to be direct, let's be direct. I like that—no BS. If *she*"—he jabbed a finger toward Allyndra—"told you a bunch of things, then here it is, the purpose of our visit is to find a new home. Ours died, and we sent ourselves into the vastness of space to find another. Somewhere—anywhere—else. I wasn't planning on *here*, but yeah, here we are.

"Yes, we've come a long way—a distance I doubt you could even imagine. But that's beside the point. We didn't know your people existed until we arrived. There were no signals, no signs of technology, nothing to suggest intelligent life. From our scans, your world looked untouched—alive, yes, but primitive. As far as we could tell, no civilization existed here at all.

"The bottom line is, we need a home—a new place—and this is it. Our ship is damaged beyond repair. Do you understand that?"

Alekelia glanced at Allyndra before answering.

When Allyndra nodded, Alekelia said evenly, "Yes. And you have several hundred of your kind in some form of deep sleep as well."

Conner's face hardened. He looked as if he had been stung. He turned sharply toward Stephen and Jane.

"Damn it! I told you to cut off some of the science sections!"

Allyndra spoke up as Conner and Jane exchanged uneasy glances.

"They did, Conner. However, the medical section was still open to me. I didn't focus on every detail, but it was easy enough to see the entries for what you call 'pods' in the inventory Stephen kept. Adding them up wasn't difficult."

Conner looked as if he'd been struck in the face.

Mother Ti'iha spoke next.

"If I understand correctly..."—she paused, searching for his name before recalling it—"...Conner, you shared information at first, but later decided there were things you did not wish to share. I'm curious—why?"

Conner's face flushed crimson as her words were translated. He clearly didn't like being put on the spot, and the men flanking him looked grim—at least, if Allyndra was reading their expressions correctly.

"Yes," Conner said at last, his tone clipped. "Because I didn't see the point. Your people don't have a concept of technology as we do, and she was there to learn the language. I wasn't aware of how fast she—or, for that matter, any of you—could learn things.

"If you want honesty, fine. Let's be honest with one another, shall we? My standing orders are to establish a new colony on this world—by whatever means necessary. From my perspective, it would be easy enough to enforce my orders, and my will, here. Instead, we've decided, in the interest of trying not to be..." He hesitated, then said the word, "...bastards."

The Mothers murmured among themselves, unfamiliar with the term.

"It means to do things without thought," Allyndra interjected quickly. "A kind of reckless behavior—similar to the way of the A'ksu."

"Whatever *that* is," Conner snapped, irritation flashing across his face.

"While A'ksu can learn very quickly, they act without thinking about the consequences of their actions. It isn't something we encourage anymore," Allyndra explained, noting

Stephen's odd look. "They caused great conflict. I apologize for the interruption."

She made a tiny curtsy.

"Okay, then—these whatever. Yeah, I suppose you could try to take us out here. That's a possibility, but..." Conner glanced at one of his men. "Sergeant Willis, see that decoration down there? Think you can hit it?"

A man at the far end of Conner's table laughed, rose, and lifted a device he'd been keeping at hand. There was a deafening bang and a flash. When everyone turned, a neat hole marked where the carving's eye once was.

Conner waited for the murmurs to die down, then continued.

"You could try, but there's no guarantee you'll succeed. We've got a hell of an advantage over you."

He jabbed a finger at Allyndra.

"But then again, maybe that lady learned way too much. Maybe we'll take a few of you with us. And before you get any ideas—my standing orders are if we don't signal back or return, take every shuttle with fully armed marines, come back here, and lay waste to the place."

The Mothers murmured. They did not know the word *marines*. Allyndra translated.

"Mothers—they're people specifically trained for conflict. From what I understand, they are very good at killing."

"What did she say?" Conner asked.

Allyndra repeated the translation.

The man who had fired the shot grinned and said, "You got that right, lady."

Conner chuckled and leaned on the table.

"That's the fact of the matter. So—what's your decision?" His final words were laced with a sneer.

Alekelia looked almost frozen in place. At last Mother Ti'iha spoke.

"As you said, I suppose there is little to decide, but let us confer privately for a moment," Allyndra relayed in English.

Conner shook his head.

"No deal. I need to report back soon, or whatever is decided here will be moot."

"Mother of Warraquim, what do the knowledge-keepers think?" Ti'iha asked.

Allyndra watched Alekelia struggle, then finally rouse herself.

"What can we do? I think we should extend to them a welcome here." Alekelia straightened. "There are some newly formed lands from Pa'hole's tears that you are welcome to."

Conner listened as Allyndra translated, then looked to the woman Allyndra knew as Jane.

"I think she means a couple of new volcanic islands," Jane said. "There isn't much there now, but some vegetation has taken hold. The seas are well stocked. I'm not sure how often the place erupts."

Conner made a face, then tapped the desk.

"All right. We'll take those—in the interests of cooperation. This place looks pretty good."

"You mean House Warraquim?" Stephen asked, stunned.

"Yes. We need a good base to work from, and from orbit this looked like one of the best—not merely barren rocks. So, ladies," Conner addressed the group, "pack your bags and move out, or I'll have you removed."

Silence fell in the House for several moments after Allyndra rendered Conner's words into their tongue.

Conner's glare softened for a moment.

"Look, I know it's a raw deal, but that's the way it is. I have the authority here. Stay peaceful from now on and you can live out your lives. Try anything else and I will bring a conflict you've never seen."

Allyndra translated every word, facing the Mothers.

When she finished, she made a deep, formal curtsy and asked in their language, "Mother, since the archives will not be available to me, I request your permission—and the permission of the other Mothers—to go to House Wussuru instead."

Alekelia blinked. Ti'iha worked hard not to smile, but a faint one danced at the corners of her lips as she nodded. The others caught her cue and nodded as well. Finally, Alekelia seemed to snap out of her stunned silence and notice them. She still looked out of her depth.

"Yes, you may go."

"What's that all about?" Conner demanded.

Allyndra turned to him.

"We keep our records here, and I've studied them all my life. Since I can no longer access them—and have no further use to the House—I've requested permission to go to a religious order in the mountains. Besides, I've no wish to interact with your kind any more than I must."

Conner eyed her warily, then glanced at Stephen.

"You understand any of what she said to them? I don't trust her."

"A little, not all," Stephen admitted. "But I understood she was asking permission to leave and go to that place. They call this the House of Knowledge, so I imagine she's telling the truth. She told me she studied old manuscripts—books, or what passes for them here. So yes, if we're taking over this place, there's probably little left for her to do."

"All right, little askew," Conner said, mangling the word. "Fine. Go be a nun, then."

He turned back to the Council.

"As for the rest of you—we'll be heading out. But you'd best be gone before too many more shuttles start landing people here."

He paused, his tone softening briefly.

"Once we're settled, maybe we can become some sort of friends. Sergeant, call the ship and tell them to start bringing people over from *New Hope*."

"Aye, Captain," said the one called Willis, turning to leave.

Allyndra watched him go, but her thoughts were elsewhere. She had liked Stephen and Jane, once—but that trust and friendship had sunk into the ocean's depths. She didn't know what Alekelia would do with the House—perhaps scatter its daughters among the others—but she had asked to go to the Wussuru because Mother Ti'iha had told her to. She placed her faith in that intuition.

I know it lies high in the mountains, reclusive, venturing down only to trade a wool-like fiber for what they need. Life is about to take a very hard turn.

Allyndra looked from the Mothers to the humans.

The storm has broken upon us all. What will the future bring now?

Chapter 9

HOUSE WARRAQUIM

STEPHEN

Stephen still felt as if he were reeling from the disaster of the meeting with the Mothers, even months later. He had raised his objections afterward, but Conner wouldn't hear any of it. The captain had all but bitten his head off, saying he had to do what needed to be done.

Stephen remembered the conversation vividly.

"Look, Doc," Conner had said, "while you were down here playing native or whatever it was—didn't look to me like you picked up much of the language—it's been a shit show back on the ship. The engineers say the vessel took a hell of a lot more damage than we knew. Shiela hoped to keep an easy orbit, but those rings up there killed that idea fast. We also had thrusters with leaking tanks. We came in hot and hard. I'm surprised the *Reliance* stayed as intact as she did. Shiela did some damn fine flying, considering everything that was failing.

"We got that settled, but as you know, there weren't enough supplies once everyone was awake. Luckily, your girlfriend—"

"She's not my girlfriend," Stephen had interrupted. "She's my teacher and liaison."

He'd sighed.

"At least she was, before that meeting went sideways."

"Whatever, Doc," Conner went on. "Anyway, she showed us we could eat a few things here, but that island wasn't big enough for the whole population, and the ship couldn't do much with all its problems. We started fishing, and Jane gave the thumbs-up on several species. I got a couple of inflatable boats out, but beyond that reef, there are things in the water that are nothing but teeth and mean. Fishing close in was fine—could've been better, though.

"There's a ton of damage to vehicles, shuttles, tools, replicators—you name it. I needed you, Doc. You damn well know the ship was supposed to be our base while we built infrastructure. Didn't pan out that way. Anyway, we showed up here, and that meeting wasn't what I'd hoped for. All right, maybe I was stressed out, maybe I overreacted. That one gal—what's her name? The one running the meeting."

"Alekelia?"

"Yeah, that's her. She got right in my face, and I snapped. Anyway, it's too late now. We'll figure it out later."

"Understood, Captain," Stephen had said quietly. "Still, it doesn't sit well."

Conner had been right that Alekelia had pushed too hard—but the damage was done.

The days back on the island came drifting to mind—the rush of fear as everyone worried the ship might erupt in a spectacular fireball. He hadn't even tried to inspect some of the sections that had taken the worst of the damage, knowing there was little hope of repairing the machinery. Most of it was a total loss. Even where the pods themselves weren't directly hit, the impact had ruined the fluids, pumps, and internal mechanisms.

In other cases, everything *seemed* to function, yet no matter what he or any of the other doctors tried, they couldn't revive the person inside. Those pods were sealed again and marked with a grim notation—*deceased.*

In the end, only about three-quarters of the original complement were brought back successfully. Even then, many of the last sleepers could barely stand before being shuffled off to a waiting shuttle, confused and dazed.

As the process dragged on, the ship itself began to fail. Lights flickered and died; and whole sections went without power. The air inside grew foul as more systems shut down. The days that followed were no easier—broken bones, heart attacks, infections, and countless other ailments kept him and the rest of the medical staff constantly occupied.

Finally, only he, Shelia, and a handful of others remained. Shelia had come down to the now-empty shuttle bay to see him off as he prepared to return to Warraquim. She would stay behind with a small contingent to monitor the *Reliance* and oversee its final shutdown.

Stephen knew Conner had no choice but to move people off the island, yet it still didn't sit right—especially after how things had gone at Warraquim.

"Geez, Shelia," he'd said, "why do I feel like Columbus again—coming ashore, greeted by friendly natives, and still standing there with a gun in hand to drive them off their land and kill them? Damn it, I thought we'd learned."

"So what, Stephen? We were going to *try!* We couldn't help it. We could all have been dead, and the natives left to pick through the wreckage and get radiation poisoning for their trouble. Conner doesn't like what he did."

She'd blown out a breath and gestured toward the half-buried ship.

"Look."

Her pretty face had scrunched in frustration.

"We'll try to patch things up later."

"If you were in their shoes, would you?"

"Oh, fuck off, Stephen. We'll *try,* I promise. As second in command, I'll lean on Conner to make peace again—once we get everyone settled in, figure out how things are, and even where the hell we are."

That had been a month ago, and Stephen had barely seen Shelia since—only glimpses when she came over from New Hope, as they were now calling the island, to confer privately with Conner. He hadn't had time to find out what they'd discussed. There was too much work: setting up field hospitals, finishing the revival of those still in hyper sleep, tending to the disoriented.

Some of the newly awakened simply couldn't cope. They couldn't grasp the reality of two suns in the sky, a world with rings, or even the basics of where they were. A few went berserk—violent, terrified, trying to flee into the wilderness. The Marines had been forced to put some down. Others weren't violent but wandered about blankly, almost zombie-like, functioning but hollow, their minds seemingly broken.

There was no time or technology to know whether the damage was temporary or permanent. Conner had them shipped back to New Hope—at least they could handle simple tasks, and it eased the burden on Warraquim. Maybe they'd recover. Maybe they wouldn't.

Thirty years of hibernation followed by a sudden, jarring return to life—it wasn't good for the body, and he doubted it was good for the soul either.

"Fuck," he muttered, rubbing his face. "Now I'm getting metaphysical."

And, he thought grimly, *I'm starting to sound like Jane.* Every other word out of her mouth these days was a curse.

The last time he saw Jane had been brief—when they gathered to watch the *Reliance* shut down for good.

Jane had actually shed a tear and whispered, "Goodbye, *Reliance.* Thanks for getting us here."

He'd stepped forward to hug her, but she'd turned away without a word and marched back to work.

For his part, Stephen shared her sentiment. *Reliance* had been a good ship. None of what happened was her fault. He'd raised his hand in a salute—and, unexpectedly, everyone else had followed for a moment before quietly returning to their duties.

It's a miracle we even ended up here, he thought. *Maybe Allyndra's gods really did intervene.* He paused and shook his head.

"Screw it. I'm getting too metaphysical again."

Stephen could only wonder what kind of relationship they would now have with the people of this world—a people who had shown them no real hostility, who had done them no harm. If their positions had been reversed, would *they* have done what Conner did? Perhaps, he thought, desperate people—any people—would do whatever it took to survive. Still, it hurt that it had come to this.

He'd heard that when the Mothers at the conference had departed, they had divided as many daughters and attendants among their Houses as possible. The skyships, heavy with passengers and supplies, had lifted off just as the first waves of shuttles landed. Conner had then ordered anyone still remaining to leave, using a bullhorn and one of the language students—Stephen's own student, in fact—to make it clear that everyone was to find someplace else.

From the accounts he'd heard, it had been chaos. Shuttles disgorged dazed, disoriented people who stumbled through the strange city, into abandoned Houses or makeshift shelters. Engineers rushed to establish temporary quarters, survey the area, and offload equipment. Supplies and machinery were hauled out and dumped wherever there was space, forming a landscape of confusion and noise.

The skyships came and went, carrying away most of the remnants of Warraquim until the native population dwindled—and then all but disappeared.

After returning, Stephen began hearing rumors. In one case, he even discovered Marines and a few civilians were keeping some of the natives as pleasure slaves. He had treated several of the men for infected bite wounds.

Damn, he'd thought, *I remember that time on the Wind Dancer. So I guess I wasn't just a random case. I said we were going to have problems, and now we do.*

He'd gone straight to Conner to complain—but the moment he entered the captain's quarters, he spotted a native girl lying in the bed.

"Captain, what the hell are you doing with her?"

Conner didn't flinch.

"What do you think? Shit, Doc, I remember that report you sent about the bite. I didn't believe it—but I had to check it out for myself. Damn, you're right. It's a kick in the balls. I'm guessing you didn't fuck your pretty little askew, did you?"

"No." Stephen's glare was ice cold.

"You should've. Not just the bite—the rest is... well, talented in other ways."

"I wouldn't know, nor do I care to." Stephen's voice was tight. "Shelia told me you've had to make hard decisions, and fine—I understand. But we still need to try to patch things up with these people."

Conner snorted.

"I'm not so sure they're that amendable. Those flying boats of theirs—"

"Skyships," Stephen corrected.

"Whatever. They've been hanging around here and near New Hope—where the remains of the *Reliance* are—even after most of their population left. I think they're testing us, seeing what we can do. I've had the Marines take a few shots at them, but I haven't sent a shuttle after any yet. I don't want to tip our hand."

Stephen remembered the skyships—flyers, really—coming near but never too close. Each time, they'd veered off when the Marines took potshots at them. It had all been so senseless. He still ached from where one Marine had struck him with a rifle butt when he'd tried to intervene. He'd shouted at the man that if he got himself hurt, he'd better find another doctor.

Now, several weeks later, things had settled into something like a routine. Still, the bitterness lingered. If Conner wouldn't reach out, Stephen would try one last time himself. That decision had led him here—standing in front of what had once been the Mother's quarters. Conner had claimed them for his own, and where servants had once stood, armed guards now flanked the doorway. A desk had been dragged into the corridor, and a uniformed man sat behind it.

He waved Stephen over.

"You on the list?"

"Damn right I am," Stephen said. "Dr. Stephen Banks, chief medical officer."

His eyes flicked to the walls, scarred with damage from the hurried occupation.

"All right, Doc, don't get your shorts in a bunch," the guard said with a smirk. "Captain's a busy man. Why aren't you over on New Hope, getting the zombies up and running? What do you need here, anyway?"

Stephen's tone went cold.

"We still can't determine what's wrong with them. Right now, I need to see what he wants to do about some of the critical cases. We only have so many resources."

It wasn't a complete lie. There were critical patients—and some, he knew, would never recover. But it wasn't the real reason he'd come.

He also knew the captain didn't trust him anymore—and Conner was probably right not to.

Stephen had often thought that if he'd known what kind of world they were landing on, he might have turned off the power to those pods himself. Somewhere along the way, he'd lost whatever connection he'd once felt to the rest of humanity.

The sergeant shrugged and turned to the other guard.

"All right, tell the captain the head doc's here."

The man disappeared inside for a few moments. Stephen could hear muffled voices before the guard reappeared and held the door open.

"There you go, Doc." His tone was flat.

Stephen stepped inside and found Conner seated behind a much larger desk. The curtains to the balcony were drawn open, letting in a salty ocean breeze. Sunlight sparkled on the waves beyond—a breathtaking view—but Stephen forced himself to focus on why he was there.

A faint noise caught his attention. He turned and saw a flicker of light reflecting off wings—a feminine silhouette that darted quickly through a side door and vanished. He paused, staring for a moment before turning back.

"What do you need, Doc?" Conner asked without looking up. "I don't have time for more complaints about the natives. They had their chance—they could've left. They stayed. So, what is it?"

Stephen wanted to say a great deal, but he knew it would be pointless. Conner had given them the option to go, and some had stayed—perhaps believing they could learn or coexist with the Earthlings. Arguing wouldn't change anything.

He studied Conner, noticing the man's sunken eyes and drawn features.

"Captain, I think you need a health check. We don't know what the long-term effects of their venom might be on the human body."

Conner set his pen down and looked up.

"So you're here to bitch about the boys having some fun? A few of them getting a little too frisky?" He leaned back in his chair. "To tell you the truth, I don't give a damn. In fact—" He stood, motioning Stephen toward the balcony, and stepped outside. "I'm fine. All right, I'll admit, maybe a few too many late nights with the little bug girls."

"They're not bugs," Stephen said sharply. "There are parallels to our insects, sure, but—"

"Shut it, Doc. I don't care. Go write a book. So, what do you want—other than to pester me about my choice of bedmates?"

Stephen could feel anger boiling inside him. He wished, fleetingly, that he had the strength to shove Conner off the balcony and see if the man could fly.

"I'd like to visit the remaining Houses—to see if we can start over," he said, bracing for the argument he was sure would follow from the way Conner looked at him.

Conner only shrugged and leaned on the railing.

"Look, I thought we could find an accommodation—and maybe we still can. I don't want to go down in the history books as the man who wiped out humanity's first intelligent contact beyond Earth. I know it was rough and brutal, but it had to be done. New Hope's shaping up, and there's plenty of land here. They never worked it very hard."

Stephen remembered Allyndra and the others speaking about the need for balance with the world.

"Maybe that's the point—they respected it. Allyndra always said something about keeping balance. You know, Conner, it was losing that balance that brought us here in the first damn place. Are we just going to destroy another planet?"

Conner gave him a sideways glance.

"No—but we have to plan for growth. We'll enforce a strict two-child policy. You're right, Doc—we do have to learn from the past. I really would like to make peace with the natives here."

He turned to face Stephen fully.

"So... how'd you like to be a diplomat again? You've spent time with them, learned more of their language than anyone else. That brings up another point—can you read any of it?"

Exactly what I wanted, Stephen thought.

"No. Why?"

Conner's expression shifted, almost excited.

"You should see what's under this place, Stephen. Knowledge gathering, indeed. There are books—writings—down there, stretching for what looks like miles beneath us. I had Tel'ia try to read some of it, but she couldn't. Said only the newer stuff was legible—the rest's buried in dust."

"That Allyndra—do you remember her?" Stephen asked. "She was the interpreter at the conference, the one who came aboard the ship."

"Oh yeah, the askew—"

"A'ksu."

"Whatever. She was a looker, all right. What about her? Went off to be a nun or something, if I remember right. Why?"

"She was the only one who could read some of the old texts. That was her job here."

"Why was she the only one?" Conner's tone had sharpened. For once, he seemed genuinely interested.

Stephen shrugged.

"I'm not entirely sure. Somewhere along the way, the language must've changed or drifted. She was the only one who could still make sense of any of those books. Even with her gift for learning, she said she had trouble understanding the older forms."

"Shame," Conner said. "Looks like they've had a long history. Well, maybe if you get the time, you can feed some of it into a computer—see if we can make sense of it."

"No key, no sense," Stephen said, shaking his head. "Now, you're serious about wanting me to play diplomat again with these people?"

"Yes, why not? They know things that could be useful to us. As a gesture of goodwill—tell you what—why don't you offer to return some of those dusty old books? Take a bunch with you and see if you can make a few friendly faces."

Stephen thought for a moment.

Why not? Those books must hold some value—they wouldn't have kept them otherwise. Maybe I could show them that not all humans are monsters. Maybe try to explain. And it'd get me away from here for a while.

"All right, Captain," he said at last. "That sounds good. I'll take some of those old books and head out—see if I can make things a little less hostile."

"That's the spirit, Doc! I'll authorize you a shuttle and a couple of Marines."

Conner gave him a light punch on the shoulder.

"Marines? Do I have to?" Stephen asked, grimacing.

The last thing he wanted was a pair of skittish, trigger-happy soldiers tagging along.

"Sorry, Doc, but yeah. You get to pick them, though—I can't afford to lose a shuttle."

Conner shrugged.

"Besides, show them what a real ship looks like. Maybe they'll take the hint and quit snooping around."

Would you, bastard, if you'd just lost your home? Stephen thought bitterly.

Conner was more worried about the shuttle than about him—but it didn't matter. If the locals wanted revenge, so be it. He could accept that as a small price for what had been done to them. Still, he knew what would follow.

I hope not. Conner would just use it as an excuse.

"Very good, Captain. I'll get out there and see what I can do. You'll draw up the orders?"

"Sure will. Take the rest of the day off, relax, find one of those bug girls. Tomorrow, I'll have the authorization ready. Now get your butt out of here—I think I want another bite and some rest."

"Yes, Captain."

Stephen knew he wouldn't be relaxing. He'd spend most of his time down in the Warraquim archives instead.

The Captain's going to get addicted if he isn't careful. Who am I kidding? He probably already is—and we still don't know the long-term effects. Well, to hell with him. Let's see if I can make a new start with these people—assuming they don't try to kill us the moment we land.

With that thought, Stephen turned and left, heading toward the archives.

I wonder what happened to Allyndra. Did she ever make it to the place she was going?

Chapter 10

HOUSE WUSSURU

ALLYNDRA

It had been a long journey from Warraquim up the main valley for Allyndra. Along the way to the mountains—where the Wussuru order, or rather *House*, she reminded herself, was said to dwell—she kept mostly to hiding, avoiding others whenever possible. She knew the one called Conner had granted her permission to go, but she no longer trusted the words of those aliens. At first, their technology had fascinated her. Their history, however, had disappointed her. Still, she hoped they could become friends.

I was a fool, she thought bitterly. *A stupid A'ksu who didn't think far enough ahead. I should never have trusted that humans had learned from their dying world. I should've known from their history that a Yahn't doesn't change its spots.*

What had happened at her old House had been nothing short of a disaster. Each night, as she gazed upon the Queen of Night's Promise, she wished her sisters—and even Alekelia—well.

As she trekked deeper into the mountains and slept under the chill of the thinning air, she often wondered why she had chosen to follow Mother Ti'iha's advice to seek out the Wussuru order. Shivering, she found comfort in the thought that Ti'iha always seemed to know more than she revealed.

It was a foolish impulse, she admitted to herself. *And now I'm trudging through the cold, carrying a few old books, nearly freezing to death.*

She shifted the volumes in her arms. To her, they were worth her life—even if unreadable. They were the oldest texts from the archives, and she had taken them because she didn't trust the aliens to respect such relics, even if they couldn't read them.

More than anything, Allyndra hoped the books might serve as a gift to the order about which she knew so little. She had heard whispers of them—a reclusive House high in the mountains that kept to itself for reasons few remembered.

Wussuru was known as the *House that Refused.* What exactly they had refused was lost to time—but perhaps, she thought, she might finally find out.

***

It took a month of weary days before a very tired, hungry, and bedraggled Allyndra finally arrived one evening at the valley that held the House of Wussuru. Snowflakes swirled through the air as she peered ahead, shivering violently in her thin clothing and struggling to keep herself from slipping into a torpor from which she might never wake. A faint memory of this happening before tugged at her mind, but she pushed it away and forced herself onward, finally reaching the great metal-bound wooden door. With the last of her strength, she pounded on it as the light faded.

The door opened, and several black-robed figures looked down at the frail woman who had collapsed on their doorstep. They gathered her up and carried her inside to a chamber carved into the mountain itself, where a fire blazed warmly in a stone inglenook. They laid her before it on soft, embroidered cushions hastily arranged on the floor and brought her food and drink.

Allyndra could barely keep her eyes open, but the warmth and the drink revived her enough to know she would live. She tried to thank the women who attended her, yet they only bowed in silence instead of offering the traditional curtsy. She was attempting to express gratitude to another who brought her a draft of warmed blood-flower juice when a new figure entered the room and seated herself in a nearby chair.

"They'll not speak to you, child."

The woman's voice was soft, yet it carried authority.

"I am Assura, Mother of this House. And who might you be, arriving at our door in the middle of a snowstorm?"

Allyndra tried to rise and curtsy, but her legs were too weak.

Assura reached out, steadying her with a hand on her shoulder.

"There's no need for that—at least, not until I know more."

Allyndra studied her. The woman was tall, nearly the height of an infertile male, with deep violet eyes that matched the streaks in her hair. Her bearing was regal, though her robes were plain.

"I am Allyndra illm Warraquim, Mother illm Wussuru," Allyndra said, pressing her palms together—the most respectful gesture she could manage. "There has been a disaster at my House. There—"

"Where the others from the sky came. Yes, I know."

Assura's tone was calm but knowing.

"We may be isolated, but we still trade, and stories travel faster than you, it seems. I've heard that your House was…" She paused, choosing her words carefully. "Dispersed across the world to other Houses. But tell me, why come here? Most have gone to the House of the Sky Traders."

"Mother Ti'iha of that same Guild told me to come here," Allyndra said. "She said that if anything went wrong, I should seek you—and offer these."

She gestured to the parcel she carried.

Assura blinked, then reached toward the bundle but stopped short of touching it.

"Allyndra, shall we see what you've brought?"

Allyndra handed her the parcel. Assura carefully undid the straps and drew out several ancient books, turning a few pages in each before lifting her brows.

"These are old, Allyndra—very old. They must have come from the deepest part of Warraquim. Things must indeed be dire for that House to let these go."

"They are, Mother Assura. I took them without permission. I no longer trust what the strangers will do to the library. They cannot speak our language or read it—and even I..." She tilted her chin toward the books. "Even I can only understand a portion. It is the old tongue."

Assura looked up sharply.

"You can read some of the old language?"

"A little. I was making progress when the strangers arrived. Mother O'lathe asked me to go to them—to learn what I could."

Mother Assura set the books aside gently, studying Allyndra's face.

"And why did she ask you specifically?"

Allyndra leaned back and closed her eyes.

"Because I bear the trait of the A'ksu. I can learn very quickly."

Assura reached out and touched her shoulder again, her voice firm but kind.

"Lift your head, child. The A'ksu were not the monsters the Houses made them out to be. That tale was twisted into something to frighten children. There is more truth behind it than most remember. You truly can learn quickly, then?"

"Yes, Mother Assura."

Allyndra hesitated at the tone—half wonder, half reverence.

"I learned the human language, both the one they use now and parts of an older one, along with some of their history, science, and how they came here."

"And how long did it take you to accomplish that?"

"Less than two days, Mother. I would have learned more, but there was too much—and then they wanted me to return."

"A little over a day, then."

Mother Assura sat back, studying her with new intensity.

"You must possess the full trait. I had thought it gone from the world. The gods must be working in our favor."

Allyndra frowned slightly.

Here, they think the A'ksu were good. Everywhere else, we're despised.

Assura patted the books and smiled.

"I thank you for this gift—and I welcome you here. But I ask that you give up your old House and become a daughter of Wussuru, Aribabitru Allyndra."

Allyndra hesitated, knowing this was what Ti'iha had meant—and her own Mother had not objected.

I have nowhere else to go. And here, at least, I am accepted—perhaps even honored.

"I will, Mother," she said softly, omitting her old House name in acknowledgment of her new allegiance.

Assura smiled.

"Rest, Allyndra illm Wussuru. You have had a long and difficult journey. I will see that you are well fed, and this—" she gestured toward the fire "—will warm you while you recover. We will speak again soon, Aribabitru."

Allyndra tried to stand, but her legs gave out again. The Mother gestured for her to remain seated.

"Rest here. I'll have the daughters prepare a proper room, get you washed, and put you to bed when you've regained your strength. The gods have guided you here."

Allyndra nodded faintly.

"Mother, if I may—what does the word *Aribabitru* mean? I've never heard it before."

Assura smiled and patted the books affectionately.

"It's an old word from the earliest days, daughter. It means *one who does quickly*—the ability to act or learn with speed. It was once a title of respect, before it was degraded into *A'ksu*."

She rose gracefully.

"We'll speak again when you've rested and regained your strength."

With that, she swept from the room. Moments later, the other women returned to tend to Allyndra.

*****

Months passed and the seasons changed. Allyndra shivered again in the cold, hard wind that swept down from the snow-covered peaks, tugging at her clothing. The air was sharp, and though she panted with exertion, her breath still frosted in front of her. She glanced upward to see how far the Twins had traveled across the sky and sighed. This high in the mountains, night would fall quickly, and soon the shadows of the peaks would swallow the valley.

She was exhausted, but she dreaded stumbling over the rocky path by Ring Shine alone. A misstep in the dark could mean a twisted ankle—or worse—and the chill that now merely bit at her skin would soon feel like warmth compared to what the night would bring.

"Come on!" she urged the Qwiklick, tugging on the lead animal's tether.

The creatures were not bright, but they were sturdy—large, woolly beasts covered in coarse, dark guard hair over a dense, silky undercoat. That fine inner layer could be woven into an almost sheer textile: soft, warm, and stronger than it appeared. The Order traded such wool with the small towns lower on the mountain plains, exchanging it for supplies. The beasts' packs were full of those goods now.

The lead animal refused to move, its four feet planted firmly, staring at her with large, placid eyes. Its head was level with hers thanks to its long neck, though its shoulders barely reached her waist. The creature might almost have been called cute—if not for the drool forming a long streamer that, caught by the wind, threatened to stain her clothes.

Allyndra turned to face it squarely and pulled hard on the tether, putting all her weight behind the effort. Her voice echoed against the hills as she shouted. The beast blinked once, bleated softly, and at last lumbered forward a single step—nearly unbalancing her. But as the lead animal moved, the others began to follow.

She trudged onward, the animals plodding behind. Darkness crept steadily down the slopes. She wondered if she had made the right choice coming here. No one had come looking for her after she fled Warraquim, and though the Wussuru had taken her in, they had put her to work almost immediately—tending animals and making periodic trading runs. There had been no further talk of her old House or her past.

She was growing weary of the endless cold and the silence of the mountains. Sometimes she thought of asking to leave again, but something—perhaps Mother Assura's knowing look the day she'd arrived, or the reverence with which she'd treated the old books—held her back. She had often wondered why these people had retreated so far into the mountains, but no one offered more than a polite word or two.

"How are the animals, Allyndra?" or "Can you bring back more blood-flower juice next trip?"

It was frustrating. She felt worn down.

"Come on," she muttered again, tugging at the tether.

The wind picked up as the Twins vanished behind the peaks. The beast snorted but kept plodding along at its own deliberate pace, indifferent to her urgency.

The path was well-worn but uneven. Rocks pressed through the soles of her heavy shoes, and as snow began to fall, she could think of nothing but placing one foot after the other, matching the slow rhythm of the pack behind her.

It felt like an eternity before the lead animal suddenly nudged her from behind, nearly knocking her over.

"First you don't want to move, and now you want to run me over!" she snapped.

She raised a fist in frustration but dropped it again—there was no use striking something that solid. The creature snorted once more, then nudged her lightly toward the slope. She followed its gaze to see the faint outline of the House ahead, and beside it, the stables nestled in a fold of the mountain.

"Well, never mind," she said. "A hearth for me and a warm stall for you."

By the time she finished bedding the animals down, darkness had fully fallen. The wind howled between the peaks, and she knew a mountain storm was upon them. The clouds that had gathered all afternoon were now releasing their burden, heavy with moisture drawn from the sea.

At last, she climbed the steps to her room, too tired even for supper. The hallway was narrow, lit by flickering lamps, and her small chamber waited at the far end. But as she walked, a figure stood ahead—tall, holding a lantern. From the height and the posture, Allyndra knew it was the Mother of the House. She sighed inwardly, wondering what Assura wanted with her at this hour.

"Allyndra, off to bed already?" The deep alto voice carried the calm authority that always seemed to silence a room.

Allyndra stopped and made a weary curtsy.

"If it pleases Mother, it has been a long and wearying day in the cold."

"We've not spoken since your arrival," Assura said. "I thought I might invite you to dine with me. I have a bit of news for you."

Allyndra straightened slightly, her fatigue giving way to curiosity.

"Yes, Mother."

Assura turned without another word, and Allyndra hurried to follow—her shorter, tired legs struggling to keep pace. They passed through narrow halls, past the weaving rooms, a small library, and finally a simple chapel dedicated to the Twins. Inside, a carved wooden table and two cushioned chairs stood in the unadorned gray-stone chamber. A pot of steaming liquid sat on the table, and two fresh tapers burned on the altar—one yellow, one red, representing the Twins.

Assura gestured to a chair before taking the other, then poured from the pot.

"Sweetened nectar tea, daughter. With herbs to revive you."

Allyndra took a sip. The tea was hot and fragrant, its sweetness lingering on her tongue. The warmth spread through her body, and she could feel her strength slowly returning.

"Daughter," Assura began, "Warraquim has survived—but only barely—the attack from the aliens."

Allyndra noted the borrowed human word.

"They've done all sorts of things to the new Tear of Pa'hole— the place where their ship came down. We can't get close for they drive us off. At Warraquim, there was activity for a time, but that too has slowed. Perhaps they're not used to the rain. For now, at least, they haven't moved further or taken up arms against us."

"The rainy season is upon them," Allyndra murmured. "I don't trust them, Mother. They said they had changed, but I no longer believe it."

"Perhaps."

Assura nodded slowly.

"I've heard one of them went to the Sky Traders, offering peace. He was not well received, though there was no violence. He was simply told to leave—and he did. But he left something behind—some old books from Warraquim. He said to give them to Allyndra."

Assura reached to her side and handed over a small bundle.

Allyndra ran her fingers over the covers. They were old—very old.

For all that I hate the humans now, she thought, *Stephen seems to have tried.* She sighed.

"I can't forgive what happened—not yet, Mother. Not now."

"I understand your bitterness," Assura said gently. "You spent time among them. Tell me what you learned, daughter. You are *Aribabitru,* after all."

Allyndra closed her eyes, letting her mind drift back to the ship.

She told Assura of the humans' dying world—ruined by overpopulation and imbalance, of a planet whose living systems had collapsed beneath their excess.

"They have great technology, enough to span the stars," she said softly. "There was little they could not accomplish—by force, if they so choose."

Assura listened in silence, her expression thoughtful, as though committing every word to memory.

I wonder if she is like me, Allyndra thought.

At length, Assura rose and gestured for Allyndra to follow her to the altar.

"Pay attention, Aribabitru."

She lifted the glass-covered tapers and began to move them: the yellow passing before the red, then circling behind as the red advanced. The candles continued to trade places, mimicking the dance of the Twins through their eight seasons. When the cycle ended, there was a soft *click,* and the altar—and the wall behind it—slid back to reveal a hidden chamber carved into the living rock. The air that flowed out was cold and dry, but even in the dim light, Allyndra could see shelves upon shelves of books.

She stepped forward, almost stumbling, and reached out to steady herself on the stone wall. Her fingers brushed across carved letters. She traced them slowly, recognizing the script.

"*Pa'ela mākouua i uā mea i hale i mea o mālamia o i ke wā e liki mai anamai,*" she whispered.

Assura repeated the words aloud, then asked, "Do you know what it means?"

Allyndra nodded faintly. The phrase was old—older than anything she had studied at Warraquim.

"It means, 'We hide away the past in order to preserve the future.'"

"Correct," Assura said, pleased. "You can hear the difference between the dialects. You truly are a student of the old language."

"It's not quite the same as the older phrase. Why?"

"It comes from the time of the *Aribabitru*—what is now called *A'ksu*," Assura explained. "They were people who could make great leaps of understanding, who learned faster than any others. But it was said they could not see the consequences of their actions."

"And thus the world fell into conflict," Allyndra said, recalling her studies at Warraquim.

"Yes," Assura agreed. "But there was more to it. They could see—they could understand—but others sought to use them. In the end, it was the *Aribabitru* who ended the conflicts. They set us on the path we follow now. They ensured the Great Houses rose—and that knowledge was locked away. But not all agreed to let it be forgotten. Our founders refused. They built this place to preserve the old ways."

Allyndra glanced at the shelves, realization dawning.

"You know how to read the old language, don't you, Mother?"

Assura smiled.

"Yes, daughter. We do. We kept it alive—and now you will learn it as well. That will be your task: to see if anything in these books, or in the ones you brought—or the ones the human brought—can help us both. We can read, but the trait of swift learning has long faded among us. Only I have a trace of it. You, though—you have the gift."

Allyndra barely heard her. This was nothing like the archives of Warraquim. The sheer presence of the old words, the knowledge, filled her with a warmth that had nothing to do with the tea.

If this Order still knows the old language, she thought, *what else might be hidden here—or back at Warraquim, if it still stands?*

She felt the old passion rekindle within her.

"Yes, Mother," she said, her eyes shining. "I will. I'll do whatever I can."

Assura smiled, placing a hand on her shoulder to steady her. "I can see the fire of the *Aribabitru* in you. Not tonight, nor tomorrow, daughter. First, you'll have a proper meal and rest. You have no duties tomorrow, but the day after, you will begin your studies. And you must not reveal this place to anyone."

"Why, Mother?"

"Because there are still those among the Houses who would rather this knowledge be forgotten—destroyed, if need be. They fear what it contains."

"Why would anyone fear knowledge, Mother?" Allyndra asked softly, gazing at the rows of books.

"Because it speaks truths about us," Assura replied, "truths that are painful to hear—even when they are true."

Allyndra nodded slowly.

I can't understand such thinking.

"Yes, Mother," she said aloud, running her hand once more over the carved words by the door.

Gratitude filled her heart as she looked at the ancient volumes before her. Almost everything she had endured—the loss, the exile—seemed to fade away. She could only thank Ti'iha, who had told her to seek those who had *refused*.

What will I discover? she wondered. *What secrets will be laid bare?*

Chapter 11

HOUSE WARRAQUIM

STEPHEN

Stephen had just received a letter from Mother Ti'iha illm La'Gave, who still sheltered Mother Alekelia illm Warraquim. It had been sent not by skyship—Conner wouldn't allow them too close—but by a single flyer, the only contact he permitted from each ship.

"While it is appreciated that you are attempting to reach out, you are not the Mother of your House," the reply read.

She's right, Stephen thought. *Unless Conner changes, nothing I do will make any real difference.*

He reported back to Conner, who promptly halted all excursions.

"Doc, there isn't enough fuel, and we don't have the capacity to make what we're burning. I'm scuttling any further missions unless they're absolutely necessary. You tried. They're not interested."

The first months had been frantic, but over the year everything slowed. Fuel for the machines was running low, and efforts to produce more faltered. Much of the equipment had been damaged, and they had planned to rely on the *Reliance* and her stores. When the ship failed, there had been barely enough time to evacuate people and grab what little they could. Lives first; salvage second. Repairs took time—time they didn't have.

Stephen stared toward the mountains rising from the flat plain where a town had once surrounded the Guild House, watching raw cuts being carved into the hills for more arable land. They had only just managed to plant those fields—and the ones on New Hope—before fuel dwindled to almost nothing. As expected, no help came from the natives. Conner threatened to send an expedition to seize stores from another island, but Jane reminded him the shuttles couldn't haul that much.

Instead—after consulting Jane and other scientists—they decided to use whatever resources remained to build makeshift sailing ships from timber and scrap, to harvest what the vast ocean might yield. The sea proved bountiful—until something dragged a ship under.

No wonder they use skyships, Stephen thought. *There are monsters in that water.*

Allyndra had warned him about predators; they simply hadn't grasped how big.

They salvaged and rebuilt, and overall the effort went better than not. Conner seemed steadier—helped, Stephen suspected, by the native girl in his bed. He seemed happier, if more distant. Stephen knew Allidian venom could induce powerful erotic euphoria; it was clearly working on the captain. Twice Stephen had to treat infected bite wounds. Conner wasn't alone; others had succumbed to the "pleasures," and those who hadn't escaped during the evacuation now seemed reduced to little more than enslaved companions. When Conner learned of the Allidians' *Iresemia* houses, he justified the practice by insisting the natives themselves kept places dedicated to sexual gratification.

Stephen had argued, "It's not a fair comparison. Those who worked there were not enslaved."

He'd tried to explain that while such houses existed—and yes, they served the needs of unmarried or widowed women—they were more than brothels.

Conner ignored him, clinging to the "sex houses" label to justify keeping those who hadn't fled.

Worse was yet to come. With the rainy season approaching and tents proving inadequate, Conner ordered the underground areas beneath the Guild House cleared for barracks. The books would have to go.

Stephen objected—Jane backed him, mildly—arguing there was value in the natives' past.

Conner only snorted.

"Put the books in tents. If they make it, they make it. I've got bigger problems. Didn't you tell me they can't even read them?"

Stephen had admitted that, while Allyndra had made progress, much was still beyond her. Conner seized on that. If their brightest scholar couldn't decipher them, what were the books good for besides nostalgia? They carted out what they could, but space ran out. In the end, Conner gave the order to burn the rest. Stephen watched smoke pour from the tunnels. Jane stood beside him, shaking her head.

"Shit, Doc. Maybe they didn't understand all of it, but what history they did have—is now ash. Imagine how we'd feel if aliens showed up, torched our archives, and then trashed the place."

"Like repeating the destruction of the Library of Alexandria," Stephen said.

Jane eyed him.

"Yeah. Something like that. Fuck. Why do I feel like this is going to come back on us?"

"It will, Jane. You can bet on it."

He gestured skyward.

"The skyships are flying closer. We've had more than one make a pass before peeling off. You don't think the Marines were shooting at butterflies, do you?"

"Not butterflies," Jane muttered. "You're damn right. They're probing us—seeing what we've got left. They have to know we're not flying shuttles, that our machinery's dead, and that we just burned their repository of knowledge. If you were them, and you knew we had little more than bodies and sticks and stones—what would you do?"

Stephen considered it. The closer passes, the testing. They were measuring responses. No shuttles sent to chase them; only sporadic gunfire. It wouldn't take much to realize the humans were in trouble.

"Jane, if they launched a coordinated assault, we'd be in serious danger."

"Damn right. So we save fuel for the shuttles to hit skyships with whatever we've got. Those things run on hydrogen, I'd bet— one spark and *boom*. But they're quiet, and the women can fly. They could mount one hell of an aerial attack."

"They've shown no weaponry," Stephen said. "But it's not hard to scale up a knife—or an arrow."

"They wouldn't need arrows," Jane shot back. "Rocks from altitude would wreck us—smash machinery we can't replace. Take out manufacturing and we're done. Once we're on our knees, what do you think they'll do? What would *you* do, Doc?"

"I'm not them," Stephen said quickly.

But as a human? I'd retaliate—maybe even wipe out the invaders.

Yet the Allidians had shown remarkably little taste for violence; their culture seemed built to avoid it. Still, corner any creature and it will fight to survive.

"God—if Conner knew this, he'd launch a preemptive strike. I'm not military, but I can see the logic of hitting first to intimidate and then negotiate."

"He doesn't talk to anyone anymore," Jane said. "He's off in his own world. Those native women have rotted half his brain."

So Jane's noticed it too. Stephen shrugged.

"Every time I bring it up, he just gets pissed."

"Last time I warned him about whatever they're injecting into him, he pulled a gun on me," Jane said flatly. "So fuck him. If this goes sideways, I'm out. I'll wave a white flag and hope they've got more sense than Conner does."

"Maybe I should check on him—medically. It's my job," Stephen said.

And it gives me a reason to go to Shelia if I have to.

"Good luck. If he puts a bullet in you, don't say I didn't warn you. Things are tense."

She slumped.

"Look—if you decide to bolt, I've got a skiff hidden behind some crates. Motor, batteries, ready to go. We're screwed, Doc. The Marines know it. That's why they're strutting around like they don't answer to anyone. As for the rest? Not my problem."

She jabbed a thumb at the sky.

"We got lucky. If the AI hadn't found this world within reach, we'd be popsicles drifting until we finally crashed into something."

It was as stark an assessment as Stephen could imagine. Conner had stepped in it, and they'd all come out stinking—if they came out at all. Without their tech, they were badly outnumbered. It was only a matter of time before the natives acted.

"Somehow," he began, "I don't think Conner's lost *all* sense. He has to know something's brewing. So does everyone else."

I hope he hasn't gone completely off the deep end.

Shelia might not challenge him—and she didn't have his hold over the Marines.

"Maybe he does, maybe he doesn't," Jane said. "There's a big push to conserve ammo. And I've heard talk about repurposing some of the ship's nuclear material. Lots of searches in the systems for launchers and the like. My guess? Someone's figuring a way to use explosives against the skyships. They're not fast, and a solid hit could blow the gas cells. Take out a few and maybe the natives pause. Even without shuttles, it could give us leverage."

She shook her head.

"Who am I kidding? It would probably unite the whole planet against us."

"In other words, we bluff," Stephen said.

"What else have we got? The one thing I can't figure," she added, "is why the trawlers haven't been hit. They're slow, exposed—perfect targets. If the natives sank the two we've got, rations would get *tight*."

Stephen nodded. It was the obvious move: starve them out without a pitched fight. The absence of attacks bothered him. There was so much the natives *could* do. What was Conner planning? He needed to find out.

The rumors about nukes made his skin crawl.

"Still—think what one nuclear blast at a House would do."

"Other than blow back on us?" Jane said. "We don't even know how interconnected their world is. Conner's addicted—end of story. You know how addicts decide things."

"Thanks, Jane. I'm going to talk to Conner. I'm still the doctor."

And if I have to, I'll go over his head to Shelia.

"If I don't make it, get out. If the natives pick you up, say, 'Ah kōkumai ʻiau'—it means 'help me, please.' With luck, they will."

"'With luck'?" Jane snorted. "Sure. I'll wait a bit."

She shook her head and sauntered off.

Stephen headed for Conner's quarters. He walked past the guards who barely glanced his way, as if anyone human could come and go. Inside, the walls were still blackened, the air faintly smoky even after nearly a year. Up the spiraling ramp he passed listless crew with little to do—machines idle, progress stalled. The reek of cooked fish overpowered the lingering smoke, and he wrinkled his nose. He realized he'd never smelled fish here when it was still House Warraquim. Allyndra had told him they "turned their eyes to the sky"—and with good reason. They'd already lost one boat to something huge that dragged it—and the crew— under. Conner had scrambled shuttles, but they arrived too late, and whatever it was shrugged off fire and vanished into the depths.

He reached the former Mother's rooms—now Conner's quarters and headquarters. An aide and a guard looked up.

"Appointment?" the aide asked.

"No. Medical check. I'm concerned about the captain's mental state," Stephen said, hoping it sounded convincing.

The aide grimaced, then shrugged. He nodded to the guard.

"See if the captain wants to see the doc."

The guard knocked, slipped inside without closing the door.

"Sir, the chief doc is here. Wants to see how you're holding up."

A beat of silence.

Then Conner's voice was heard saying, "All right, send him in. Couldn't hurt—and I want to see if he's made any progress."

The guard held the door and jerked his head.

Stephen entered.

Conner lounged in bed. Someone else lay beside him, asleep. In the dim light Stephen caught a glint of wings, the reddish metallic streaks of an Allidian. He kept his face neutral.

"Captain, I wanted to check on your stress levels," Stephen began. "There's been a lot to handle. I should've done this sooner."

"Really?" Conner said. "You're right—there's a lot. You know most everything is shut down. Sorry about cutting flights, but we need to keep shuttle fuel in reserve."

"Understood, Captain. I assume the plant's not producing enough for the machinery, either. Looks like most operations are on hold."

As if I didn't already know.

"Yeah. The rain makes it worse. Might as well stand down," Conner said, sitting up and lacing his fingers behind his head.

"Good call," Stephen said evenly. "I'm hearing more skyships are coming closer. I hope they're not planning anything."

"You hearing tales?"

"I spoke with Jane," Stephen said. "She's worried. We're vulnerable if the natives get bold."

Conner snorted.

"And what've you heard? Any luck patching things up?"

"No," Stephen admitted. "Nothing hostile—just… no interest in talking. I can't blame them. It could be diplomatic theater, but I doubt it. They strike me as straightforward."

"That's good to know," Conner murmured, reclining again.

"So, in your assessment—are we safe enough? A coordinated air attack could take out the boats and damage our remaining equipment."

"You've been talking to Jane," Conner said. "She's a worrier. Did she tell you what her little science club cooked up?"

Stephen shook his head.

"Well, Doc—these people here—" he patted the sleeping woman's hip; she barely stirred "—they breed in the ocean. Lay eggs—"

"Nymphs," Stephen said quietly. "They call them *K'tareth*—'precious.'"

"Whatever. They're vulnerable then, and for the next year, out there with the predators. Jane came up with a poison. Kills them straight off—"

"You *let* her experiment on their babies?" Stephen could barely breathe.

"Damn right," Conner snapped, sitting up. "We had to pull back. Those boats are vulnerable as hell. If the shoe were on the other foot, I'd use it. So I made sure they knew that if they hit us, I'd wipe out generations—poison the breeding grounds. We get a few curiosity flights, sure, but I send word by courier where things stand."

He placed a hand possessively on the figure beside him.

"Ultimatum's clear. You attack us, we take your brood stock and blow your spawning grounds to hell."

Stephen couldn't get past the fact that Jane had gone along—had experimented on what were essentially infants. No wonder he'd been kept away. He drew a breath. Arguing now was useless. He'd talk to Jane—and Shelia—later.

"I see," he managed. "About those bites—I hear you've had a couple more infections. Want me to take a look?"

Conner shook his head and jerked his chin toward the door.

"Nope. You can get the hell out now, Doc."

Stephen held his ground for a heartbeat.

"Now, Doc."

Conner's hand slid to the bedside table and came up with a pistol.

"Can't decide if I want to get frisky with this one—or do a little target practice. Not sure of the order."

To hell with you, Conner.

Stephen gave a half-salute and left. He couldn't reason with the man—but he would damn well find out what Jane had done. If necessary, he could wring the truth from her himself.

The Allidians know, he thought. *Conner admitted he warned them. He's backed them into a corner. And when that happens— the storm breaks.*

Chapter 12

HOUSE LAGAV'A

ALEKELIA

Alekelia had spent the year bouncing between Houses, trying to keep up with her scattered daughters around the world. Most of her time was with House Lagav'a, the weavers. The rest she split with the skyship guild that sailed the world. She had spent so much time near Mother He'a's quarters that she felt she might choke if she saw another Trillium-silk garment. Rare elsewhere, the fabric was common here; the looms clattered without pause, the noise driving her half mad. Still, between here and the skyship guild lay what remained of Warraquim.

That was not what troubled her most since exile. What gnawed at her were the reports—from skyships, flyers, and outlying settlements in Warraquim's former territory. She and Mother He'a, along with visiting Mothers, listened to tales of aliens terracing the mountains, carving them into steps. There was much debate over what to do, how long the aliens would confine themselves, and what would come next.

Alien, she thought, testing the borrowed word. They had picked it up easily enough.

Most skyships had been driven off—either by the aliens' weapons or by their flying machines. The same with the flyers: shot at, some badly hurt, a few killed—though most, thankfully, recovered.

Then, with the rains came the worst news of all. The aliens had carted out the books from the archives and burned the rest. The books were the very reason Warraquim existed.

Any need for us to exist as a House has been erased in a day.

Alekelia sent flyers pleading to salvage what remained, but her requests were ignored—as they had ignored that one human's plea for peace. *Human* had crept into their language, too. Alekelia wondered if, in some distant age, it might come to mean the same as *A'ksu.* She almost hoped it would. She did not hate— it was a foreign emotion—but she was beginning to understand it.

Reports followed. Human skyships no longer ventured out. The machines scarring the land had stopped. Two hastily built ships now trawled the seas, hauling in the ocean's bounty.

Alekelia set down her blood-flower juice and rose as Mother He'a entered the weavers' main hall.

"Mother," Alekelia said, nodding.

He'a waved, poured herself a mug, and sat.

After a deep swallow, He'a spoke.

"The other Mothers are coming. I know this has been hard on you. I cannot fathom such wanton destruction of knowledge. We must decide what to do."

Alekelia nodded.

In talk after talk, every Mother agreed the aliens had shown little regard for them. She could have ripped the wings from those who still counseled patience. Patience had passed.

And now they threaten the K'tareth—the breeding reefs.

She had told the Mothers the humans likely didn't know all the reefs. Poisoning the K'tareth could taint the wider sea and return to haunt the humans.

A commotion at the entrance announced the other Mothers. It was the first full council since the parlay with the aliens. Formalities done, they took their seats and waited for Mother He'a to speak—it was her House. The reminder of how far Alekelia had fallen stung.

"Council," He'a said solemnly. "Thank you for coming. There is much to discuss. We must gather our wisdom on the problem of the aliens."

Ti'iha spoke first, dispensing with ceremony.

"Indeed. You have seen that these aliens do not seek to live *with* us, only to take *from* us. But they are weak now. Their machines have stopped. Their flights have ceased. From flyers who learned some of their tongue, we know their fuel is low, and the device that makes more has limited capacity. They have built boats—may the waves swallow them—to harvest the ocean. They are short of food."

"How do you know so much, Mother Ti'iha?" Alekelia asked. "We cannot get so close."

Ti'iha snorted.

"Their men fancy our women—and cannot tell one from another. I asked for volunteers to share their beds and bring back news. Thanks to that alien's lessons, we know some of the language. I wish Allyndra were here. She would know more. But it is not to be."

Murmurs rippled—admiration mixed with disapproval. Trading favors for information was bold, but to many, it was not ethical. Mother He'a raised a hand.

"Enough. All were volunteers. Without them, we would know even less. So—given their current weakness?"

"As weak as they will be." Ti'iha said. "We can starve them by destroying their ships. If fortune favors us and we can destroy their fuel-making, we blunt their air advantage. If we can damage their skyships, so much the better."

Mother Nehia rose halfway and shook her head.

"We received a message from their 'Mother'—or whatever he is. We too, have, like Mother Ti'iha's House, sought to engage the aliens."

"Well, Mother?" Ti'iha snapped, impatient.

"That leader says if we attempt anything—especially against the sea-boats—he will poison the K'tareth and destroy the breeding reefs. He threatens our future generations. We cannot risk that."

"And what do you think will happen if they gain the upper hand *again*?" Ti'iha shot back. "Yes, we may lose a generation— we can find new reefs, and they do not know them all. They have already burned our knowledge, carved our lands, and ravaged the sea. From what I learn, their nets take everything—including K'tareth—and let it die."

She pointed—unthinkably—at Nehia.

"Tell me, Mother, when *they* breed, what then? They will expand and take what they want. What should we do?"

Nehia faltered, silent.

Mother He'a spoke.

"What you say is true. I do not believe we can negotiate— certainly not from weakness."

Alekelia rose, but Nehia spat, "I am surprised you are even here, Warraquim. There is no House left for you to Mother."

"And when they come for *your* House, Nehia?" Alekelia replied, keeping her voice steady though fury burned within. "Will you sit silent then?"

"We are artists—not keepers of old books no one can read."

Alekelia conceded the point with a sigh.

Warraquim had failed. They had allowed the old knowledge to fade until only Allyndra could decipher scraps.

"The aliens will have no use for you either," she said. "Perhaps Warraquim failed—let the books die. Fine. Let the House die. Those volumes are ash now, scattered on the wind. But I, for one, will not be the same."

He'a nodded and motioned her to sit.

"She is right, Mothers. They will not stop. We must take our chance now, while we have one. As for the K'tareth—they are not safe even now. Those boats haul everything in. What they don't want, they throw back dead. Do you think we will be better off later? When they breed and expand, what becomes of us? We act *now*."

The Mothers muttered, then stilled.

"Shall we vote," He'a asked, "or are we agreed?"

"No need," Ti'iha said. "We all hear the ring of truth. The question is *how*."

Ideas sputtered and died.

At last, Ti'iha said, "At the end of the rains, for a time, the winds shift off the western mountains near Warraquim. We will gather our skyships, sail to the island's west, then wait—after the Twins set, before Ring Rise. With full sail, we ride the wind over the western ridge into the valley leading down to Warraquim. The wind will be high so the ships will be swift. With the gods' blessing, we strike before Ring Rise."

"The mountains are high," Nehia said. "Can the ships clear them? And we have no weapons. What then?"

"We strip the ships to the decks—lighter, higher," Ti'iha replied. "Crew them with women, save perhaps a few infertile or fertile males. We carry dark lanterns. At the moment, we dive—set the ships on fire."

"On fire?" Nehia gasped. "The silk... the gas..."

She stopped, understanding dawning.

"Yes," Ti'iha said, face grim. "We burn them out as they burned Warraquim."

Alekelia allowed herself a thin smile at the vision, but a question remained.

"How do you ensure they hit the targets? Once abandoned, a ship may veer."

Ti'iha nodded.

"We will ask for a helmsman to stay—a volunteer. An infertile male first, then fertile, and if need be, a woman. It will be a suicide course. May the Twins bless them. The rest abandon ship.

We've been told a sharpened ruaru stake, dropped from height, pierces much. One wave of ships targets their shuttles and landing field at Warraquim. Another hits the fishing vessels. The last, lightest, and swiftest goes for the wreck of their own ship."

Silence followed.

Many would be hurt; some would die. To volunteer for death... and yet they all knew there was no other plan with better odds.

Alekelia nodded, then another thought struck.

"What if we use the aliens' own instincts against them?"

"In what way?" Ti'iha brightened, hoping Warraquim had some hidden leverage.

"Their healer—the one who worked with Allyndra—seemed to want peace. Invite him to negotiate."

Ti'iha snorted.

"And why would he help?"

"We make him," Alekelia said coolly. "Or see if he can fly. Their blood is said to be thick."

She smiled—a hard, unfamiliar curve.

Silence—then Ti'iha laughed.

"You are getting ruthless. Perhaps the next A'ksu. I will stand with you. We can also send a few ahead to kill and sow trouble before the skyships arrive. We have a plan, Mothers."

She turned to Alekelia.

"And how do you propose to bring this healer here?"

"I'll send my daughters. As you say, the aliens struggle to tell one of us from another. In familiar places, they'll be taken for women who stayed behind. A few speak the language well. We accost him, ask him to come—if he agrees, four of us can, under darkness before Ring Rise, carry him far enough to reach a small sky skiff."

"Good," Ti'iha said. "One more thing...where is the Voice?"

"The Voice? Why?" Alekelia frowned.

"If the Voice of Warraquim called to the Houses, it would rally volunteers," Ti'iha said.

Alekelia shrugged.

"No idea. I've lost touch."

A lie. We don't need him. I should have arranged his first flight long ago.

He'a spoke, and Alekelia felt a flare of fury.

"I thought you spoke to him just before the rains—House Irsa, wasn't it?"

Alekelia kept her face smooth.

"Ah. Yes. I've been forgetful, worrying about Warraquim's loss. House Irsa. There you are, Mother Ti'iha."

"House Irsa is out of the way," Ti'iha mused. "Perhaps another time—if there is one. For now, I ask leave to begin training. Lagav'a will not carry the full burden alone."

Mother He'a stood and nodded.

"Yes. Very well, Mothers—we begin preparations."

"One last matter," Ti'iha said, her gaze sweeping the council. "We should involve *all* Houses. We seldom summon House Wussuru, and they rarely come—but this is too important to exclude them."

"Wussuru? Why?" another Mother asked. "They're small, reclusive."

"Allyndra went there," Ti'iha said. "She had the most contact with the humans since she went aboard their skyship. She knows most of them. We must summon all resources. She can judge whether this healer lies. Perhaps she learned something useful."

"Oh?" He'a nodded. "I had forgotten."

"We don't need her," Alekelia snapped. "She chose seclusion."

"I disagree," Ti'iha said. "Shall we vote?"

There was brief discussion before He'a concluded, "We are agreed."

"I am not—and she is of *my* House!" Alekelia stood, heat prickling under her skin.

Ti'iha had another game in play.

"Are you so sure?" Ti'iha asked mildly. "The tale I hear is that she pledged to Wussuru—like others before her. Our custom for ages allows any daughter to change allegiance to Wussuru—the only House so honored."

Alekelia swallowed her retort, then sat with a dismissive wave.

"Fine. Call her—if they'll let her come."

"Very good."

Ti'iha smiled briefly, then stepped back and dipped.

"Then we are pledged—all one to the other."

The Mothers rose and dipped in answer.

"All one to the other."

As Ti'iha turned to go, Alekelia called, "Luck, Mother Ti'iha."

Ti'iha paused, nodded.

"Luck to you as well, Alekelia. We hope to see many daughters of Warraquim."

She departed. The omission of *Mother* did not go unnoticed. Alekelia wondered what game Ti'iha played.

What does it matter? she thought bleakly.

Warraquim was scattered—bits and pieces without a home, their only knowledge what lived in their heads. And yet... there might be a chance to rebuild. Alekelia allowed herself the smallest smile.

Chapter 13

HOUSE WARRAQUIM

STEPHEN

To Stephen, the days seemed to blur together. The rain fell, but the temperature, never cold, cooled a little as the humidity climbed. He felt he scarcely had a job. Sometimes he wished he were back on the *Reliance*, checking the pods—boring, yes, but a steady duty that carried him year after year. Here, not even a year in, there was little to do beyond the occasional stomach bug, bruise, or minor emergency—and other doctors were awake now to handle those. In a few months things might pick up—there were several pregnancies underway—but unlike some, he refused to join the betting pool on who would deliver the first baby born here.

He was still angry with Jane, yet he had listened.

Conner had threatened her with bodily harm. She hated it. She had protested and nearly been shot for it. When Stephen raged about the dead nymphs, Jane had agreed—then gestured at the fishing vessels.

"What do you think is happening out there, Stephen? Those nets don't care what they haul up. The nymphs get swept in with everything else. We've been baby-killers since long ago, and I doubt that changes soon."

He had to admit she had a point, though deliberately making a poison still went too far.

Jane had pulled him aside and whispered, "It only works for a short while, not long-term. I don't want to be the destroyer of a species. It's just enough to get Conner off our backs. If we seed the ecosystem we're eating from with poison, we might kill ourselves. Conner can't see past tomorrow. He's so damn addicted."

Stephen wasn't comforted, but he couldn't deny the captain was fraying. Stress, perhaps—but Jane was right. Conner had become addicted to what the natives called the blood kiss. Months earlier Stephen had warned them that no one knew the long-term effects of repeated bites.

He paused over a few charts and stared out the window at the planet's majestic rings.

Magnificent, he admitted. *This world is magnificent.*

Then he looked left and down at the scarred hillsides and the silent, skeletal machines.

"I wish we had never come here," he muttered.

"What's that, Doctor?" asked Alicia, one of the nurses, glancing up from her paperwork.

"Oh—just admiring the rings," he said, knowing she wouldn't share what he was feeling.

"They lend a special magic to New Earth, don't they?" She turned to the window.

"Alliadia," Stephen corrected gently. "The world is called Alliadia."

"That's the old name. It's New Earth now." Her tone was confident.

Stephen's mouth tightened.

"I didn't know the natives agreed to change it for us."

She shrugged.

"Doesn't matter what *they* call it. It's our home now, Doctor."

The casual certainty hit him like a slap—ownership assumed, the locals reduced to inconvenient squatters.

"And what about *them*? Do we stick them on reservations eventually? We've got about fifty pregnancies now. How many more? How soon before we outgrow this island and the others?"

Alicia set down her folder and shook her head.

"I hope we can work things out, but they have to be flexible, too."

"Tell me, Alicia—how would you feel if someone walked through a maternity ward, took all the babies, suffocated them, and threw them in the trash?"

She stared at him, appalled.

"Who would do something so horrid? I can't believe you'd even say that."

"Why not?" Stephen pointed toward the window. "Those boats are hauling up the equivalent of their babies. The nymphs suffocate in the nets, and the fishermen toss them back like refuse."

"They're just tadpoles—nymphs—and there are hundreds. And those people—if you can call them that—don't care for them until they come back a year later. If they don't care, why should we? We take care of our young. They don't. I don't get you, Doctor. Good night."

She locked her desk, pulled on a rain jacket, grabbed an umbrella, and left.

He wanted to argue more, for he remembered the pain in Allyndra's eyes when she spoke of losing her husband and children. Though Alicia was long gone, he called after her anyway.

"They *care*. They also know the world must be kept in *balance!*"

He felt torn.

Everyone wanted to live, have children, leave a legacy—but here, there would be only one winner, and he knew who. He yanked open a drawer, shoved his papers inside, locked it, and headed out. He had no coat or umbrella. The rain was warm, a mist more than a downpour. He stalked into the night, away from the tower that had been House Warraquim and toward the surrounding town.

He was staring at the wet pavement when a feminine voice said, "You want blood kiss?"

He stopped. An Allidian woman stood in the shadows, with at least three others behind her, all in light garments.

"No," he said.

Some of those who'd stayed were trading favors for a taste of human blood.

"I give you deep kiss. My venom real good," she said in halting English.

"I said no. I don't do that. Do you understand?"

He turned to go.

"Perhaps," she replied—then, in far better English—"but for us, Doctor Stephen, you may wish to change your mind."

She knew his name and title.

Not a leftover opportunist, he thought, whirling back.

"Who are you? Not a random Allidian, I'd wager."

She stepped into the light.

"I learned some of your English here. I remember you from the classes. It is not perfect. Doctor Stephen, the Mothers would like to speak with you. They sent us to bring you. Perhaps we can begin again."

He studied them. These women—or others like them—had likely slipped in and out of the city for some time. At last he nodded.

"I'll go. How?"

"We fly you," she said, pointing to herself, her companions, and then him.

Stephen shook his head.

"Too chancy."

She didn't seem to understand.

"Risky," he tried.

No better. He mimed shooting at something in the sky. One woman nodded and replied in the native tongue too quickly for him to catch. He remembered the skiff Jane had hidden away. The motor was quiet and if he kept to the shore, they might avoid attention.

"Boat," he said. "Water ship."

They conferred briefly.

"Show," the woman said, gesturing.

"This way."

He led them through alleys to the stash. He pulled off the tarp, checked the motor, and nodded. Again there was a rapid exchange he couldn't follow; then two women leapt, caught the air, and skimmed off low over the water. The other two climbed in. The speaker slipped an arm around him and rested her head on his shoulder.

He raised an eyebrow.

She murmured, "Effect."

Clever.

If any guards saw them, a human out for a night ride with two Allidian girls—one draped on him—might pass. Four would draw notice.

They're so damn smart, he thought.

He backed the skiff out, turned, and followed the flyers, weaving slightly and going slow—as if tipsy.

Once they were well away, the woman sat up. He caught the faint sweetness of her scent and felt a brief, human pang. He was oddly relieved when she moved. If she hadn't, he might have been tempted by the bite.

"Headland," she said, chin-pointing at a thin ridge jutting into the water.

He altered course. Ten minutes later they rounded the point. A small airship lay moored in darkness, unlit and nearly invisible in the pre–Ring Rise night.

"There."

She indicated a landing spot. He could make out several figures, including the two who'd flown ahead, and another woman he didn't recognize. The skiff ground into the shallows. All three jumped out, hauled the boat up, and tucked it behind rocks.

Stephen glanced back at the skiff.

Sorry, Jane. I borrowed your escape.

A well-muscled woman approached.

"Stephen—we meet again. I am Captain Hila'ar of the *Wind Dancer*, if you recall."

"Captain. I'm glad it's you. This isn't the *Wind Dancer*, though."

Hila'ar nodded toward a small open hatch.

"No—just a skiff. No time. We must hurry. Ring Rise is near. I'll explain later."

Her English was much improved. Stephen didn't interrupt. In the silver light of the rings, sails would glow like beacons. Even without pursuit, he couldn't fault her caution.

Within minutes, the crew had raised sail, cut loose, and sealed the ship. With a lurch, the skiff surged skyward, banking just as the rings began to brighten.

Stephen stared, awed, until the captain returned.

"Stephen, I'm sorry—I need you in a cabin. Many aboard are not pleased with your kind. I won't risk trouble."

"I understand, Captain. Lead on—or have someone show me."

He offered a small bow.

She exhaled.

"I appreciate the courtesy, but there's no formality here."

"Very well. Thank you for coming to bring me to your Council," he said, following her down the steps toward the cabins.

"I'm doing Council business," Hila'ar said. "Truth be told, when my Mother asked for a ship to fetch you, I volunteered in a heartbeat."

Emotion flickered in her voice.

"If it were any other, they might toss you overboard to see if you could fly."

"I understand," Stephen said quietly. "It means something that the Mothers are trying to talk."

He hesitated.

"You know we're not all alike."

"Nor are we. The original captain of this skiff had a husband from Warraquim. He couldn't fathom the destruction of the library there and decided to fly. As you can imagine, many here hold little regard for your kind. Trust is hard—unless one has truly come to know the other."

"That's an excellent observation, Captain. I'm hoping things can be better between our peoples. I'd like to see more of this world, and to sail the skies with you would be wonderful."

"I would love to show you. For now, the Council has asked you to come, and I'll see you arrive safely. Here's your cabin, Stephen. It should be stocked, but admit only me, understood?" Hila'ar opened the door.

Stephen nodded.

"I'm sorry for many things. I know it may not mean much, but my condolences to the other captain."

He searched his memory of nearly a year ago.

"May the Twins bless."

Hila'ar gave a tight smile.

"It's appreciated."

The flight was long enough and uneventful. Hila'ar checked on him periodically and sometimes sat to talk—ostensibly to practice human speech. He obliged and suspected her curiosity was genuine; it also gave him time to learn more of her language. As a skyship captain, she was fascinated by how a ship could travel between the stars. She spoke of distances vast beyond imagining. Stephen agreed and tried to explain the basic principle. He wrinkled a napkin to show how the ship shortened the *distance* by warping space. Captain Hila'ar grasped the idea readily, but when she asked *how* the ship did it, he could not say.

"You might ask Allyndra," he said. "I think she learned more than anyone else aboard the *Reliance*."

Hila'ar snorted and slapped his knee.

"I'm not surprised. She's A'ksu."

"I learned a little about the A'ksu. I wish I'd had more time, but as you say—this isn't the time."

Hila'ar stood.

"Me too. Pleasant night, Stephen."

"And you, Captain." He switched to Allidian. "May the Twins bless."

Hila'ar pursed her lips.

"And to you."

She started out, then paused to fix him with a look.

"You intrigue me, male."

The door closed.

***

Two days later he woke to crew shouting and realized they were descending. He freshened up and peered through the cabin window. They were dropping slowly. The commotion was the crew trimming sails for landing. A knock sounded. He cracked the door and saw Captain Hila'ar standing there. He opened it fully and made a small bow.

"Save that for the Mothers," she said with a wave. "You're up already. We're nearly at House La'Gave. Freshen up if you need to. If you'd like to watch from the deck, I'll stay with you. While I'm near, no one will say or do a thing."

"That would be lovely, Captain. I'm amazed by what these vessels can do."

"Then let's go."

Stephen stepped into the narrow corridor, choosing to follow rather than blunder about alone. Hila'ar moved with the practiced gait of a woman at home on a swaying deck. He braced against the bulkhead to keep from sprawling. Soon they reached a wider passage and the stair to the open air. Warm, humid sunlight washed over them.

"Beautiful day," he said—in Allidian, as much for the crew's sake as hers.

"That it is," she replied in the same tongue. "I'm guessing the A'ksu taught you?"

"Yes. I studied a while at Warraquim with Allyndra."

"I remember her. Quite the water dancer. Do you know what became of her?"

"She left Warraquim for another House. I'm not sure—started with a W. Wu—"

"Wussuru. Interesting. I wish her well. They are reclusive."

He wanted to ask more but decided this wasn't the time.

"Your English is much improved."

"Perhaps I've tried," Hila'ar snorted. "She is A'ksu. I am not. Now—grab the rail. You're none too steady, Stephen. I may have come to like you, but I'm not ready to test whether you can fly."

Her face held for a heartbeat, then she laughed.

"A joke—perhaps it doesn't translate well."

"I get it," he said. "Among my kind are those who think this world is theirs by right and might. Others want peace and coexistence. I'm of that mind."

"We'll see what the Council says. I care about getting my ship and crew safely from port to port. Strangers among us—and what to do about them—is beyond what I want to ponder. I'm a simple skyship captain."

Before he could answer, she was barking orders—descent, sheets, a hundred details—to settle the skiff. Wind buffeted the hull and Stephen hung on as it lurched. Soon they were moored. The crew, too busy with lines and cargo to bother him, spared only a few glances.

Slow, yes, he thought, *but a marvelous way to travel.* Wind for power, materials easy to source and repair. It embodied what was right with this world: a people who didn't hold high technology but had enough—and in harmony with the land. Perhaps that was where his own kind had gone wrong: bringing their tech, bending this world instead of learning to live with it. *We could learn so much—if we had the sense.*

"What was that?" Captain Hila'ar asked behind him.

"Oh—I was musing that we could learn a lot from your people."

"Probably," she said. "Come. A Council envoy is waiting."

He followed her down the central staircase, noting how the hull sides had folded out for loading. At the ramp's end stood a woman of medium height, blonde hair streaked with red, wearing a formal sash bearing a sigil.

She dipped.

"Doctor Stephen, I'm Marryll of House La'Gave. I hope the flight was pleasant. Thank you for coming."

Her English surprised him. He bowed.

"Pleased to meet you. It was, and I thank the Council for the invitation."

She regarded him briefly, then gestured for him to walk with her. He turned to Hila'ar and bowed.

"Fair winds," he said in Allidian.

Hila'ar blinked, dipped in turn, and replied, "Fair winds to you."

She returned to the ship.

As he fell in beside Marryll, she said, "I'm told you know some of our language. Your pronunciation isn't bad—only a little off. I hope mine in yours is acceptable."

She moved with the easy grace common to her people.

"Forgive me. I'll keep working on it. You speak English as if you've always known it. Your people seem to learn faster than mine."

"It's said that traces of the A'ksu linger in us all—some more than others," Marryll said, as if reciting a truism.

"I'm intrigued. My teacher from House Warraquim—Allyndra—said she was A'ksu. She learned our language to native fluency in two days. I once asked her what 'A'ksu' meant, and she told me something I can't recall."

They walked through bustle—ships and people busy with what looked like construction. Stephen had visited once but never saw such activity. Marryll answered a question he hadn't voiced.

"*Ha'iela mākouua i uā mea i hale i mea o mālamia o i ke wā e liki mai anamai?*" she asked, the words trilling musically.

"Yes—I think so."

"It's the old language. No one speaks it now—or reads it."

"A student told me that phrase is taught to all. If I recall, it means, 'We put away the past in order to preserve the future.'"

"Indeed."

Marryll's stride never faltered.

Stephen ventured, "I gathered there was a time your people fought one another—and that your ancestors chose a different path."

"Yes. We fought," she said. "You know the rings that gird this world?"

He nodded.

"We call them the Queen of Night's Promise. One tale says the gods vowed never to interfere again. Another—less comforting—says the A'ksu, in anger at our wars, tore the moon apart and fashioned the rings so we would remember—never again."

Stephen almost stumbled.

The A'ksu tore the moon apart? That implied a technology far beyond anything he saw here. *What if they once had it?* The rain of debris alone—unimaginable devastation. No wonder a culture might choose to lock such power away—and remember the wielders as dangerous. He found his voice.

"Fascinating. I would like to learn much more."

Marryll spared him a glance.

For the first time he noticed the deep emerald of her eyes, bright in the twin sunlight.

"Perhaps, had your people not burned the writings at Warraquim, you might have."

It hit him like a blow. He wanted to protest he hadn't lit the fires—but what good would that do? He shared the guilt.

"We're here," Marryll said, extending a hand toward the doorway. "The Council is inside. You will be called shortly, Stephen."

She dipped.

"Fair winds to you."

He bowed and repeated the phrase, working to match her cadence.

"Much better."

She flashed a quick smile and strode off.

Stephen watched her go, then turned to the door. There was so much they could teach each other. Why did it always come to strife? Perhaps there was still a way forward. Marryll's story churned in his mind.

What was in those books Conner burned?

An attendant appeared and beckoned.

Inside, the Mothers were assembled. Stephen bowed deeply.

"Greetings, Mothers," he said in his most polished Allidian.

Still, his mind circled the old phrase. He had always assumed this was the height of their technology.

But if they once shattered a moon... I made a terrible assumption. Then another thought came to him. *'We put away the past.' What if they hadn't destroyed that power—only chosen not to use it? God. If they still have anything like that—Conner would finally sit up and listen.*

Chapter 14

HOUSE LA'GAVE

ALLYNDRA

Allyndra stood behind Mother Assura as she and the other Mothers awaited the arrival of the human doctor. Her thoughts drifted back a week. A letter had come up from the nearest village—astonishing in itself, with snow still clinging to the upper hillsides in Low Spring. Ordinarily, a letter would arrive from House Warraquim up-valley by courier or via traders moving between communities, then finally to a Wussuru daughter who came down to barter fine woolens for supplies.

This time, as the messenger told it, the letter had come by skyship directly to the village. The ship had scaled the rugged western heights and drifted carefully down into the narrow valley. From there, a flyer had borne the message the rest of the way. A letter by skyship and flyer to Wussuru could only mean something important.

Allyndra remembered being called from the library by We'ela, Mother Assura's right hand. She had come reluctantly. Within the library of the House that Refused were books—and, more importantly, the preserved old language, enough to unlock the past. While aboard the human ship, she had turned her gift toward learning all she could. Many volumes were fascinating, but none more than the ancient books she herself had brought. She had just begun to work through them when summoned to Mother Assura.

She recalled the walk to the Mother's office—corridors hewn from mountain rock and worn smooth by many hands. The place was perpetually cold, the light barely pushing back the gloom. At times she had almost volunteered to run pack animals again, as when she first arrived, simply to see the suns. Unlike Warraquim, there were few openings to the outside and certainly not the terraces and balconies where one might breathe open air. The tall peaks kept the suns out of sight, but in compensation, when the snow melted, rivers and falls flung themselves around the valley in spectacular threads. She had taken short flights for respite, but the tug of the mind always drew her back to the dim light and the words of long ago.

Then the letter came, and she found herself in the Mother's chamber when Assura said, "Allyndra, the Council is calling us, and you specifically. In my life, and perhaps even my predecessor's, I've never received such a summons. We've always had a seat but rarely taken it. What could move the Council to call us—and you by name?"

"It must concern the humans," Allyndra had answered. "I know them best—at least, I did. I've no idea what or who remains of the old House."

Assura pursed her lips.

"That makes sense—and important enough to call even our small House. Sending a skyship on such a perilous route says as much. Very well. We'ela," she said to the attendant, "make preparations. Allyndra and I will travel to House La'Gave. Inform the flyer; we will meet the skyship in the valley as soon as we can."

We'ela looked surprised but obeyed with her usual efficiency.

***

A day later, the two of them descended the valley to where the skyship lay at anchor. The sight caused a stir. The captain, visibly relieved, came forward to greet them.

"Captain Vera'in of House La'Gave," the woman said with a curtsy.

Her hair was storm-cloud black with red streaks, long but bound, her dusky amber eyes steady. Muscled like an infertile male, she clearly worked alongside her crew. Allyndra eyed the vessel. It was smaller—and curious. The rigging remained, but there were no rails, ornaments, or niceties. Stripped to essentials, even the crew seemed few for its size. She remarked on it, and the captain shrugged.

"Can't enter at Warraquim anymore, so we had to come over the western rim. We lightened everything. I want to be underway before the Twins set since we'll have to pass near Warraquim. The valley winds run one way. With luck, we'll be in darkness before Ring Rise, build speed, then furl and drift to turn around the headlands before the strangers spot us. Then full sail and away. I'm told most of their watch is seaward."

She and Assura barely saw their stripped-down cabins before the ship lifted, catching the winds spilling down from the high peaks. With Assura's leave, Allyndra went up to the deck and watched the countryside, bracing with her wings as the skiff sped down-valley.

After a time Captain Vera'in joined her.

"We're making good time. Strong winds. About an hour to sunset, another half to full dark. We'll hit the valley mouth soon after. So—Wussuru. First time on a skyship?"

Allyndra considered what the captain had shared. The speed came not just from the wind, but from what had been stripped away.

"I was of Warraquim before Wussuru, for quite a while," she said, then glanced over. "Tell me, Captain—beyond clearing the heights, why strip her so bare? I suspect this is also a test of how fast the run from the village to Warraquim can be made. I would judge someone is thinking of taking skyships down this valley where the humans won't expect them."

Captain Vera'in chuckled and shook her head.

"You must be Allyndra. I was told to expect the Mother and an A'ksu called Allyndra. Well, A'ksu, you're right on all counts. We're testing—seeing how it goes. You can fly, I hear. Do so if things go wrong. Yes, the Council is planning how to counter the humans."

She eyed the narrowing walls ahead.

"It will be a hard passage. No harm in telling you. The plan is to send several ships over the west like this, weigh anchor, set full sail, and, under darkness before Ring Rise, come in from where the strangers look least—then fire the ships and ram their infrastructure to destroy it."

"An interesting plan, well thought," Allyndra said, "but it depends on many factors. If the humans—"

"Is that what they call themselves?"

Allyndra nodded.

"If the humans catch wind of it and launch their shuttlecraft—" she amended, "their own skyships—then the plan fails. They'll take the ships down easily."

"Perhaps. But we must try. We've no other way. Maybe we take a few of theirs with us," the captain said, grim.

Allyndra shook her dark, blue-streaked head.

"Their craft endure stresses you cannot fathom. You'd need to catch one between a skyship and Warraquim's walls, perhaps. The fire you can muster is nothing like what they're built to withstand."

"Well then, A'ksu, what do *you* offer?" Vera'in asked, almost a sneer.

"If this is the Council's course, so be it," Allyndra replied calmly. "I would take the majority to shield and draw off and strike their fishing vessels. Send a few like this to distract. Take most and wave-dance across the whitecaps to hit the trawlers and the structures on the island of their first ship. Last I knew, most of their shuttles were here. There must be a way to cut power to those skycraft and their machines."

"Fishing vessels—those slow water-ships?" Vera'in asked.

"Yes. They lack food for their numbers. That blow would be hard to recover from. But it will also make them desperate, and I can only imagine they'd take their own skyships to raid farms and Houses in retaliation. A people with little to lose will do terrible things," Allyndra said, staring ahead.

She had another idea, but that was for the Council, not here.

"And are *we* not desperate as well, A'ksu?" Vera'in said through her teeth—then nodded. "Still—a good thought. Distract with one fleet, strike with another. I hear they're bringing a... what was the word... a human to the meeting. Maybe there's more afoot than I know. Maybe you, A'ksu, have some other surprise. Isn't that why they call you that—A'ksu, dangerous?"

She laughed.

"In the old days, one like me was called *Aribabitru*—an honorific," Allyndra said at the captain's puzzled look. "It meant the ability to do things quickly."

"Truly? Interesting. Well—let's hope we make this run, Allyndra illm Wussuru. If you can find a way to spare lives—and save *Water Dancer*—I'll be grateful."

"*Water Dancer?*" Allyndra echoed, surprised.

"That's her name."

The captain patted the mast as one might a friend.

"Do you know the *Wind Dancer?*"

"Indeed. She's at La'Gave under Captain Hila'ar. The Mother has ordered her not to depart any port without permission. How do you know her?"

""She was the captain who sailed with me to the human ship. Ah, *Water Dancer*, may you be light and poised on wind and wave."

"Interesting choice of words."

"I used to do that—water dance. It feels ages ago. I was told I was as good as, if not better than, most in the House of Artists."

"Is that so? Well, if we all survive long enough, I'd love to see you water dance, Allyndra illm Wussuru."

"Warraquim."

"What?" The captain looked puzzled.

"*Allyndra illm Warraquim.* I hope one day to reclaim that House. I know"—Allyndra held up a hand—"that almost all the records there have been lost, but not all knowledge is gone. Not yet."

The captain gave her a strange look, then shook her head.

"You've a poor ship's captain confused, but if there's something to it, then *Aribabitru* Allyndra illm Warraquim, I'll pray to the Twins that it be so."

"I do have something—but save *Aribabitru* for later. What I have in mind could be dangerous for all of us."

"Something an A'ksu would do?"

"Yes."

The captain rested a hand on her shoulder for a moment.

"You sound as if treacherous currents lie ahead. May the Twins guide you."

She turned as the valley widened toward Warraquim.

It reminded Allyndra of what Captain Hila'ar had told her less than a year ago, though it felt like many more.

True to her word, the captain sailed the skyship in complete darkness and, as soon as the valley allowed, turned her toward the headland. Before the last bend, the crew swarmed the masts and furled the sails. The ship kept much of her speed as the wind rushing down the valley still pressed her on. The turn was brutal—several crew lost their grip and had to take wing to catch up. Allyndra rode the deck the whole way, clinging tight through the hard swing. Once clear of the valley's wind, the ship bled speed quickly, but the crew moved as one. She climbed back into steadier air, the sails dropped again, and the captain found a favorable set moving the opposite direction. They were well away before the first silver touched the sky as the rings caught the

Twins' light. No human shuttles rose to intercept. From the dim glow of the partially ruined town, there were no lights or signs of heightened activity. It seemed their passage had gone unnoticed as the skyship bore away toward House La'Gave.

The rest of the trip was uneventful.

At La'Gave, Allyndra and Mother Assura noted the number of skyships in port and the flurry of work. The plan was clearly moving forward. Allyndra relayed her discussion with the captain—and her misgivings about its chances. Mother Assura listened, then echoed the captain by saying, "What else are we to do, Allyndra?"

Allyndra had no answer.

Now she stood again with a Mother—though a different one than at the last Council. Alekelia cast glances her way but otherwise tried to ignore her. Plainly, she disliked her current standing; seated near the end of the table, she was far from the place nearer the center that Warraquim would once have held even here.

At last Mother Ti'iha rose.

"The ship with the human has been sighted and will arrive within the hour. Now is the time to settle our final plans with this being. First, another matter."

She signaled an attendant, who nodded and slipped away. Ti'iha straightened.

"A matter has come to my attention that must be resolved before we proceed. Alekelia."

She fixed the woman with her gaze.

Allyndra felt the room sharpen. Ti'iha had not used the title *Mother*.

"Here before the Council," Ti'iha said, "who witnessed Mother O'lathe naming you her successor?"

Alekelia flinched, then masked it, keeping her voice even.

"Allyndra—and the Voice, certainly."

"Allyndra, is that correct?" Ti'iha asked.

"Yes. Mother O'lathe said that if I did not survive, Alekelia was to be Mother of House Warraquim."

"Then why aren't *you*?" Ti'iha leaned forward and tapped a finger on the table.

"I was injured by the humans. Then the *Wind Dancer* needed repairs. I was long in returning. By then, Mother O'lathe had gone to the arms of the gods."

"And when you returned?" Ti'iha pressed.

"Mother Alekelia told me O'lathe had passed, that she had been named successor, and that the Voice had witnessed it."

Allyndra frowned, unsettled. She had given Alekelia her obedience. Why would Alekelia say otherwise now?

"Council," Ti'iha said, standing tall as her gaze swept the hall. "I propose we call the Voice of Warraquim to speak."

The Mothers traded puzzled looks, then nodded one by one— all but Alekelia, who glared.

Two attendants brought forward a fertile male.

"Lo'hia, you are—or were—the Voice of Warraquim, correct?" Ti'iha asked, tapping her finger like a gavel.

Lo'hia bowed deeply and held it.

"Yes, Honored Mother. Last I knew, I was still the Voice."

"You may stand. Now—clarify this…in the turmoil at the end, did you personally hear Mother O'lathe name Alekelia her successor and change her original admonition?"

Ti'iha's tone was cool.

"That is what Mother Alekelia told me, Honored Mother."

He darted a nervous glance at Alekelia. Ti'iha tapped once, sharply.

"So—you did not *personally* hear the change. Is that correct?"

"I've no reason to doubt the Mother of my House, Honored Mother."

He swallowed.

A hum rippled through the Council. Only Alekelia and Assura were silent. Assura merely observed, a small smile playing at the edges of her lips. Allyndra noticed and wondered if she and Ti'iha had corresponded over the winter while she labored in the library.

"Ah." Ti'iha clapped once to still the room. "There we have it. I claim to this Council that there was no witness to any change in

Mother O'lathe's pledge beyond the original. Allyndra has returned. I ask the Council to recognize her as the legitimate Mother of Warraquim."

Alekelia sprang to her feet.

"You say I did not tell the truth?"

Mother Ti'iha regarded her calmly.

"Perhaps you did. But without a reliable witness, you know your succession would be questioned. When a Mother dies without naming a successor, the Council may determine who in that House is best qualified."

She narrowed her eyes.

"I have spoken with many of your House while they were here. To a person, they say it was known you two competed—and that your ethics were not of the highest standard."

Mother He'ea spoke.

"I see no reason to continue. If what has been said is true, and the only two witnesses confirm that Alekelia's succession was at best provisional and without proof, then—" she turned to Alekelia—"the legitimate Mother of Warraquim is Allyndra. Does anyone here object?"

One by one, the Mothers—though shocked—shook their heads.

"Very well, Alekelia. I ask that you give up your seat. The Council recognizes Allyndra illm Warraquim as the Mother of the House of Knowledge Keepers."

Alekelia looked up from her end of the table, then stood.

"Very well—the House of nothing, anymore. She's welcome to it."

She turned and walked out of the hall.

Allyndra was stunned, still standing beside Mother Assura when Ti'iha spoke again.

"Mother Allyndra, take your seat, please, and let's discuss our plans."

Allyndra moved to the chair and sat, realizing she now faced Mother Assura directly. The definite smile on Assura's face told her more had been in motion than she'd realized.

An attendant hurried to Ti'iha and whispered in her ear.

"Ah—the ship with the human is docking."

Ti'iha looked around the table.

"Now, how far are we prepared to go to obtain more information? And, Allyndra, are you familiar enough with the proposed situation?"

"I am. It's an interesting plan—but I'm worried."

Murmurs broke out as Mothers conferred in low voices. Mother Assura raised hers above the rest.

"Even if we gain only a little more information—so be it. I have spoken with Allyndra, and is that not why you summoned her? To advise us on these humans and what they are capable of? She was aboard their great skyship. Before we go further, we should ask her. She already has insights."

The hall fell abruptly quiet. Ti'iha nodded and smiled.

"Of course. That is why you're here—and you're right, Mother Assura. Please, Mother Allyndra, tell us what you think. Our plan is based on what you told this Council nearly a year ago. How will the humans respond?"

So the word *human* has crept into our tongue, Allyndra noted.

"Overall, the plan is sound—strike where they're most vulnerable. But I believe it's ultimately doomed to fail."

"Oh? How so?" Ti'iha sat, puzzled.

"As long as they have their skyships—*shuttles*, as they call them—they remain dangerous. A burning skyship crashing into them will likely do little. Their craft are designed for stresses far beyond anything a skyship can inflict, and for far more fire than wood and gas can produce. Damaging infrastructure may be possible. Sinking their water-vessels would hurt them—but it will also make them more dangerous. From the history I studied, fear makes them highly aggressive. If their shuttles still function, they will raid for what they want, perhaps even destroy a House outright. The key is neutralizing their shuttles. Do that and you strip away much of their advantage. Another key is the people who can operate them—there are few. You might learn who they are from this human."

Conversation broke out again, sharp and overlapping, until Ti'iha restored order—just as the human appeared in the doorway. Heads turned.

Allyndra recognized Stephen at once. She wasn't sure how she felt. He had seemed earnest, yet he was still alien, and she wondered where his loyalties truly lie.

Two large infertile males escorted him to the table.

He bowed deeply, holding it in their fashion, and said in their language, "Honored Mothers."

"Little time for formalities, human," Ti'iha said with a wave. "Is your grasp of our tongue sufficient, or shall we speak yours?"

"In mine, please," Stephen replied. "I haven't learned as much as I should. Why have you asked me here?"

Ti'iha was blunt.

"We sought peace and were met by violence and destruction instead. Tell me, human—how would *you* respond?"

"I would be angry, frustrated, and want to retaliate. Is that why there are so many ships outside?"

The Mothers reacted—several muttered about seeing if he could fly.

"Enough," Ti'iha thundered. "Yes, if you must know. And yes, you must also realize you will not be allowed to return."

Stephen nodded.

Allyndra spoke gently.

"Stephen, that means only that we cannot trust you not to reveal what you learn. You are correct. The Council is considering sending ships to attack. You must understand—we fear your kind will expand, disregard us and this world, and that you are now vulnerable. From what I learned, your history is full of agreements broken and promises not kept. Am I wrong?"

He met her eyes and shook his head.

"No—you're right. I hoped we'd changed, but perhaps not enough. Some of us try. Some still think our needs justify anything. There's another side, though. The *Reliance*—the big ship you were on—was far more damaged than we realized. Its orbit was too low, dragging through your rings. We had to land quickly. With more time, a slower approach—perhaps none of this would have happened. And..." He trailed off.

"And?" Allyndra prompted, still gently.

"Conner—he was overbearing, but it's as if he's lost his mind, and some others as well. They've... slept with some of your people."

"*Slept?*" Ti'iha frowned. "What does sleeping have to do with anything?"

Allyndra smiled faintly.

"A human expression, Mother Ti'iha. It means *to have sexual relations*."

She turned back to Stephen.

"You mean the Blood Kiss, don't you?"

"Yes."

He nodded, a little sheepish.

"From others' descriptions, your bite—your venom—has an erotic effect. It also appears addictive to some of us. I don't know how many. There's been no time to study it, but continued exposure seems to change behavior. Conner, our captain—like a Mother of a House—has become dependent, and erratic. That hasn't helped."

"I see," Allyndra said, shaking her head. "Then you understand why I've warned the Council that if we don't neutralize the shuttles, your captain will likely use them against us. They're armed. From my reading, their shuttles are built to withstand a great deal. Your fishing vessels are vulnerable. Other infrastructure, less so. I fear any attack that doesn't disable much at once will fail and provoke sharp reprisals. Am I wrong?"

"No. Conner will likely order full retaliation against as many Houses, places, and skyships as he can. Many on both sides will die, and we'll be enemies for generations."

Allyndra raised a hand, halting the rising murmur.

"And though your technology is superior, we have numbers. In the long run, I believe we would still lose."

"More than likely," Stephen agreed. "Still—if Conner dies, and enough damage is done, Sheila—our second in command— might be far more willing to make peace."

"Then it's decided," Ti'iha said. "We do what we can. Some daughters already slip in and out. Perhaps we can remove this Conner as well. As you say, Allyndra, we must act while we can. Otherwise, they will build more, breed more, and think nothing of the future or of living in balance. In a few days' time we'll be ready. We'll gather what we can, continue preparations, and ready ourselves."

The other Mothers—all but Allyndra—indicated their assent to the plan that had been laid out.

She watched Stephen for a moment as he merely shook his head. When the commotion died down, Allyndra rapped the table lightly for attention. She waited until every eye turned toward her, a small, knowing smile playing on her lips.

"What if there were another way?"

Her voice was so soft that the others had to strain to hear. It was Mother Assura who finally rapped on the table again.

"Allyndra, what do you mean? Have you found something in your readings?" Assura's tone was cautious but hopeful.

"Yes—and perhaps no."

Allyndra inclined her head respectfully. Then, glancing briefly at Stephen, she turned back to the Council.

"Who among you can tell me the story of the Queen of Night's Promise?"

The Mothers exchanged puzzled looks. Mother Ne'ha frowned. "Why are we discussing an old myth about the Twins? Mother Allyndra, this has no relevance!"

Allyndra's smile widened.

"It does—but not that version of the story. There is another one, a much older tale—one that involves the A'ksu."

It was Stephen who spoke next, brows knitted.

"A woman I met while waiting for the ship that brought me here told me that long ago, when your people were more like us, they fell into strife. The ones you call A'ksu became angry and tore your moon apart, changing your destiny."

Allyndra nodded slowly.

"Indeed. That is exactly what happened."

She turned back to the Council.

"It was our ancestors—the *Aribabitru.* I see the name means nothing to you now. Allow me to explain. It meant 'the ability to do things quickly.' After the great destruction, they became known as the A'ksu."

She let the words sink in before continuing.

"Long ago, it was discovered that certain individuals could learn with astonishing speed and combine ideas from many disciplines to create entirely new things. This gift—this trait—was inheritable. Breeding one Aribabitru with another could strengthen it, sometimes even beyond the parents. And so, among the early clans, a race began—to see who could produce the most, the strongest, the most gifted. No one considered the consequences. Competition turned to rivalry, and rivalry to war."

She paused, her voice lowering.

"The Aribabitru foresaw what was coming, though no one heeded them. As the world descended into chaos, the greatest among them took action—terrible, decisive action. To stop the madness, they destroyed the moon that circled our world. Its fragments rained down, driving the oceans into monstrous waves. Volcanoes awoke. The ice sheets melted and drowned the land. How many of you know the tale of *Pa'hole's Tears?*"

Several Mothers nodded solemnly.

"Only a few A'ksu survived the cataclysm," Allyndra continued. "Those who remained gathered the survivors and divided them into groups by skill—some to weave, some to navigate and fly, others to create art or record knowledge. Thus were born the Great Guild Houses. The A'ksu decreed that each would depend on the others. They warned of further destruction if we strayed from balance. In time, the A'ksu themselves died out—choosing not to reproduce—but their teachings endured. The Houses learned to live in harmony with the world."

She paused, her gaze distant.

So much preserved in those books, and yet so much lost. If only I had known all this before the Warraquim archives were destroyed.

Taking a breath, she went on.

"Much vanished beneath the waves. The machines and weapons of the A'ksu were to be locked away, never again to be used. They left us a phrase—a promise: *Ha'iela mākouua i uā mea i hale i mea o mālamia o i ke wā e liki mai anamai.* 'We put away the past in order to preserve the future.' And indeed, they preserved it."

Silence filled the hall. Even Stephen seemed struck dumb, his mouth slightly open as the meaning settled in.

Allyndra knew she had their full attention.

"However," she said softly, "perhaps they had more foresight than we believed. For in one of the oldest texts I found that phrase was *not* what was originally written. The true phrase was: *Pe'iela mākouua i uā mea i hale i mea o mālamia o i ke wā e liki mai anamai.*"

She looked around at their blank faces—only Mother Assura would recognize the old words.

"It does not mean *we put away the past*, but *we hide the past in order to preserve the future.*"

A collective murmur swept through the chamber. Allyndra pressed on.

"And that is precisely what they did. They hid things away. Artifacts of the old world—machines, knowledge—sealed for a time of need. Perhaps they foresaw that others might come, as the humans have, or that one day we would again require what they once achieved."

When she finished, silence reigned.

Stephen was the first to find his voice. His expression was one of pure astonishment.

"You're telling me something powerful enough to tear apart a moon might still exist?"

"Yes." Allyndra's eyes shone. "This has been my life's work—to understand those books. Now I believe I finally do."

Ti'iha blinked rapidly, clearly overwhelmed.

"And you've found this—this information—in one of the books?"

"Indeed, Mother. The clues were cleverly hidden, and I have not yet fully deciphered them. But something happened to me long ago, something I once thought a fever dream. Now I know otherwise. I *have seen* the old things."

"You've seen them?" Ti'iha asked, almost incredulous.

Allyndra nodded.

"At the time, I dismissed it as delusion, but with the help of Mother Assura and Mother We'ela, I have recovered the memory in full. Would you like to hear the story?"

Both Ti'iha and Stephen answered at once—an eager, resounding *yes.* Realizing his breach of decorum, Stephen bowed hastily. Ti'iha waved a hand impatiently.

"Please, Mother," she said. "Tell us about the old machines."

Chapter 15

HOUSE LA' GAVE

ALLYNDRA

Allyndra sat back in her chair and closed her eyes.

"Let me relate the tale."

She let her mind drift sixteen years into the past. The memories had returned after the help of certain techniques taught to her by Mother Assura and We'ela at House Wussuru.

"My friend Mysima and I had just earned our wings. I remember her running a finger along mine and teasing, *You're really going flying with those new wings? There are far more pleasurable pursuits to be had down at the Iresemia House.*'"

"*I'm sure there are,*" I told her, "*but not for me. I like flying. Did you know I've always wanted to be a water dancer?*"

"*Then you were born into the wrong House, Allyndra illm Warraquim,*" Mysima laughed, attempting a pirouette like a water dancer—and nearly falling over.

"I caught her arm before she could tumble.

"'I know, but it's what I'd like to learn someday.' I flexed my wings. 'But today, I want to feel these on the wind!'"

"Mysima shook her head, grinning. 'You've always been the best of us—top of the class in everything, not just books, but flight. I remember Mother Jer'iha saying, *The ground is a harsh mistress.*' I don't think you ever had to learn that lesson.'

"'Oh, I had my share of bumps and bruises,' I protested.

"'Not like the rest of us.' Mysima made a face.

"'I did study dancing beforehand—and practiced a little. Maybe it paid off.'

"'Ah, I should've known! You've always had a knack for learning fast. I think Alekelia resented that. That's probably why she started that rumor that you were A'ksu.'

"It was my turn to grimace. *And those rumors still linger. Mother O'lathe has never said anything, but I hope it's not true. To be like one of those…*

"My thoughts scattered as Mysima traced my wings again, feather-light, making me shiver. 'Be careful, Allyndra,' she said softly. 'You're still new to these. This time of year, storms rise quickly, and you've never flown in those kinds of winds.' She took my hands. 'The Twins bless you.'

"'The Twins bless you too, Mysima. Just don't make too much of a spectacle of yourself down at the Iresemia House!'

"'Oh, if I don't, I've failed my mission!' she called, laughing. 'Safe flight!'

"I waved after her and then turned toward the cliff overlooking the ocean near the main house. I ran, leapt from the edge as if diving into the sea below, and let gravity take me. Speed built quickly—and with a thought, I flared my wings. They caught the air with a snap, and I soared upward, the wind lifting me higher and higher until House Warraquim was a tiny speck below. From this height, I could see the curve of the horizon over the vast ocean. The air was cool but not freezing, and the sunlight of the Twins warmed my wings. I followed the coast, gliding more often than beating, conserving my strength. The sensation was exhilarating—freedom itself.

"Before long, I had flown beyond familiar landmarks. The sea stretched endlessly northward, while to the south, mountains rose like jagged teeth. The beaches vanished, replaced by dense vegetation clinging to steep, broken slopes.

"Then, in the span of a heartbeat, the Twins vanished behind roiling clouds. The sky darkened, and fierce winds howled up from the sea. Mysima had been right—storms formed in moments. I searched for a place to land, but there was none. The slopes were too sheer. Each time I tried to descend, an updraft caught me and hurled me skyward, driving me inland toward the mountains. I had to fight just to stay upright in the air. The peaks loomed ever closer, snow gleaming on their summits. The wind grew colder, biting through me until I could barely feel my limbs.

"The mountains reared up before me—grey cliffs of stone. I couldn't fly against the gale without shredding my wings. So, I made a choice. I stopped resisting and let the storm take me. A violent gust flung me toward a mountain face streaked with snow, shaped like an arrowhead. I braced for impact, but at the last moment, the wind lifted me—just enough to shoot through a narrow pass between two peaks.

"On the lee side, the winds eased. Below me lay a broad field of snow. It was my only chance. I folded my wings and dove. I struck hard, crashing into the snow and sinking deep into its softness. The cold bit like a thousand needles. I gasped, breath stolen by the shock.

"For a moment, I lay there stunned, fighting the urge to sleep. The chill crept into my bones, whispering of rest—of torpor—but I knew that would mean death. My training forced me on. I gathered what little strength I had, staggered upright, and immediately began to shiver violently. Wrapping my arms around myself, I fanned my wings gently to shake off the snow. Nothing seemed broken—small mercy. Scanning the slope, I spotted a dark patch in the mountainside. A cave, perhaps. Shelter. It was my only hope.

"Each step was agony, the wind stealing my warmth as I trudged forward through the drifts. At last, I reached the opening and stumbled inside. The stone was cold, but at least it shielded me from the wind, which howled outside like a maddened beast, plucking at my thin flight dress.

"I moved deeper into the darkness, one hand tracing the wall to guide me. The floor was uneven at first, rough stone beneath my feet—but soon, it changed. Smooth. Polished. My brow furrowed. Someone—or something—had carved this place. Why here, so high in the mountains?

"The passage curved, hiding the faint glow of the entrance behind me, yet there was light ahead—soft, diffuse. I stepped toward it carefully. Then I stumbled, catching myself against the wall—and froze. My hand was no longer on plain rock. I could feel carvings—incised lines forming patterns and symbols. I traced them slowly with numbed fingers. Recognition came with a jolt: they were words. The old language. Ancient, but familiar. The same phrase all children were taught in their youth.

"I ran my hands over it again and again, awe overtaking the cold. *Why here?* I wondered. *What did this place hide?*"

Now, back in the present, Allyndra opened her eyes and looked around the chamber at the assembled Mothers—and at Stephen.

"It read," she said softly, "*Pe'iela mākouua i uā mea i hale i mea o mālamia o i ke wā e liki mai anamai.* I now know what it means. And now, so do you."

There was a commotion as the Mothers began speaking all at once. Ti'iha rapped sharply on the tabletop until the noise subsided.

"Mothers! Please."

Her voice cut through the murmurs.

Fixing her gaze on Allyndra, she asked, "Then it is true—there are old things from the past?"

"Indeed," Allyndra replied calmly. "But allow me to finish my tale, if you would permit."

She inclined her head slightly.

"Yes," Ti'iha said before the others could respond. "Continue."

Allyndra closed her eyes once more, letting the recovered memory surface.

"Finally, I took the last step, and before me, the passage opened into a vast cavern—or rather, a chamber. It was far too smooth, too precise, to be natural. The stone walls and floor were covered with some kind of artificial surface. In the dim light, I saw objects—countless objects—stored away. I cannot say how long they had been there, yet the place felt both ancient and untouched, as though someone might have walked through only yesterday, not generations ago.

"At one wall stood a tall, oblong structure that gave off a soft white glow, as if something within it still lived. I approached and touched it—it was warm. I walked around it, studying every angle, but could not fathom its purpose, nor that of the other artifacts scattered throughout the chamber. I could only wonder how they had come to rest in this hidden place—and why."

Her voice softened.

"I was cold, hungry, and exhausted. My body begged for rest, so I curled up on the smooth floor beside the glowing object, which at least gave off some warmth. I fell asleep quickly, the deep, dreamless sleep of complete exhaustion. I do not know how long I slept, but when I woke, I was stiff and chilled. The artifact still glowed. I remember wrapping my arms around it for warmth and realizing then—it wasn't a fever dream. It was real.

"I traced again the inscription carved at the entrance to the tunnel, wondering what it truly meant. I wished I could know how long ago the chamber and its contents had been made. But my body reminded me how weak and hungry I was, so I left the cavern and made my way back to the surface.

"The storm had long passed. The Twins shone bright in a clear, cold sky. I warmed my flight muscles and took to the air once more. I barely remember the journey home, but later I was told a Blood Flower farmer found me delirious in his field."

Allyndra opened her eyes and looked around the table.

"The machines are still there. Though more than a few decades have passed, if one was still active after so many centuries—since the time of the Aribabitru—I doubt it has ceased to function since."

Ti'iha sighed, her tone heavy with resignation.

"You said yourself, you do not know exactly where you were, nor what the objects were, nor how they worked. So we are, more or less, back where we began."

"Yes, Mother Ti'iha," Allyndra replied evenly, "that was *then*. Not now. The library at Wussuru holds much—enough, I think, to awaken the machines again. I found in one of the old books both a phrase and instructions for reviving the ancient artifacts. As for *where* they lie—well, for that, we have Mother Assura's assistant, We'ela, to thank. When I described the peak shaped like an arrow of snow, she knew the place. She said she once glimpsed it while chasing a Qwiklick calf one high-spring day."

Ti'iha shook her head slowly.

"We are still uncertain, Mother Allyndra. However—" she raised a hand to forestall interruption—"I propose we divide our efforts. Mother Assura, this region lies near your House, and our resources are already committed here. If you and Mother Allyndra are willing, I would ask that you work together to find this mountain and, if possible, revive what lies hidden there. Just in case, we will continue with our existing plans—and hope."

Mother Assura nodded.

"I would gladly seek this place. As you may recall, our House has always been one that questions, that disagrees. We keep to the way of the world, yes, but if there is even a chance to reclaim what was lost, I would welcome it."

She turned to Allyndra.

"Mother Allyndra, would you be willing to retrace your flight once more? Perhaps, Mother Ti'iha, you might lend us a small skyship—the journey by wing would be arduous, if not impossible."

Before Ti'iha could respond, Stephen stepped forward.

"I would like to go as well."

He hesitated, suddenly aware of himself—an outsider, a human, and a male. He quickly bowed.

214

"Forgive me. But I ask it, nonetheless. I'm driven by curiosity. If I could see this for myself—perhaps I could convince Conner that you are not to be trifled with and avert bloodshed. Restrain me if you must, but please, let me go. Even showing him proof that such things exist might make him think twice. It's worth the risk."

Ti'iha exhaled heavily, her displeasure clear—as was that of several Mothers at the table. But she fixed Stephen with a hard gaze.

"Very well. Your fate, then, I leave to Mother Allyndra. She knows you—and your kind—better than any of us. As for a ship, you shall have the best of the small skyships. A larger vessel would never navigate the narrow passes, but the one I have in mind is agile, sturdy, and captained by an experienced hand. I have kept her here, awaiting just such a need."

Mother Assura inclined her head in thanks, then turned to Allyndra.

"And what of *this one*?" She nodded toward Stephen.

Allyndra regarded him for a long moment, fingers tapping lightly on the table.

"You, not your Conner—or whatever title he claims—have shown some willingness to listen. Very well, Stephen. On your honor, if you have it, and on your life, I will allow you to come."

Stephen bowed deeply.

"Mother Allyndra illm Warraquim, I, Doctor Stephen Banks, pledge on my honor not to act against you or commit sabotage. I only wish to learn, as you do. And if I can—if there's even a chance—I'll send a message to Conner urging him to stand down. If ever you doubt me, you may test whether I can fly."

Allyndra laughed softly, the sound like distant chimes.

"You may rise. Very well, Stephen. Let us see what the ancient Aribabitru have left behind."

She stood, inclining her head to the assembled Council.

"Then, Mothers, if we are agreed—time is of the essence. As soon as the skyship is prepared, Mother Ti'iha, we shall depart.

May the Twins bless us—especially if this journey fails and war comes instead."

Mother Ti'iha nodded, then rapped the table sharply, signaling the assembly to rise.

"May the Twins bless our endeavors—especially yours, Mother Allyndra—if you truly believe we can avoid death and loss."

Her gaze shifted briefly to Stephen.

"For all our sakes."

The other Mothers bowed their heads and responded in unison, "May the Twins bless."

Ti'iha stepped closer to Allyndra and Assura.

"The ship I've held in reserve is one of the finest—and one you'll find familiar. It's the *Wind Dancer*, under Captain Hila'ar."

Allyndra smiled, a flicker of fond memory softening her features.

"Excellent. I remember her well. It was the *Wind Dancer* that carried me to the human ship. I told the captain it might prove to be a fine adventure."

Ti'iha tilted her head slightly and pulled a small pad and stylus from her pocket. She leaned over one of the tables, scribbled a few quick lines, then tore off the page and handed it to Allyndra.

Allyndra read the note: *Captain Hila'ar—The Mother of the House requests that you lend all aid you can. —Mother Ti'iha.*

She inclined her head respectfully.

"Thank you, Mother."

Ti'iha waved a hand dismissively.

"Forget the formality, Allyndra. Go quickly. I've got a bad feeling in my bones."

"In what way?" Allyndra asked, concern edging her voice.

"Hopefully," Ti'iha said with a sigh, "Alekelia will do nothing worse than drown her loss in a tavern—or at an Iresemia House. But—"

"She's impulsive and quick-tempered," Allyndra finished for her. "I only hope she doesn't go to the humans..."

"Indeed." Ti'iha's expression hardened. "We may have to move even faster than we'd planned. Now go—all of you. And may the Twins bless us all."

They echoed her words, even Stephen, who spoke the blessing in the Allidian tongue. Ti'iha regarded him for a moment, something unreadable flickering in her eyes.

"Perhaps," she said softly, "there is a way forward for all of us."

Then, with a shooing motion of her hands, she added more briskly, "Now get out of here—before disaster finds us first."

As Allyndra turned to leave, she couldn't help but think: *Mother O'lathe used to do the same—and her intuition was always right.*

Chapter 16

HOUSE LA'GAVE & WARRAQUIM

ALEKELIA

Alekelia walked away from House La'Gave as fast as she could without actually running.

The Mother of this house embarrassed me—then stripped me of my title.

The heat burning through her wasn't from the Twins but from her own anger.

Yes, perhaps Mother Ti'iha was right in her way, but it was never meant to be Allyndra. It should have been me.

Allyndra—the bookworm. Allyndra—the widow. Allyndra—the Twins-forsaken A'ksu. Allyndra, who would lead them all to ruin if they were foolish enough to listen.

She didn't know where she was going until she found herself among the skyships—some being repaired, others loading or unloading cargo. The air was full of shouts, tools, and the smell of oils and fabrics. The fleet was busier than ever, every vessel being readied for the coming strike against the humans.

Those *creatures* had invaded her House, forced her out—and now Ti'iha had taken even her title from her.

She stopped, still seething, her hands clenched at her sides.

There has to be a way to make her pay.

She imagined Ti'iha losing everything—her home, her authority, her precious skyships. Then, a thought began to take shape.

What if the humans learned what this House—and the others, but especially this one—were planning?

She could picture it clearly: the humans discovering the stripped-down ships, the preparations for war. They would descend on House La'Gave in fury, tearing it down stone by stone. Ti'iha's arrogance would be her own undoing. And perhaps, if Alekelia played her part well enough, the humans would see her as useful—a cooperative Mother rather than a threat.

Maybe I could convince them that a friendly hand guiding the ships is better than a hostile one. Perhaps they'd make me the Mother of this House.

The idea thrilled her. The more she considered it, the more it made sense.

The islands can't function without the skyships. If I control them, I control everything.

Her pace quickened. She began scanning the docks for a vessel preparing to depart. She knew no ship would be permitted near Warraquim, but if she could get close enough, her own wings could carry her the rest of the way. The humans had grown lax with the daughters who came and went—they saw them as harmless. It would be easy enough to slip in.

I'll tell them I've come to make peace, she thought. *That I've brokered a treaty between our peoples—and that it's all thanks to me. Once they've destroyed Ti'iha, they'll see I'm the better choice to lead.*

At last, she found a small, narrow vessel being loaded with bolts of Trellium silk bound for the Artists' Guild—a perfect cover. That island was close enough to Warraquim that she could glide the remaining distance. Her excuse would hold—the Mother of Warraquim seeking to visit the Artists' Guild to inquire about one of her "daughters," a dancer of some renown. Few would question it. No one outside the Council even knew yet that she'd been removed from her position. She still wore her sigil, after all. Traveling without attendants might seem unusual, but not impossible, especially now that her House was in disarray.

"Captain," she called to a burly woman shouting orders to her crew.

The woman turned, puzzled. Her gaze dropped to the sigil Alekelia wore, and she made a hasty curtsy.

"Mother of Warraquim! What brings you here?"

"Ah, I know—it's unexpected," Alekelia said smoothly, slipping into the tone of authority that still came easily. "I seek passage to the Artists' Guild. I've recently learned that one of my daughters—whom I believed lost in the attack—still lives. She's a water dancer of some skill. I thought to send her as a gesture of gratitude to House La'Gave, to dance for Mother Ti'iha…and the humans."

"The humans?" The captain's expression hardened. "They destroyed your House."

"It was a misunderstanding," Alekelia replied quickly, pressing a finger to her lips. "We've reached a mutual understanding—one brokered by the Mother of your own House. But it's not yet common knowledge, so I'd ask that you keep this to yourself."

The captain rustled her wings uneasily and straightened.

"I see. And there's no one traveling with you, Mother illm Warraquim?"

"Alekelia is fine, daughter of La'Gave," she said with a practiced smile. "No, I travel alone. There's much that's irregular these days—nothing is as it once was since the strangers came. Still, I've lingered here long enough. I've nothing else to offer the Mother of your House in gratitude, save this—one of my daughters to entertain and honor her. And…" She paused, lowering her voice conspiratorially. "I wished it to be a surprise. So, again, I ask your discretion, Captain."

The captain blinked and gave a small shake of her brown-and-orange-streaked head.

"I see. It still seems a bit odd—but then, as you said, Mother, these are odd times."

She turned and nodded toward the ship.

"The *Blossom* doesn't have much in the way of quarters. She's small."

"Small, but fast, I would imagine—especially with a good captain like yourself and a capable crew. And since I wish this gift to be presented soon, a little speed is a blessing. I'm sure you understand, Captain. My comfort is of little consequence."

At least for now.

"I suppose so. I'm just a simple skyship captain, Mother of Warraquim."

She hesitated, then turned and shouted to her crew.

"Belay the final closing! Ready a cabin for our guest!"

She motioned for Alekelia to follow.

"Well, Mother of Warraquim, I am Captain Feli'a of the *O'nathe Blossom*. Welcome aboard."

She gave a slightly awkward curtsy.

"Thank you, Captain Feli'a."

Alekelia tilted her head graciously and made her way toward the boarding port. She entered the ship, where a young crewwoman met her and showed her to her quarters. Before they reached the small cabin, there was a loud thump as the boarding door shut, followed by a gentle lurch as the ship rose into the sky.

"Apologies, Mother," the crewwoman said with a laugh, catching hold of a rib in the wall to steady herself. "The captain's in a hurry to catch the wind before the Twins rise too high."

"It's quite all right—in fact, commendable," Alekelia replied smoothly. "Tell the captain I wish her fair winds and a swift journey."

"Yes, Mother," the crewwoman said, dipping her head before hurrying off to fetch what Alekelia might need.

Alekelia sat on the narrow bed and allowed herself a small, satisfied smile.

If luck holds, no one will even notice I've gone. They'll assume I'm sulking in my rooms.

Captain Feli'a proved to be skilled, driving the small vessel hard through the winds—even weathering a storm. Still, it took three days' flight before they reached House Hi'ili, home of the Artists' Guild.

Once the *Blossom* docked, Alekelia disembarked, her demeanor calm and composed, as though she were simply paying a social visit to the Guild. But once she had walked far enough from the docks, her eyes began to search. She was looking not for the Guild proper but for an Iresemia House—and as expected, she found one nearby. There was always one close to a Guild House.

She had no real intention of indulging in its usual pleasures, though the thought crossed her mind. A bath, a massage, a meal—and perhaps, *perhaps*, a little diversion. The flight to Warraquim would be long, and she would need her strength. Besides, a visit to an Iresemia House drew little attention. Such places were as much rest stops as they were retreats of pleasure.

She approached the entrance and stepped inside. Immediately, she was greeted by a tall, well-muscled infertile male.

"Mother," he said with a deep bow, his voice low and resonant. "How may I be of service to you today?"

His tone was rich, pleasing. He glanced up at her, then bowed again.

"House Warraquim—and of high rank, if I read that sigil correctly. I am Ma'iu."

She placed a finger to her lips.

"Yes, House Warraquim. I've been traveling for days on my way to House La'Gave. I'd rather avoid the formalities of House Hi'ili—I just need to relax. A good bath and massage, nothing more. I've no desire for all the fuss and ceremony."

Ma'iu smiled.

"Of course, Mother. Somewhere private, quiet, away from distraction. I'll prepare a room for you immediately. Would you like an attendant to assist you in the bath? I myself am quite skilled in both water and dry massage—and it would be my honor to serve you."

She nodded approvingly.

"That sounds perfect. And afterward, perhaps something lighter to wear—a flight dress would do nicely. Have chilled Blood Flower juice brought as well... and perhaps some company later."

Ma'iu smiled again and bowed, leading her through the corridors to a softly lit room. He opened the door and stepped aside.

"I hope it pleases the Mother."

Alekelia looked around. The chamber was much like others she'd seen—well-ventilated, a broad bed draped in gauzy pink curtains, simple but tasteful. As she surveyed the room, Ma'iu went to the adjoining shower. She soon heard the water begin to flow. He returned after a moment.

"If the Mother would like to begin, I'll fetch the chilled Blood Flower juice," he said politely.

Alekelia turned her back to him.

"Undress me first."

Ma'iu came forward without hesitation. His hands were deft and gentle as he loosened the lacings of her dress and let the fabric fall away. His touch was firm, practiced—a servant who knew his craft well. In moments, her garments lay in a soft pool at her feet.

He lingered just long enough to knead her shoulders in a brief, teasing massage.

"Your bath awaits, Mother," he murmured. "I shall return shortly to attend you."

Alekelia turned and nodded, then stepped into the room. Warm water cascaded over her, washing away the humiliation that clung to her like dust. She let the heat soak into her skin, closing her eyes as if it could cleanse not just her body but the sting of defeat.

When Ma'iu returned, she glanced over her shoulder. He had set aside the formal trappings of service, and his expression was calm, reverent even, as he approached. His presence filled the small space, steady and unhurried. Without a word, he began to tend to her, letting the water flow between them as he carefully worked the tension from her shoulders and along the delicate arches of her wings. His hands were practiced—gentle where care was needed, firm where her muscles knotted.

The touch was soothing, almost hypnotic. The room filled with the sound of running water and the faint scent of Blood Flower oil. For a moment, Alekelia allowed herself to forget her anger, to feel only the steady rhythm of breath and pulse, of warmth and release.

But beneath that calm, her purpose remained. The moment stretched—then shifted. Her eyes opened, clear and resolute now. This was no longer a moment of indulgence but necessity. When it was done, she would have what she needed: strength, focus, and the vitality to fly again.

When at last she stepped from the water, the storm in her chest had quieted. The weakness and shame of La'Gave were gone, washed away. She felt renewed—dangerous again.

Now, she thought, *let the Twins bear witness. I will not be cast aside.*

***

Hours later, after the Twins had set and she had relaxed, Alekelia felt invigorated. One last relief before the flight, then a change into a simple flight dress — a thin, gauzy white thing that tied at the neck and waist, left the back open, and came just above the knees. She looked in the mirror, tied her hair, and then nudged Ma'iu's body. He was dead.

She squatted and whispered, "Sorry — you served your purpose. May the Twins bless you," and rose.

It was late. The House seemed to have settled into sleep with occupants tucked away with clients or alone. Alekelia tiptoed through the dim corridors, slipped out into the warm night, and headed for the docks. She warmed her flight muscles, then ran and flicked into the air, angling toward the island now outlined by the Queen of Night's Promise.

The flight was long, but she had supped well and wasn't as exhausted as she might have been. She flew low over the water, skimming so near that she could have brushed the surface. The Promise had faded; it was fully dark before the Twins rose. Ahead, the silhouettes of the town and the hastily erected human structures around the House of Warraquim showed only a few scattered lights — far fewer than when the House had thrived.

Rather than approach the town, she aimed for the promontory and planned to come up to the House from above. The waves masked the sound of her wings. She knew the route by heart; she had occupied the Mother's apartments long enough to know every balcony in the dark. Veering upward, she dropped gently onto the chosen balcony. The curtains drifted in the breeze; only a faint light came from within. She took a step — and froze.

A deep voice came from the shadowed doorway.

"Hold it right there, or I'll blow your head off."

"Conner, I'm Alekelia illm Warraquim, and I intend no harm. In fact, I've come to bring you a gift. May I enter, please?"

"Put your hands on your head and walk into the light—slowly," came Conner's voice.

Alekelia obeyed, stepping carefully into the dimly lit room. After a moment, she could make him out, lounging in bed with something held steady in his hand.

"Do you remember me, Conner? I was the Mother of this place before you took it over."

He sat up a little straighter, though his grip never faltered.

"Yeah, I remember. Well, *Mother*"—he twisted the title into mockery—"what sort of gift are we talking about? Unless it's you gracing my bed. My usual girl didn't show, and I'm missing that little blood kiss your kind's famous for."

Alekelia kept her expression pleasant. She had no desire for him, but she had heard that some human males were addicted to the effects of the *H'oni A'likoa*.

I'll do whatever it takes to be a Mother again, she thought. She began to lower her hands.

"No, you don't," Conner snapped. "Keep 'em where they are until I say otherwise. Got that?"

"Yes, Mother," Alekelia replied sweetly, her tone that of someone humoring a child.

Conner gave a small nod.

"Better. Now—go on."

"It seems Allyndra and Mother Ti'iha decided I was not the legitimate Mother of this House," she said evenly. "They displaced me. But with your help, I can return the favor. I know what they're planning against you."

Conner studied her, the weapon unwavering.

"And why should I believe a word of it? Even if I did, why should I care? I could make you talk if I wanted to."

"You could," she admitted calmly. "But I'll tell you freely. The Houses plan to move against you—led by La'Gave. They intend to strip down skyships for speed, sail them under cover of darkness, set them alight, and crash them into your ships and settlements. Their goal is to destroy everything they can, including your surface vessels."

Conner frowned.

"Is that so? And how exactly are they supposed to pull that off? We'd spot 'em miles out."

"They'll come from the west," Alekelia explained. "Over the ridges. They'll gather in the valley, launch between the setting of the Twins and Ring Rise, furl their sails near the edge, and let the down-valley winds carry them to the sea. Then they'll ignite their ships and guide them into your skycraft and fishing vessels. Some may even turn toward your base on the main island."

Conner gestured for her to lower her arms, setting the weapon loosely on the bed but keeping it close.

"Sounds damn well planned. Didn't think your kind had it in you."

He scratched his chin, then barked, "Sergeant! Get in here!"

Moments later, a stocky man entered.

"Sir? Is she bothering you?" He jerked a thumb toward Alekelia.

"No," Conner said curtly. "Get a pilot and a shuttle. Check the western valley and the ridge—now. Report back as soon as you see anything."

The sergeant blinked.

"Now, sir?"

"Now!" Conner snapped. "ASAP. Move!"

"Yes, sir."

The man saluted, giving Alekelia a wary glance before leaving.

Conner turned back to her, smirking.

"Let's see if your story holds up. It'll take a few hours. So—honey."

He threw back the covers and patted the space beside him.

"Keep me entertained while we wait. If your story checks out—and if you keep me happy—maybe I'll see about granting that little request of yours."

Alekelia studied him. Broad-shouldered, heavyset—closer to an infertile male in build, though more imposing. This wasn't what she wanted, but revenge demanded sacrifice. And if he truly was addicted to the *H'oni A'likoa*, then a taste of it would make him pliable.

She took a steadying breath, then smiled and crossed the room.

"You will believe me, Conner," she said softly. "And you will be very happy. That I promise."

He grinned.

"Good. Then we understand each other."

As she slipped into the bed beside him, Alekelia reminded herself of her purpose. The tiniest bite was all it took—just enough to make him hers.

Chapter 17

WIND DANCER

STEPHEN

It was almost two days before the group finally departed to see if what Allyndra had said was true — whether something from her people's distant past still lay hidden away. The idea was maddeningly intriguing, and Stephen wanted desperately to ask more, but he knew it was wiser to stay quiet. He was tolerated here, not welcomed, and he could hardly blame them for that.

He had spent the past two days under what amounted to house arrest, trading his uniform for the more comfortable clothing provided to him. A sigil of House Warraquim was embroidered on the garment — a quiet reminder, he suspected, of whose protection he was under. He was permitted to go out on deck; there was nowhere else to go, after all. Unlike Allyndra, he couldn't simply fly away.

From the deck, he could watch the preparations below — ships being loaded, repaired, or stripped down — yet commerce still flowed, masking the signs of greater activity.

Clever, he thought.

House La'Gave was not committing all its resources at once.

He liked standing out there, feeling the breeze and watching the calm sweep of the ocean beneath the skyship as it glided toward Warraquim. He sipped gingerly at a cup of Blood Flower juice — a deep red liquid, sweet enough to make syrup taste tame. Still, he'd grown accustomed to it.

Just not too much at once, he reminded himself.

After the Council meeting, he had been escorted to a room where clothing was laid neatly on the bed. A brief note in English instructed him to change and wait. When he finished dressing, there came a sharp knock. Opening the door, he found a daughter of the House accompanied by two tall, broad-shouldered infertile males. The woman gestured for him to follow. He started to bow, but she shook her head.

Straightening, he did as asked.

Without a word, she turned and strode briskly down the corridor, her long stride forcing him to nearly jog to keep up while the two towering males followed behind. They descended the spiral walkway into the lower halls where the Council had met. There, Mother Ti'iha and Allyndra waited, both looking tense.

Allyndra made a quick dip in respect, and Stephen followed, bowing with the males. Ti'iha waved it off impatiently.

"No time for that, Mother Allyndra. You must be away. I wish you fair winds, and may you find the old things — may they be worth the search."

"Thank you, Mother Ti'iha. May the Twins bless you as well," Allyndra replied, returning the gesture before turning sharply and striding off again, so quickly that Stephen had to hurry to stay beside her.

Questions burned in his mind, but he knew this wasn't the time.

Perhaps later, he told himself.

When he saw where they were headed, he smiled. It was a familiar vessel — the *Wind Dancer.* On the deck, Captain Hila'ar paced restlessly, her wings twitching in agitation.

"Are you ready, Captain Hila'ar?" Allyndra called as they approached.

"Aye! And I'm glad you're here, water dancer," the captain shouted back. "It'll take longer than I'd like, even with fair wind, Mother Allyndra."

Then, catching sight of him, she grinned.

"Well, if it isn't the man I once wondered could fly. Hello, Stephen. Hurry along — same place as before. Once we're away, if the Mother permits, you can come topside."

Stephen bowed slightly.

"Yes, Captain Hila'ar."

He glanced at Allyndra but said nothing, boarding quickly and finding the same small cabin he had used before. Within minutes, the ship lurched skyward, and he had to brace himself against the wall.

They're in a hurry, he thought.

Once the motion steadied, he stayed below — there wasn't much to see through the narrow window anyway.

The following morning, just after the Twins rose, there was a knock at his door. One of the crew — a short-haired woman with a brisk, no-nonsense air — stood waiting.

"You know your way?" she asked, jerking her chin toward the ladder.

He nodded.

"Good. We're short-handed, so you're on your own."

She turned away, already calling orders as she disappeared down the corridor.

Stephen made his way up through the narrow passages between holds, cabins, and the massive gas bladders that filled the ship's interior. The moment he stepped onto the deck, a warm, stiff breeze hit him. He widened his stance for balance and looked around. Much of the vessel's weight had been stripped away.

They've lightened her for the mountains.

He turned to gaze at the horizon — the sweep of clouds and sea below — and admitted to himself that Allyndra had been right. Traveling this way made one feel the world's vastness in a way no machine of his own kind ever could. It stirred questions he couldn't yet voice.

After some time, Allyndra came to stand at the prow, her poise serene despite the ship's occasional sway. He envied the way her wings caught the air and steadied her so effortlessly.

The day before, there had been little conversation; but today felt different. The frantic urgency had ebbed, replaced by quiet focus. The pace had slowed, if only a little.

Stephen found his gaze drawn to her — the breeze pressing the thin fabric of her dress close to her form, her hair streaming behind her like a storm cloud streaked with blue lightning.

God, he thought, *she's beautiful. Exotic as hell — even the eyes. Especially the eyes.*

Two faceted sapphires that caught every glint of light. A pang of guilt hit him.

*Sandra...*He forced the thought away. *If things were different — if this were another time — I could easily fall in love with her.*

The realization unsettled him.

"If I may, Allyndra," he began carefully. "That statement you made before we left — about the Aribabitru and the old machines — it took me by surprise. I take it you found some way to read those old texts?"

"I did," she said. "The Wussuru have a library — not as large as Warraquim's, but they kept a way to read the old language. There was much there, and much still missing. But those machines from long ago — I think I understand them better now."

"So the Aribabitru — the ones like you, quick learners — they really did destroy this world's moon?"

"Yes." Her tone was even. "They did it to reset society — to give the world a new beginning before it collapsed entirely. It was terrible, but it saved what could be saved. They were thought reckless, blind to consequence, but as I read more, I learned how wrong that story was. They saw too much — and acted anyway. The tales of the dangerous A'ksu were created later, to warn against arrogance and detachment from nature."

She turned her gaze to him.

"Do you remember, Stephen, when we first met on this ship a year ago? I said it was unfortunate that you aged as you did — that you found it strange we did not. And that I had regrown these fingers?"

She lifted her left hand, flexing it.

He nodded.

"I remember. Even our scans showed nothing amiss — no sign they were ever missing. Why bring it up now?"

"Because before the Aribabitru, we were like you," she said softly. "We aged, grew frail, and died. But they gave us a gift — to grow to maturity and then remain as we are until the very end. When they hid their machines away, they put away medicine, too, but they couldn't undo that gift. It would have been... unethical. So they wove it into us."

Her brow furrowed slightly.

"If I understand your science correctly, they *engineered* it — altered us."

"You're right," Stephen said quietly. "Modified your genetic code."

She nodded, looking out at the horizon again.

"They also knew we shouldn't live forever. So they ensured that when our time comes, we end all at once. No slow decay, no lingering."

Her voice grew distant, almost reverent.

"They gave us life — and a graceful end."

"Impressive," Stephen murmured. "How they managed it — we never did. But even more remarkable is that they *chose* to do it. To have the foresight and the ethics to alter life itself because they knew they would take advanced medicine away — that's extraordinary."

He sighed, his gaze distant.

"If one lived forever, or even for centuries, the world would eventually drown in its own population again. Their foresight is... stunning. Just enough technology to live comfortably, but still in balance with the world. Everyone dependent on one another, connected — and yet still living long, healthy lives. For all our technology, Allyndra, for all we achieved to cross the stars, it means nothing without the wisdom to see ahead, to plan for the consequences. You and your people are far superior in that regard. I can only hope — and pray — that mine can learn the same."

He nearly lost his grip on the rope, so lost was he in thought.

"Perhaps," Allyndra replied softly. "But I think it isn't within your people quite as deeply as it is within us. Different roads were taken. Even though I'm called *Aribabitru,* I don't know if I have that much foresight when it comes to your kind."

She stared straight ahead, her expression unreadable. To Stephen, it seemed as if she were trying to peer into the future itself.

Is that what the A'ksu could do? he wondered. *See the threads of possibility and choose the one that led to the outcome they desired? If so, it was a gift humanity sorely lacked.*

"Maybe," he said at last, "more than we realize. Different roads, as you said. But I'll tell you one thing, Allyndra — as a medical man, I'd love to study how that regenerative gift of yours works. We were only beginning to unlock that secret back home, but it was always destined for the rich and powerful. I wonder how your people avoided that — how you kept it for everyone. Still, I think we could learn a great deal from one another."

He glanced at her, trying to read her thoughts.

What might humanity have become if we'd chosen the path her people took? he wondered. *If, instead of serving the powerful, our scientists had worked for the good of the world — to preserve it rather than exploit it? Perhaps then they wouldn't be here now, intruding upon a civilization that had found its balance.*

Another thought struck him — unsettling, but persistent.

Some would call this stagnation, he realized. *No progress, no innovation, no ambition left.*

He frowned. He would have to ask her what she thought of that — to see the world through her eyes.

"Some might say what you have is admirable," Stephen began, "and others would call it stagnation. That your society has stopped progressing — turned inward, shutting itself away from the wonder of the stars."

He glanced at her. The wind caught her hair and pressed the thin fabric of her dress against her form. For a moment, he was struck again by just how stunning she looked — even by human standards — and a flicker of desire stirred within him. He forced it down.

Allyndra turned her head, studying him as a teacher might a pupil.

"You speak of progress," she said. "But what *is* progress? How is it measured? By how far one can push the next machine? By finding new lands or claiming new territories? Perhaps true progress is measured by the satisfaction of one's people — whether they are cared for, whether they are happy, whether they have enough, and whether the world remains in balance."

She looked out toward the horizon.

"When your ship came, we first thought it was a meteor," she said quietly. "There have been others before. But what if it had brought disaster — as the Queen of Night's Promise once did? What if we had not survived? A dead world would offer nothing to grow again. But a living world, even if *we* vanished, might still give rise to something new. On your world, there was once another dominant species — and in the blink of a cosmic eye, it disappeared. If it had not, your kind would never have had its chance."

Stephen marveled at her insight.

Yes — if the meteor hadn't wiped out the dinosaurs, we wouldn't exist.

She was suggesting the same for her own people — that even their extinction could serve life's greater continuity. It was an almost alien way of thinking—to place the world above oneself.

She continued, her tone reflective but steady.

"Perhaps that is what makes our paths different. Your people think only of themselves — never of the whole. Is our culture stagnant? If you mean we no longer build machines beyond what is necessary, or that ours are crafted from what nature provides

— perhaps. But our artists still create new songs, new stories, new paintings. Our weavers craft new designs. If anything, it is my own House — the House of Warraquim — that failed the most. We gathered knowledge but did little to share it. We lost the ability to read the archives. In that sense, yes, we stagnated. We stopped thinking and teaching as we once did. Perhaps we did lose some of that wonder."

She turned back to him, her gaze keen.

"But tell me, Stephen — given what you know of us, and of your own history, who do you think has chosen the better path?"

There it is again, he thought. *A different way of measuring worth.*

They judged his people by their values, just as he judged them by his. Perhaps the two sides would never find a true common ground.

He nodded slowly, considering his words.

"There's so much in your culture that I find remarkable," he said at last. "You live in peace. People are cared for, content, and live good, healthy lives. That's something my kind has never mastered. We always take — a little more, a little faster — without thinking who we hurt or what we destroy.

"Still, maybe it's just my human nature, but I can't help wondering if your way could use... a little flexibility. The Houses seem so rigid, so bound by tradition. Maybe there's a balance to be found — a bit of your harmony with a touch of our ambition. A blend of both worlds. But unlike you, Allyndra, I'm no A'ksu. I can't see that far ahead."

Allyndra nodded slowly, thoughtful.

"I will have to think on that," she said. "But your words mean little if I can't counter your people's technology. I fear the plan the Council has made will not succeed — hence our haste."

Stephen frowned.

"You say haste. Is there another reason?"

Her sapphire eyes met his, a faint smile touching her lips.

"Are you looking to fly, Stephen?" she teased lightly, then grew serious again. "Yes — there is another reason. Alekelia left

House La'Gave without telling anyone. It's... unusual. No one knows where she's gone. She would have been furious about being removed — that much is certain. We can only hope she learns to master her anger, but we cannot depend on it."

Stephen's eyes widened.

"You think she'd go to Conner?"

"I've no idea," Allyndra said at last. "Perhaps she simply wanted to leave — to go somewhere far enough that few would know she's no longer a Mother. Maybe she just wishes to enjoy whatever prestige that title still brings. Still, we must plan for the worst — that she might betray us, or that what we seek will not be found. Either way, there is enough to do."

She closed her eyes for a moment, let the wind catch her wings, and rose briefly into the air. Then, folding them again, she landed lightly and walked away down the deck.

Stephen watched her go, shaking his head.

If Alekelia really did go to warn Conner, then any attack is doomed before it begins.

He had no doubt that Conner wouldn't hesitate to make a preemptive strike. This mission — this search for ancient power — was already a long shot.

Still, one thing gave him pause. Alekelia had left before Allyndra had even mentioned the possibility of finding some kind of ancient weapon — something powerful enough to tear a moon apart.

That'd be enough to scare anyone, he thought grimly. *And if Conner learns of it, there's no telling how he'll react. More likely than not, he'd strike first — to make sure he held all the cards.*

***

The next day passed without incident. They saw no movement from the human bases — no patrols, no shuttles in the air. Only the island of Warraquim looming ever closer on the horizon.

It was larger than Stephen had expected — perhaps the size of the Big Island of Hawai'i — but sharper, more rugged, its cliffs rising in jagged spires from the sea. After hearing Allyndra's story of *Pa'hole's Tears* and how the ice had melted, he wondered whether this land had once been part of a great mountain range — its peaks carved by time and tectonic fury rather than volcanoes. It was far outside his field, but fascinating, nonetheless.

If anything survives all this, he mused, *there's enough here for generations to study.*

The *Wind Dancer* made steady progress, and by the next morning, the mountains of Warraquim loomed like monstrous teeth rising from the sea — their jagged peaks dusted with snow, their flanks stripped bare of trees.

Stephen stood at the prow, staring at them in awe, when Captain Hila'ar joined him.

"Good day, Captain," he said. "They're certainly... nasty looking."

Hila'ar gave him a sideways glance and nodded.

"No one's crossed this way before — not even to test the run to Warraquim. These peaks are higher than the others, and I'm not sure we'll make it. The *Dancer's* near her limit. See anything that looks like a tall mountain with an arrow-shaped patch of snow?"

Stephen shaded his eyes, scanning the horizon. All he could see were ridges of gray stone and white peaks, forbidding and immense. Then something caught his eye off to the left — almost hidden in a fold of rock but angled just as Allyndra had described. He tried to recall what Mother Assura had said about the valley that connected to the village near Wussuru. If he was right, this might be it.

"Over there, Captain," he said, pointing. "See that mountain? There's a patch of snow along the side. From this angle, it's hard to tell if it's arrow-shaped, but it seems about right."

Hila'ar followed his gesture, then patted his shoulder briefly.

"Stay here. Keep it in sight. I'll see what the Mothers think."

Without another word, she leapt into the air, her wings catching the updrafts. The *Wind Dancer* rocked as she passed overhead. Stephen gripped the railing to keep his footing but kept his gaze locked on the mountain.

He barely noticed when Allyndra and Assura landed beside him.

Assura spoke first.

"So, Stephen — you say you've spotted something? Show me, please."

He pointed again.

"We're nearly side-on to it, but there — that mountain with the snow patch. If I understand correctly, Mother illm Wussuru, it could be in the right direction from your House."

Assura stood behind him, her height allowing her to easily see over his shoulder. She rested a hand lightly on his arm as she peered into the distance.

"I think you are correct, Stephen," she said at last. "That looks like the upper end of the valley where our House lies. If that's true, then the cave entrance would be on the far side."

She turned to Allyndra, shaking her head slightly.

"I'm surprised you survived that flight, Allyndra. There's hardly a clear passage through those peaks."

Allyndra gave a small smile.

"The Twins must have decided it wasn't my time."

Not long after, Captain Hila'ar returned, landing lightly on the deck. The four of them — captain, scholar, and Mothers alike — gathered to discuss their options. Formalities were forgotten. There was only the shared urgency of the moment. It was decided that they would attempt the crossing.

Hila'ar adjusted their course, turning the *Wind Dancer* to line up with the distant valley, watching carefully to see if there was any safe passage through the peaks — or if Allyndra could spot the place she might have been carried by the storm all those years ago.

For several hours, they sailed back and forth across the rugged terrain, the air growing thinner and colder. The captain's expression grew increasingly tense.

"If something's gone wrong elsewhere," she muttered, "we can't risk being spotted up here."

The others said nothing, but Stephen could feel the unease settling over them all like a gathering storm.

A sudden boom cracked through the air — then another, closer this time. Stephen turned sharply toward the sound and spotted two white contrails slicing the sky.

"Damn," he muttered. "Two shuttles — those were sonic booms. They're going faster than sound. Looks like they're turning. If they're starting to search for us, we're in trouble."

"There!" Allyndra cried suddenly.

All four turned to follow her gaze.

"See? There's a fold in the mountains — it runs right up the side of the arrow-shaped peak. That might be it — the passage to the valley beyond!"

Stephen followed her pointing hand. The narrow gap between the jagged ridges looked impossibly steep and confined. Thin sheets of rock jutted down like blades, and the cliffs rose sheer on either side. Yet there — near the center — was a narrow, crumbling path, as if a portion of the mountain had collapsed long ago to make a way through. For a fleeting moment, he wondered if the *Aribabitru* had done it deliberately, leaving a hidden trail for their descendants to rediscover. Then, shaking his head, he decided it was just the work of nature and time.

Captain Hila'ar stared grimly at the gap.

"That's going to be one hell of a passage. The updrafts might help us — it's nearing evening — but they'll also make for wild winds and unpredictable drift. Well," she said, flashing a brief smile, "trust to your wings."

She clapped Stephen on the shoulder.

"As for you — I'll raise a glass to you at the next port if we make it."

Then she gave a quick, musical laugh — more spirited than pleasant — and shouted over the roar of the wind.

"Toss it all! Anything not tied down or absolutely needed — overboard! Everything! We've got to make the *Dancer* as light as she'll go. Furl those sails — toss them if you have to! We'll ride the currents and steer with what we've got. Move!"

The crew erupted into motion. Though the ship had already been stripped nearly bare before leaving House La'Gave, they threw off the last of her fittings — spare planks, crates, even doors — until she was little more than a skeleton drifting on the wind.

Mother Assura turned to Stephen.

"When we make the turn into that fold, you'd best be below. The air will be rough, and you can't fly."

He shook his head, heart pounding as the mountains loomed ever closer.

"No, Mother Assura. Give me a bit of rope, and I'll lash myself to the front mast. I have to see this. I'd rather face my fate with my eyes open than wait in the dark, wondering."

Assura arched a brow but smiled faintly.

"As you wish. Braver than I gave you credit for."

She called to one of the sailors, who fetched a coil of rope.

Before she could help him, Captain Hila'ar arrived, motioning for Assura to return to her station. She came over herself, testing the knots.

"You're sure about this? If we hit the rock and come apart, there'll be nothing you can do."

"Yes, Captain. I'd rather meet my fate head-on — even if I have to stare death in the face."

Hila'ar studied him for a heartbeat, then shrugged and tied the last knot herself.

"There. You impress me, male. Not many do."

She squeezed his shoulder and hurried back to the helm.

Slowly, the *Wind Dancer* turned to align with the narrow gap and began her approach. With nearly no sail left, she drifted more than she flew, carried by shifting currents as the suns sank toward the horizon.

The temperature dropped sharply. The snow-covered peaks cooled faster than the sea below, and warm air from the ocean began to rise, feeding turbulent winds that battered the ship. The *Dancer* lurched and shuddered, buffeted from one side to the other as the mountains closed in.

Stephen gritted his teeth, gripping the mast. He felt like Odysseus lashed to the ship's mast — helpless but defiant.

"Climb, *Dancer*, climb!" he shouted into the wind.

Twilight deepened into gloom. Ahead, the gap loomed, dark and narrow, the last of the light fading from the snow. Then came a bone-jarring scrape as the *Dancer's* hull dragged against rock — a terrible groan of splintering wood echoing through the mountains. For a moment, Stephen thought the ship would tear apart.

Then, with a sudden blast of icy air, they were through. The *Wind Dancer* shot out into the open, gliding above a snowfield that glittered faintly in the starlight. A final lurch — and then the ship shuddered to a halt.

He hung from the mast, dazed, until Captain Hila'ar herself came to untie him.

"We made it," she said, her voice rough with relief. "We're moored. In the morning, we'll look for the cave. For now, we need warmth — and we tossed most of what we had. Come on."

A low boom echoed across the peaks. Both turned toward the sound in time to see one of the human shuttles streaking back toward Warraquim. It didn't pause, didn't alter course.

They both exhaled in unison.

"Whew," Hila'ar muttered. "If they'd caught a glimpse of us on their screens, this expedition would be over."

"I agree," Stephen said quietly. "And I think we know where Alekelia went — and what she's done. Let's just hope she hasn't caused too much damage... or too many deaths."

"Indeed," the captain said.

She extended her hand — a rare gesture among her kind — and Stephen took it. Her palm was rough, calloused, and cold to the touch. He had forgotten that her people did not carry their own warmth the way humans did.

She led him below decks, where what remained of the ship's interior had been stripped bare — doors gone, fittings torn away. The air grew colder as they descended toward the hold, where a low, rhythmic humming grew louder.

When they entered, Stephen saw the crew gathered in a wide circle. The women stood on the outer ring, wings beating steadily, the sound merging into a deep, droning thrum. In the center, the others huddled close together, resting in the shared warmth.

Hila'ar guided him inward.

"You'll stand in the center with the rest of the males, Stephen. It won't be warm, but it'll keep you alive. If one of the women looks too tired, bring her inside and give her juice from that cask."

She pointed to a barrel with mugs hanging from its rim.

Stephen smiled faintly.

"Aye, Captain."

At least I can be useful again — even if only as a doctor.

Hila'ar touched his arm briefly before taking her place among the outer ring, her wings joining the steady rhythm that kept them all from freezing.

Stephen worked with the other males, passing mugs of the sweet red drink, keeping watch on the exhausted flyers. Once, he had to bring the captain herself into the circle; for she was shivering so violently she could barely stand. He held her close, sharing his body heat until her breathing steadied. She whispered a faint word of thanks before drifting into sleep.

Stephen looked around the darkened hold, listening to the steady drone of wings and the sigh of wind outside.

Twins bless us, he prayed silently. *Let us see morning — and grant that Allyndra finds what she seeks. But if she does... gods, let her have the foresight of the Aribabitru to see the cost before it's too late. We don't need more death. No more destruction.*

Chapter 18

THE CAVE OF THE ARIBABITRU

ALLYNDRA

It had been a long, grueling night, and Allyndra, like the rest of the crew, was exhausted. Still, morning had come. Though the air was biting cold, the Twins had risen above the peaks, casting their light and warmth over the frozen valley. It was High Summer — the season of renewal — and yet here it felt like the edge of winter.

To her, it seemed an age ago, though barely a year had passed since she had danced on the waves, thinking of nothing but the water, the sky, and the joy of movement. Back then, she had cared little for ancients, aliens, or even the mysteries locked away in old books. She sipped from a mug of Blood Flower juice, feeling the sweet liquid replenish her strength. Soon they would have to start searching for the cave entrance. They could not remain here long — not before their stores ran out and the cold claimed them all.

She looked up as the human came stamping down the corridor into the hold, rubbing his arms and shivering.

He can endure the cold better than we can, she thought, *but even for him, this is harsh. Still, he had volunteered to help despite the night's ordeal. The crew had accepted him — perhaps even admired him now. A hopeful sign,* she mused.

"Damn, it's cold out there!" Stephen exclaimed, blowing on his hands. "And that sheet of ice out in the valley doesn't make things any easier."

"Did you see anything?" Allyndra asked, taking another sip.

Stephen nodded, his breath fogging in the chill.

"Oh yes. Just as you said — there's a cave mouth. The captain managed to set us down almost beside it. It's a steep climb, but I think I can make it. I'm guessing the rest of you will... fly?"

"Of course." Allyndra smiled faintly. "You still wish to come with us?"

"I can't fly," he said, "but if you can get me close, I'll climb the rest of the way."

"You're not equipped for the cold," she warned. "You wouldn't last long out there on your own — and we can't wait for you."

Stephen's expression fell.

"I see."

"Mother Assura and I have a plan," Allyndra said after a pause. "While we can't lift you outright, between the two of us we might manage a glide down to the entrance. If you're willing to take the risk. But if we lose our grip..." she met his eyes, "we can't wait."

Stephen's brows rose, but he nodded.

"I'll take the chance."

"Very well, then — drink."

She handed him her mug.

"I know it's too sweet for your taste, but it's all we have. Better than nothing — it will give you strength. Go on."

He hesitated, then lifted the mug.

"I should leave this for the crew. I saw the cask — it's more than half empty. Last night took a lot out of them. I had to practically force some of them to drink. I'm sure a few were angry at being handled by a male — and an alien male at that."

"I think you'll find otherwise," she said gently. "Many would have died if you hadn't done what you did."

He smiled faintly.

"My instincts as a doctor took over, I suppose. I didn't want to lose anyone. No one's said much — just a few nods, a few quiet thanks."

He took another sip and grimaced.

"No thanks needed. Just duty."

"Ah, a Mother after all," she teased, chuckling softly. "I believe they're more grateful than you think — especially the captain."

She raised a finger as he hesitated with the mug.

"More."

Stephen laughed.

"Now who's the Mother here? I feel like a child being scolded."

He gave a small, mock bow.

"Yes, Mother."

He drained the mug quickly before the sweetness overwhelmed him and made a face.

"All right. Ready. Who's coming?"

Allyndra hung the mug back on the edge of the barrel.

"Just me, you, and Mother Assura. The captain will remain here. We can't linger — it's cold even in High Summer, and the nights will only grow worse. This is the end of our supplies. We can't stay another night. Are you ready, Stephen?"

He nodded.

Together they climbed to the deck, waiting until Mother Assura joined them. Allyndra explained the plan. Assura gave a short nod, then smirked.

"Well, male, it seems you're going to fly after all."

She took one of his hands in both of hers, and Allyndra did the same on his other side. The two Allidians began to beat their wings in unison, the powerful strokes lifting them into the air.

With a final nod to each other, they rose — then lunged forward off the deck, carrying Stephen with them.

The drop was immediate.

Stephen cried out, "Oh, shit!" as the three of them plunged downward.

The women strained against the air, wings hammering hard to slow the descent.

Allyndra could feel the strain in every muscle.

We can't keep him aloft for long — he's too heavy.

It was less flight and more of a controlled fall.

Perhaps next time four of us could manage it, she thought fleetingly. *That's what we suggested to get him away from Warraquim — awkward, but possible.*

Even so, it took careful coordination. They had to angle sideways to keep their wings from tangling, balancing his weight between them. Allyndra found the rhythm — wind and body in harmony, like a water dance in the air. Assura wasn't as graceful, but she was stronger, compensating through sheer power.

After several tense minutes, Stephen's boots brushed the snow, and then the three of them landed in the ankle-deep drift beside the dark maw of the cave.

Allyndra glanced skyward.

"We must hurry. The Twins won't stay long on this side of the range."

She led the way toward the cave, motioning for Stephen and Assura to follow.

"It's exactly as I remember. See — the walls here are rough and damp, but soon they become smooth and dry."

She pointed ahead, where a dim, ghostly light glowed around a bend in the tunnel. As they approached, she stopped beside the carved wall and gestured.

Stephen ran his fingers across the surface.

"This is machine-made," he said, awe in his voice. "It's too precise, too clean. Not something done by hand."

"I have to agree with him," said Assura, stepping back to take in the chamber. "This is unlike anything—even the finest artist could not have achieved such precision."

She paused, then recited softly, "*Pa'ela mākouua i uā mea i hale i mea o mālamia o i ke wā e liki mai anamai.* We hide away the past in order to preserve the future. It's the same phrase found in the old books."

Mother Assura dipped her head in respect.

"The ancients had great foresight. Come—let's see what they hid away, and whether we can use any of it."

Stephen turned toward her.

"I hope there's something here that might make Conner stop and think. Still, I'd urge caution. If he learns about this place, he might try to destroy it."

"Understood," Allyndra replied evenly. "But remember, Stephen—though I like you and you've done much to understand our ways, you're here by tolerance alone."

She gestured toward the floor.

"Now—step there."

The tunnel curved downward, the air growing colder as they descended. When Stephen reached the bottom step, he froze and blinked.

"What was that? It felt like we just passed through something."

"No idea. Come," Allyndra said, motioning Assura forward.

Assura descended the last step and shivered slightly.

"Nothing much—just a chill, perhaps. I'd call it a draft."

"Maybe a way to keep the place sealed?" Stephen suggested as he turned to look around.

His voice trailed off, "Oh..."

The room stretched out before them, lined with smooth, gleaming surfaces—just as Allyndra remembered. She stepped beside him, awe reflected in her own eyes.

"Do you recognize anything?"

Stephen shook his head.

"No idea. But that—" he pointed toward a large, oblong object glowing faintly from within—"that's something."

Allyndra's breath caught. It was exactly as she had seen it before. Stephen approached it carefully, reaching out a tentative hand as if expecting to be shocked. When nothing happened, he pressed his palm flat against it.

"It's warm," he said quietly. "Warmer than the rest of the room."

He turned toward her.

"Any idea what it is? Was it mentioned in your old books?"

Allyndra shook her head.

"No. But there should be writing on one of these devices…"

She scanned the room.

"I don't see anything, do you, Mother Assura? The texts said there would be a word—something to awaken them."

Assura moved reverently from one artifact to another, fingertips brushing the smooth surfaces. Finally, she straightened and shook her head.

"No, Allyndra. Beautiful, yes—but meaningless to us without knowing their purpose."

She raised her voice and called out the ancient phrase into the chamber, but nothing stirred.

Allyndra began her own search, moving slowly along the rows of relics.

"The books insist there should be writing," she murmured. "But I see nothing…"

She turned to Stephen.

"Please—help us. Tell me if you see anything unusual."

He began to inspect the devices one by one.

"Sorry—nothing yet…"

He stopped abruptly, squinting.

"Wait. Here—there are faint symbols. Glowing red, just barely."

The two women hurried to his side. Allyndra ran her fingers along the surface but felt only smoothness.

"Are you certain?"

Stephen nodded.

"Very faint—but yes, right here."

He traced the lines with his fingertips.

"No wonder you can't see them. Your visual range extends into what we'd call ultraviolet, but it's poor in the red spectrum. This would be invisible to you."

He leaned closer, frowning.

"I can't read it, though. It's not in any language I know—it must be one of your ancient scripts. Whatever power source it has must be nearly drained. It's barely glowing."

Assura stepped closer, pulling a small pad and pencil from a pocket sewn into her sleeve.

"Can you draw the symbols you see, please? Allyndra may recognize them."

He nodded and carefully sketched what he saw, with Allyndra leaning over his shoulder. When he finished, he handed her the paper. She studied it for a long moment, then looked back at the object.

Raising her voice clearly, she spoke the word aloud, "*Ala'ae.*"

At once, the oblong device blazed with white light. The three of them stumbled back as a shape began to coalesce before it— flickering, shifting, until it steadied into the form of a tall woman.

Assura leaned toward Allyndra, her voice low.

"What did you say?"

"It's the old tongue," Allyndra replied, eyes fixed on the glowing figure. "The word means *awaken.*"

The form solidified to become a woman with long black hair streaked with metallic blue, her eyes a pale, luminous azure. Her clothing was strange—like a dress, but close-fitting and made from some smooth material that shimmered faintly in the light.

She spoke first.

"Ah... how long has it been?"

Her gaze swept over them, pausing on Stephen. Her expression shifted from curiosity to intrigue.

"And... a human? How very interesting."

The three of them stood frozen, stunned not only that she spoke but that she seemed to recognize him for what he was.

At last, Allyndra gathered herself and made a respectful curtsy.

To her surprise, the figure returned the gesture.

"Unknown Mother," Allyndra said softly, "it has been a very long time. And yes—there is a human among us. How do you know of his kind?"

The figure smiled faintly.

"Ah. I am—or rather, *was*—Feli'a. What you see is only a projection, a reconstruction of my likeness in life. Do you understand?"

Allyndra shook her head slowly, but Stephen stepped forward, eyes wide.

"Are you... a hologram? A three-dimensional projection of light?"

"A little simple—and more than that—but good enough, yes." Feli'a smiled faintly.

"Oh my, humans have come such a long way since we last visited them."

A flicker of puzzlement crossed her features.

"But tell me, how do you come to be here, human?"

"Uh... well," Stephen began awkwardly, "we traveled across the stars—in a ship."

"A *ship?*" Feli'a's eyes widened. "Oh my goodness, all that way! How long did it take you?"

"Thirty of my years," he said. "But how is it that you know us—and can even speak our language?"

"We visited your world long ago," she replied, as though it were the most natural thing in the universe. "And it's easy enough to read the engrams in your mind and interpret your speech. Now then..." Her gaze shifted away from him. "Which of you spoke the word?"

She dismissed him with a glance, focusing on Allyndra and Assura.

I have a thousand questions, Stephen thought. *She looks as real as any of us—and she knows humans. That means her people crossed the stars long before we did. Incredible.*

Allyndra steadied herself and stepped forward.

"I did. I've learned the old language at last—but it was Stephen who could read the writing. It was too faint, too deep in the red for me to see. I am Allyndra of House Warraquim, and this is Mother Assura of House Wussuru."

Feli'a frowned slightly, then froze, as if computing.

"At least several thousand years," she murmured. "And how fares the world we tried to save from destruction?"

Allyndra smiled.

"Very well, Mother. We've lived in balance with the world—each House working with the others, each person free to pursue what they love. That harmony has endured... until recently."

Feli'a closed her eyes, but a broad smile touched her lips.

"Then it was worth it—to make the moon fall. Tell me, how fare the House of Knowledge and the House of the Keepers?"

Allyndra's face darkened.

"House Warraquim has been burned... the library destroyed. We've lost everything."

Feli'a's smile faded.

"Destroyed? By whom?"

Her gaze flicked sharply toward Stephen.

"Not the humans, surely?"

Allyndra lifted her head.

"Unfortunately, yes—but *not him*. Stephen has been an ally."

Feli'a's expression remained cold. She waved a hand dismissively toward Allyndra.

"And why, human, did you come here to bring such ruin?"

Stephen straightened.

"I argued against it. I never supported the destruction. It wasn't right to seize House Warraquim."

Feli'a frowned more deeply.

"That's not an answer. Why are you here? Why was this done?"

Stephen cut in before she could speak, hearing the rising tension.

"Our world died," he said softly. "We fled into space aboard a great ship. The journey took thirty years. This was never our intended destination—something failed in our drive systems, and our AI shifted course to save us. The ship was damaged when we arrived. We had nowhere to go, and too many lives to protect. In desperation, things were done that should not have been."

Feli'a regarded him in silence, then turned to Assura.

"And what of the House of the Keepers? You were entrusted with relics—artifacts to be preserved in case of need. Why come here, if not for them?"

Mother Assura looked confused and offered a curtsy.

"Ancient Mother, what artifacts? We have some of the old books, and a few remnants of the language, but nothing like these. The House of the Keepers? We are known as the House that Refused."

"Oh, my." Feli'a shook her head, clearly surprised. "One moment."

The figure froze, utterly still for several seconds, then came to life again.

"They're still there," she said at last. "Somehow, your House has forgotten where they are stored—or even what your purpose was meant to be. We tried to plan for the future, but I suppose no one can foresee everything. Still, it seems much went as we hoped—and that pleases me."

She smiled faintly.

"Now, perhaps I understand why you came to this remote place rather than to House Wussuru. I assume there is… conflict with the humans?"

"Yes, Mother Feli'a," Allyndra replied, bowing her head.

"Ah. Tell me." Feli'a raised a hand before Allyndra could begin. "No—wait. Rather, let me *see* for myself."

"It's a long journey, Mother," Allyndra said cautiously. "The skyship may be fired upon."

"No need, Allyndra."

Feli'a turned toward the tall, glowing frame.

"Let me show you some of what we accomplished before the moon fell."

She placed a hand against the oblong device, and it brightened steadily until it filled the room with light.

"Come, Allyndra. Touch the frame—and think of where the humans are now."

Allyndra obeyed, pressing her palm to the smooth, warm surface. As she focused on House Warraquim, the center of the frame shimmered, thinned, and then vanished—replaced by a vivid image of the ruined House, its great courtyard littered with debris, only a few shuttles parked amid the wreckage.

She stepped back, eyes wide.

"A picture—one that shows another place?"

Feli'a laughed lightly.

"Oh no. Step through, Allyndra. Go on."

Allyndra hesitated, then took a cautious step forward—and suddenly she was there.

The Twins blazed above her; the air hot and heavy with moisture. She turned to look for Feli'a and the others—then flinched as a shout rang out. Gunfire cracked through the air. She stumbled backward—and found herself back in the chamber, unharmed.

"What—how?" She patted herself down, astonished to find no injury.

If I'd known how to use this, I wouldn't have ended up delirious in that field... and the humans could never have done what they did.

"A portal device!" Stephen exclaimed, eyes wide. "Your people figured out how to create portals through space-time!"

"We did," Feli'a said, nodding proudly. "It was how we once visited your world—so many, many years ago. And now you say your world has died?"

She turned back to the glowing frame and touched it again. The surface rippled, thinned, and opened once more—this time revealing a dying world bathed in sickly gray light. Towering, skeletal vegetation stretched across the wastelands. Crumbling cities stood half-submerged in rising waters, silent monuments to a civilization long spent.

"Stuff of legends!" Stephen exclaimed. "I spent ten years frozen and another twenty trying to get from Earth to here—and with this, I could've just walked through!"

He reached toward the device, sliding his hand partway into the shimmering surface, then pulled it back quickly.

"It's cold! Damn, they actually did it. They used nukes. Maybe… maybe it'll heal someday."

Feli'a let the portal close and turned to study him.

"Well, that answers that. Your kind destroyed its own world."

She sighed, the sound heavy with centuries of regret.

"We should have watched more closely—but our ethics forbade interference. It was not our world to guide."

"Yes." Stephen lowered his head. "We didn't learn. We had no one to teach us as you once had."

"Perhaps," Feli'a said quietly, "in a few hundred years, your world might heal enough to live again. But you can't wait that long, can you? And now you wish to take this one?"

She didn't wait for him to answer.

"I see what has happened, Allyndra, Assura. We feared something like this might come to pass—that's why we hid these relics away instead of destroying them. They were meant for contingency."

She turned her piercing gaze back to Stephen.

"Your kind cannot stay here. It will only bring conflict."

He raised his head, protesting.

"What if we learned to live like the Allidians? To build our own Houses, to live in balance?"

Feli'a shook her head.

"It's not so simple. Two sentient species—two ecosystems— competing for the same space. Even if peaceful, you would change this world merely by existing. We debated this long ago when we first discovered how to open portals. We realized we could reach any world we wished. But what if that world—like yours—was already alive? What if, even without intelligent life, we disrupted its natural course and prevented new life from forming?

"A sentient species always reshapes its environment. An alien one does so even more dramatically, bringing foreign flora and fauna with it. We saw other worlds like yours, Stephen—worlds that rose, burned bright, and destroyed themselves. A few escaped, as you did, but they only repeated the same mistakes until they ruined the next world as well. Worlds like yours—and ours—are rare gems. There are not many left."

"We had no choice!" Stephen's voice cracked with emotion. "Our ship barely survived the journey. We lost so much. But Mother—" he used the title instinctively "—with this device, we could go to the world we meant to reach, the one we called Big Blue. We could all just walk through!"

Feli'a's tone turned cold.

"No. If you did, others would learn of this place. How long before they send more ships? How long before war breaks out for control of the device—or this world itself? As much as I pity you, my duty is to protect the balance of this world and the culture we built here."

"Now, see here—" he began, but Feli'a cut him off with a sharp look.

"Quiet."

She regarded him for a moment, then turned to the Allidian women.

"As I said, we debated whether to travel to other worlds—and chose not to interfere with those already bearing life. But we did allow ourselves one exception. We considered remaking or reseeding worlds that once had life but lost it. Our morals found that acceptable. So, before we ended our own decline, we experimented. One such world was *Hulibri*."

Feli'a turned back to the portal and activated it again. The light shifted, revealing a new world—bright beneath twin suns. Vast plains stretched into the distance where herds of creatures ran, and strange birds wheeled in the sky. The wind was crisp and cold, but not cruel.

"Ah," she said softly, "it fares well. Too cold for us, but perhaps perfect for your kind, Stephen. A world that never truly lived—or where life once was, but long since faded. Allyndra, Assura—would you gift this world to those who have lost theirs?"

Allyndra met Assuri's eyes. The elder Mother gave a small shrug.

"I would, Feli'a—but only if they, like us, learn to live in true balance with it. No shuttles, no higher technologies. Let them build their own Houses as we once did."

She lifted a hand as Stephen started to speak.

"And you, and we, will guide them."

Feli'a inclined her head.

"Then I will help as much as I can."

Stephen looked between them, struggling with the enormity of what he was hearing.

"You have regeneration. You have knowledge. You have the wisdom of balance—and you would send us to a harsher world with nothing?"

Feli'a tilted her head.

"No. You may take what you can carry. But when your shuttles fail—and they will—when your machines break and your technology fades, it shall not be replaced. You will have generations to adapt, and we will guide you. That is the offer. No more, no less.

"We, the Aribabitru, enforced this law here, and it will be enforced there. You will learn to bend—or you will break. But we will not let you destroy another world."

Her gaze hardened.

"Know this, Stephen—the universe grants few second chances. This is yours. Perhaps, in time, there will be commerce again—between two peoples, two worlds."

Feli'a turned to the Allidian women.

"House Wussuru must reclaim its ancient duty as the Keepers—guardians of what was. And you, House Warraquim, must become once more the Teachers of Knowledge. That was your intended role. I charge you to fulfill it again. One day you may need what is stored here. Do not lose it. But remember—if balance is threatened, I will enforce it myself. There are tools here, and at Wussuru, that can help you preserve it."

Allyndra and Assura both bowed, acknowledging the command.

"Now," Feli'a continued, "Allyndra, Assura—after Stephen and I have gone through the portal, you must return to House Wussuru and share what I have said. The future depends on it."

One of the glowing constructs nearby shimmered, flowing over Feli'a's form and resolving into a sleek silver gown that made her seem even more solid—almost alive. She extended her hand to Stephen.

"Come now. It's time for you to rejoin your people. Your part in this world's story is finished—for now. Tell them what I have offered... and what will happen if they refuse."

Stephen's shoulders sagged.

"Allyndra... what I've seen here makes everything we have look crude by comparison. You're centuries ahead of us. I only hope Conner will listen."

He stepped forward and took Allyndra's hand.

"Well, Allyndra," he said softly, his voice heavy with emotion, "it seems this is goodbye. There's still so much I wish I could have learned—and perhaps you from us. Maybe someday, if we're given that second chance."

"Not goodbye forever, Stephen," Allyndra said. "I am Mother of House Warraquim—the gatherers and teachers of knowledge."

She smiled faintly.

"That means not only gathering what lies within this world but also learning from others beyond it. I've never heard that we shouldn't."

Feli'a activated the portal again, and the view shifted to the courtyard of ruined Warraquim. She smiled approvingly.

"I will hold you to that, Mother of Warraquim—and you as well, Mother of Wussuru."

Stephen gave a deep bow, then turned to go, but Allyndra called out, "Mother Feli'a—one moment. Stephen, if you see

Alekelia, remind her of the phrase we all know. But tell her to replace the first word with *Ho'oulu.* It means 'to revive.' Tell her it's true."

He repeated the word under his breath several times and nodded.

"Yes, Mother."

Turning to her, he added softly, "I hope to see you water dance again someday."

Then he followed Feli'a through the shimmering gate. For a heartbeat, their shapes were visible within the light—and then both were gone. The portal closed.

Allyndra rolled her shoulders, her wings rustling softly, and took a long, deep breath.

"There is still much to do," she murmured. "Come, let us leave this place and do as the Aribabitru asked."

Assura nodded and started back up the tunnel, only to pause when she realized Allyndra had not followed.

"Is something wrong, Mother Allyndra?"

Allyndra shook her head slowly.

"No."

She looked back once more at the dark, ancient room and whispered, "*Ho'oulu mākouua i uā mea i hale i mea o mālamia o i ke wā e liki mai anamai.*" *We revive the past in order to preserve the future.*

Assura shook her head.

"You're right, Mother of Warraquim. *We revive the past in order to preserve the future.* That's what you want Stephen to tell Alekelia if he sees her."

"Yes," Allyndra said softly. "Maybe she'll realize things are about to change—and quickly. Ah well, Mother Assura, it's time we left before anyone else finds this place. We should also see if we can locate the other devices that Feli'a said are hidden within your House."

Mother Assura nodded.

"Yes, Allyndra—Mother of Warraquim—just in case."

The two began the trek back toward the skyship, but Allyndra paused once more and bowed deeply toward the cavern's depths.

"May we all have the foresight to plan wisely—for the good of all."

Assura smiled.

"Indeed. Come, Mother. Let's get back to the ship before the captain and crew have to endure another freezing night."

"Yes, Mother."

Allyndra glanced back at the now-dormant portal.

"At least we no longer have to figure out how to make the male fly."

Assura laughed aloud, the sound echoing down the icy corridor.

It was a short flight back to the slender skyship. Captain Hila'ar wasted no time turning her vessel, steering through the narrow mountain pass and then down the long valley that led toward House Wussuru. The crew was bone-tired, as was the captain herself, but she listened wide-eyed as the two Mothers recounted everything that had occurred in the cavern.

"So, I'm just a simple skyship captain," Hila'ar said at last, "but you're telling me that this ancient Mother—or whatever she was—just stepped through that... thing to Warraquim with the human male? Without a care in the world? As if she knew no one could stop her?"

Allyndra nodded.

"Yes. I think the humans there will be in for quite a surprise. They believed us backward, but they've made a mistake—and now the situation has reversed. With luck, there will be peace at last, and all of us will be safe."

Captain Hila'ar looked down into her nearly empty mug—the last of the Blood Flower juice—and swirled it idly.

"I hope you're right. And I hope that human male survives. I liked him, after a while."

Allyndra smiled faintly.

"Indeed."

The ship drifted on the air currents, descending from the jagged peaks toward the green valleys below. Allyndra stood by the railing, watching as they passed the mountain marked by its distinctive arrow of snow.

Twins grant that I may have enough wisdom to see far ahead, she prayed silently. *So many things could go wrong... yet so many could go right. Bless us all that it may be for the good.*

"Twins bless you, Stephen," she whispered.

Chapter 19

House Warraquim

Alekelia & Stephen

It was morning before the sergeant returned and knocked on the door. He had to rap several times and was about to force it open when Conner's voice finally came, rough with sleep.

"Yeah, yeah—come in."

The sergeant entered and glanced briefly at the slim-figured woman in the bed before focusing on Conner.

"Right as rain, sir. There were at least six of those floating boats up the valley and a couple more on the west end, trying to climb higher."

"And?" Conner's tone was sharp, impatient.

The man shrugged.

"The ones on the west side turned tail when they spotted us and went full sail. We didn't have a chance to chase them, so we hit the ones in the valley instead. By the time we got there, most of the crews had scattered. I ordered them put down. Circled the village too—several houses and ships were already burning."

Conner rubbed at his shoulder, where a set of angry red marks stood out.

"Good work. Get any other shuttles in the air and start a patrol. If you see one of those damn skyships within a hundred miles, you take it down—no questions asked. Got that?"

"Sir, yes, sir." The sergeant saluted and turned to go.

"Hold on," Conner snapped. "I didn't dismiss you. You get the pilots off New Hope—assuming you can find any sober enough—and head over to..."

He trailed off, frowning.

"Hell, can't remember the name."

He tossed the covers back, grabbed a pair of shorts, and pulled them on while the sergeant politely averted his gaze.

"La'Gave," the Allidian woman in the bed offered, sitting up languidly.

Conner shot her an annoyed look, then went to the desk and rifled through scattered papers.

"Right. Here we are."

He motioned the sergeant over.

"We're here."

He jabbed a finger at the map.

"And that place is over here—another island, few miles east. Another House, similar to this one. Probably loaded with skyships. You take out everything—docked, flying, or under repair—and then broadcast that everyone in that House has twenty-four hours to clear out before we do it for them. Got that?"

"Sir, yes, sir," the sergeant said, nodding crisply.

"Well then, get moving," Conner gestured toward the door.

The sergeant needed no further prompting. He left at a jog, already shouting orders for pilots and Marines to rouse.

Conner turned toward the bed where Alekelia still reclined.

"Well, honey, your intel was damn good. And yeah—you did a fine job keeping me happy last night, though you bit hard enough I almost throttled you. Still, a deal's a deal. I'll boot that old bitch of a Mother out, and you can have the place—for a while."

"For a *while*?" Alekelia sat up, frowning.

"Sooner or later, we'll need to expand. That'll be the next target."

Conner stretched, unconcerned.

"That's not what I bargained for!" she snapped, anger flashing in her voice.

"Guess you should've thought that through," he said, smirking. "Sooner or later, sweetheart, *we'll* be running this world, not you. Do as you're told, play nice, and put out when I say—and maybe I'll see you get some comfortable accommodations when the rest of your kind get pushed off."

Alekelia threw off the covers and rose, fury blazing in her sapphire eyes.

"The Twins blast you," she hissed, baring her teeth to show the four small, sharp fangs. "I want to be *Mother of a House*, not your plaything!"

"Ah, too bad, it's—"

He never finished.

Shouts and gunfire erupted outside, swelling into chaos. The bursts came faster, then sporadically.

"What the hell's going on out there?" Conner barked.

He yanked on a shirt and pants, grabbed his weapon from the desk, and pointed it briefly at her. Then another volley cracked close by, and he turned toward the door instead.

He ran down the spiral staircase and caught a Marine rushing past.

"What the hell's happening? I thought we took those skyships down! Are they attacking anyway?"

"Unknown, sir!" the man shouted over the din. "Last transmission said some gal in a silver suit just *appeared out of nowhere*—taking down soldiers left and right. I was heading there myself!"

"Call the shuttles! Tell them to get their asses back here! I want to see this myself!"

"Tried that, sir," the Marine replied. "Comms are down. The shuttles aren't responding at all."

Conner shouted his displeasure and, in a fit of rage, shoved the Marine aside before storming toward the main entrance of Warraquim.

"Not a damn fit soldier among you lot!" he barked as he disappeared down the corridor.

Above, Alekelia dressed quickly in the flight gown she had worn when she arrived. Unlike Conner, she went straight to the balcony, vaulted over the rail, and caught the air beneath her wings as she dropped toward the waves. She glided out to sea for a moment before circling back, keeping low over the water just as she had when she first came to this place. Curiosity—and an uneasy sense of foreboding—pulled her toward the commotion. She skimmed around the curve of the great House, landed lightly, and made her way inland to see for herself.

How could the daughters of the other Houses have managed anything? she wondered. *I made sure to foil their plans—unless this was some kind of suicide mission.*

Keeping to the shadows, she moved toward the square. From her vantage point behind a half-collapsed wall, she finally saw it: a lone woman standing in the open plaza, wearing an outfit unlike anything Alekelia had ever seen. It was tight-fitting, fluid, and silver—shimmering like living metal. It reminded her vaguely of Trellium, but more refined, more alien.

Several Marines had taken cover and opened fire, but their weapons had no visible effect. The silver-clad woman didn't flinch. The bullets—or whatever projectiles they fired—struck her and vanished, leaving only faint ripples that danced across her form. Even as Alekelia watched, the woman seemed both there and not there, as if the eye couldn't quite decide where her edges ended.

Then Alekelia noticed movement nearby: the human doctor, Stephen, ducking for cover behind a pile of crates and equipment.

The woman advanced calmly, heedless of the gunfire. When she reached the center of the square, she lifted one hand. A moment later, the air itself seemed to tear open. A void appeared—black, impossibly black—and the atmosphere around it roared to life. Winds whipped outward and then inward, spiraling toward the opening. Loose debris was snatched from the ground and sucked into the darkness.

Alekelia braced herself against the crates as the gale intensified. The pull wasn't just wind—it was something deeper, like invisible tendrils grasping at everything nearby. She watched as two soldiers dropped their weapons and tried to crawl away, their screams snatched by the storm. The unseen force dragged them into the black void, which then collapsed in on itself and vanished as if it had never existed.

When the woman lowered her hand, the wind died instantly. Silence fell, broken only by the groaning of the damaged structures around the square.

Who is she? Alekelia thought, her pulse racing. *How did she do that?*

"I wish to speak to Captain Conner of the *Reliance*, please," the woman announced, her voice calm, resonant, and utterly unshaken.

The square remained still for several seconds before Conner burst onto the scene, red-faced and furious, weapon drawn. He fired without hesitation.

The shots had the same effect as before—none at all. The woman didn't even blink. She stood motionless, patient, as though waiting for a child's tantrum to end. When Conner's weapon finally clicked empty, she spoke again, her tone firm but almost gentle.

"Are you Captain Conner of the *Reliance*—the leader of the humans here?"

Conner lowered the weapon, still breathing hard.

"Yeah, I'm Captain Conner, lady. These pop guns might not do much, but I've called the shuttles—if you even know what those are—and when they get here, they'll toast your shiny ass."

The woman merely shook her head.

"I don't think so. Your shuttles to the west—and the ones heading toward the other House—have already met the same fate as those soldiers. They won't be returning. Now then, I am Feli'a, an Aribabitru. And you, Captain, and your kind are no longer welcome here."

"Is that so?" Conner sneered. "Well, screw you, Arbi-whatever."

He spat on the ground and yanked another device from his belt.

"I'll blow this place to hell before I let you throw me out."

"Conner!" Stephen's voice cut through the tension.

He emerged from cover, hands raised.

"Conner, stop! You don't know what you're dealing with!"

He approached quickly, glancing toward Feli'a.

"These people—this being—she has technology we can't even begin to understand! Do you know what that was? That was a *gateway*—a portal through space and time—and it led straight into a black hole!"

Conner's eyes narrowed.

"So? Toss me into your damn black hole. I'll still burn this place down before I let it happen. We've got one of the cores from the damaged ship rigged and ready to blow, while you've been off playing native."

He tossed his sidearm aside and lifted a different device from his belt.

"I might go down, but I'll bet this fancy lady of yours can't handle a blast like that."

"Conner, don't!" Stephen shouted, stepping closer. "You'll condemn us all! We fought and sacrificed everything just to get here. You said your duty was to keep humanity alive—and now you're ready to wipe us all out? If you detonate that core, you'll kill every human here and on *New Hope!* You have to listen to me!"

He pointed urgently toward Feli'a.

"You can't kill her, Conner! She's a construct—some kind of advanced holographic entity. Whatever she's made of, it's beyond us. You'll burn, I'll burn, and she'll still be standing when it's over. Then she'll erase the rest of the colony, and everything we've done will have been for nothing!"

Conner didn't waver—he only shrugged.

"I'm willing to take the chance she's not that well-built. I'm calling your bluff, Stephen—yours and whatever *she* is."

"You're not thinking straight, Conner. That bite of theirs—it messes with your head. And you've gotten addicted."

"Fuck off, Doc."

Conner turned his glare toward the silver-clad woman.

"As for you, bitch, get the hell out of here. My finger's gettin' tired."

Alekelia, hiding nearby, had been willing to sacrifice a House—perhaps even Mother Ti'iha herself—but what Conner was threatening was far worse. If he was serious, he would destroy everything: humans, Allidians, and their fragile world together.

Who is that woman? she wondered. *Did Allyndra actually find something?*

She straightened, stepped out from her hiding place, and called, "No need to worry, Conner. I am Mother of Warraquim once again—and I know how to handle this."

Conner's head snapped toward her.

"You knew about something like this?"

"Well, not exactly," Alekelia admitted, walking toward him with an easy, almost teasing smile. "Such things have been all but forgotten. Isn't that right, Stephen?"

She turned her gaze toward the doctor.

"You've heard the phrase *'Ha'iela mākouua i uā mea i hale i mea o mālamia o i ke wā e liki mai anamai'*, haven't you? Is this from then? Did Allyndra find something in her dusty old books?"

"Yes, she did," Stephen replied. "She told me to tell you to replace the first word with *Ho'oulu*. She said it means 'to revive.'"

Alekelia bowed her head, hands on her thighs, and began to laugh softly.

"What the fuck is so funny?" Conner demanded, irritated.

She looked up, smiling faintly.

"It's an old phrase. We're all taught it as children."

"So?" Conner snapped. "Can you do anything or not?"

They both want to see if I can control whatever this thing is, she thought. *Oh, how I wish I could—but I can at least pretend.*

"Yes," she said simply.

"Well then," Conner said, impatient, "if you can shut her down—or whatever the hell it is—then do it. I'll make sure you're one of the last to survive after we burn the rest down."

Alekelia ignored the venom in his words.

"We revive the past in order to preserve the future," she murmured, glancing between Feli'a and Stephen.

Where's Allyndra? she wondered. *She found something—something from the past—and she brought it back. Mother O'lathe, you were right all along. As much as I hated that bookworm A'ksu, she may have saved us all.*

"She's still standing there," Conner barked, breaking her thoughts.

Alekelia turned to face him squarely.

"Then what has been revived—I can also put away again."

"Fine by me," Conner said with a dismissive wave. "Do what you have to."

"As you wish," she said.

Then she moved—swift as lightning. She leapt, slamming into him and knocking the detonator from his grasp. He stumbled, cursing, as she sank her fangs deep into his neck. Conner howled, punching and clawing at her, finally wrenching her loose and clutching the bleeding wound.

"Bitch!" he roared.

Alekelia staggered back, gasping. Pain seared through her chest; every breath burned. She knew several ribs were broken—and one wing. Still, she didn't cry out. Instead, she turned her gaze toward Feli'a.

"*Ho'oulu mākouua i uā mea i hale i mea o mālamia o i ke wā e liki mai anamai,*" she said, voice trembling but steady. "Do it. It's my penance. I welcome the arms of the gods."

Feli'a raised her hand, and the air split open once more. The black void returned, dragging the wind and that terrible unseen pull with it. Alekelia didn't resist. She let the force take her.

Conner dove for the detonator, but as she was pulled past him, Alekelia grabbed hold of him. He clawed for the device—but before he could reach it, both were swept into the darkness. The void swallowed them whole and then vanished, leaving only swirling dust and fluttering scraps of paper.

Feli'a lowered her hand.

"May the Twins bless her—and grant her peace," she said quietly.

Stephen turned to her.

"Then that's the end of them? You said you could control the portal without being physically present. I assume that one led into a black hole."

Feli'a's expression dimmed. "Yes. I didn't wish to do that—but there was little choice. I only hope there will be no more deaths. We killed enough when we altered this world's path, and even now... each loss weighs heavily."

They stood in silence for a long moment before Feli'a's luminous form brightened again.

"Now, Stephen—who commands after Conner?"

"Shelia," he said. "She's second-in-command. Let me see if there's a comm link—I think she's on *New Hope*."

"No need," Feli'a said, raising her hand. "We shall go ourselves."

"Wait."

Stephen knelt briefly beside the scorched floor where Conner had stood.

"Conner... it's over. I'll do what I can with Shelia to make sure what's left of us survives."

He turned slightly, voice softening.

"And Alekelia—let me echo what a skyship captain once told me...*fair winds, and the Twins bless.*"

He stood.

"Ready."

Feli'a regarded him for a long moment.

"There is hope yet," she said. "That is why we did what we did. Hope is a powerful thing."

Stephen nodded.

"It is. Hope for a new life brought us here. I only hope we can make it right—and maybe even become friends."

He gave a short laugh.

Feli'a tilted her head.

"What amuses you in such tragedy?"

"I once told Allyndra there was beauty in this world," he said. "Now I see there's not just beauty—but wisdom and wonder, too."

Feli'a smiled faintly.

"I only wish you hadn't learned it the hard way. Now come— there is still work to be done."

She extended her hand.

"Think of the place where this other Mother resides."

Stephen nodded and focused.

Feli'a gestured, and another rift opened—this one overlooking the green but scarred island where the *Reliance* lay grounded. Together, they stepped through. They emerged to find Shelia and a group of Marines staring in shock. Stephen held up a hand.

"Hold your fire, Shelia. We need to talk. A lot has happened— and you need to hear it."

"We lost all contact with the shuttles and Conner," Shelia said cautiously. "What's this?"

"This," Stephen replied, motioning to Feli'a, "is Feli'a—an Aribabitru. We made a massive mistake, Shelia. We all thought these people had nothing more advanced than those skyships. But long ago, they had technology far beyond ours. That—" he pointed to the shimmering portal "—is a space-time gateway. A bridge between here and there."

Shelia's stance remained firm, but unease flickered across her face.

"What are you saying, Doc?"

"I'm saying," he said grimly, "that if it came to it, this Aribabitru could sweep every one of us away like dust. But it doesn't have to come to that. They're offering us something else—a new world."

Shelia hesitated, then gestured for the Marines behind her to lower their weapons.

"All right. Tell me everything. A whole new world? How do we get there?"

Stephen nodded.

"I will. But listen, Shelia—the universe doesn't give many second chances. And we've just been given one."

He paused, then added softly, "Maybe even our third."

Chapter 20

HOUSE WARRAQUIM

ALLYNDRA

This would not be the first time the portal had opened between House Warraquim and Hulibri—the third planet from the Twin Suns, where the humans had lived for the past ten years. There had been many exchanges already: of materials, information, and aid. The Aribabitru Feli'a—or whatever form she now took—had traveled several times between the two worlds to help. But this time was different. This was an *invitation*.

It had been ten years since the humans first landed on Allidia, and now things had long since settled. In fact, over the years, a modest but steady trade had developed between the two worlds beneath the Twin Suns.

Allyndra felt content at last. The daughters of her House thrived; she was welcomed at every other House; and the bond between House Warraquim and House Wussuru had grown as close as that of twin sisters.

As it should have been all along, she thought. *We have found the path once more.*

After the exile of the human contingent to Hulibri—with Feli'a's guidance—she and Mother Assura had rediscovered the lost passageways that led to caverns full of ancient machines. Between their two Houses, daughters had worked tirelessly to transcribe recovered information into new books.

Yet even with this rediscovery of the old technologies, the Council had decided that the existing way of life was more than sufficient. To depend too much on the relics of the past was not in the best interest of Allidia. They would study them, learn from them, yes—but not rely on them. The Houses would preserve this knowledge as guardians, just in case it was ever needed again, so that the mistakes of forgetfulness would not be repeated.

As she reclined on the Mother's balcony, Allyndra mused aloud.

"I told the world what we had once possessed. Each House examined its own members, but when we gathered as the Council, all agreed—the life we have now is enough. Our people are content."

A few were curious, of course. As she had once told Stephen, there was always a place for those whose curiosity ran deep, and Wussuru still held its ancient privilege as the one House to which anyone could transfer allegiance freely.

As promised, she had reshaped Warraquim itself. The record halls were filling again—not only with recovered history and rediscovered knowledge, but with new achievements as well. She ensured that what humanity had learned was also recorded and preserved.

But that was not my only promise, she reminded herself.

Now, new buildings flanked the square—schools where daughters of Warraquim taught history, art, and language—both Allidian and human, ancient and modern alike. She had kept her word to Feli'a. Ten years on, the first generation of children born not on Earth but on Hulibri had come of age. Some would come here to study beside her own people.

Tonight's celebration was for them—the beginning of a new tradition—daughters and sons, human and Allidian, learning side by side within House Warraquim.

From the Mother's balcony, Allyndra watched as the last of the skyships from the other Houses arrived for the evening's festivities. She smiled and lifted her face to the setting light of the Twins. Life felt good. And though she was a Mother—and some still whispered that it was scandalous—she fully intended to water dance tonight.

She could still recall the old murmurs of disapproval.

It isn't dignified for a Mother of a House, least of all a Great House, to perform such things.

She didn't care. She had practiced for years now, and she would dance again. Let some of the old stiffness fade away. Respect would remain—but the rigidity that had once bound them could vanish with the setting suns.

With a sigh, she went to change. She chose a simple flight dress like the one she had worn long ago—thin, tied at the neck, the hem falling just above her knees, the back left open for her long translucent wings.

It was a perfect High Summer evening—warm, clear, and bright. Her attendants helped her change quickly, fastening the ties and smoothing the fabric before she made her way toward the portal chamber.

The gateway itself was a duplicate of the one she and Assura had discovered on that remote mountaintop ten years before—a gift from Feli'a and House Wussuru.

Mother Assura had already arrived at Warraquim. Allyndra had met with her old mentor earlier in the day, saddened to see how age had finally caught up with her. The once-tall woman now walked with a cane; fine wrinkles lined her skin; and the bright color had faded from her hair. Yet her eyes still gleamed, and her mind remained as sharp as ever.

They had shared a meal and reminisced about the past. Captain Hila'ar had personally ferried Mother Assura to Warraquim but had begged off joining the two, saying the meeting was for them alone—and that she needed to attend to her crew.

"And to whom do you leave House Wussuru, Mother Assura?" Allyndra had asked as they sat together on the balcony earlier that afternoon.

"We'ela," the older woman had replied with a fond smile. "She has been loyal, capable, and wise. And she left a message for you, Allyndra illm Warraquim."

Allyndra arched an eyebrow, and Assura chuckled, imitating the younger woman's tone.

"She says the Qwiklicks miss you—and their stable still needs mucking out."

They had both laughed at that, remembering the exhausting chores of their youth.

"Perhaps when I find the time," Allyndra had said with amusement. "There never seems to be enough of it these days. But that's good, I suppose—so much new, so much to look forward to. It feels as though a new course has been set. I only hope I can see far enough ahead."

Mother Assura had taken her hand, her grip gentle but firm.

"You are Aribabitru, child. They gifted us foresight—and in you, that legacy endures. I trust your judgment. You do not act lightly. You seek the best path for us all."

She patted Allyndra's hand with a faint smile.

"Now, I am an old woman, and I need my rest before tonight. I want to be alert—for I hear there's a very talented water dancer performing this evening."

"I'm not sure about talented," Allyndra had replied, laughing. "But I've been told she's not *too* bad."

"Ah, good. And what, if I may ask, will this talented water dancer perform tonight? Please—an old woman would like to know. It will be our secret," Mother Assura had laughed softly as she spoke.

"La'u meke nao nukou," Allyndra replied with a small smile. "I think it's appropriate. But what do you think, Mother?"

Mother Assura raised her brows.

"That song—*a gift to you?* That's difficult, but it's so moving. Indeed, I think what you have tried, what *we all* have tried, is to give a gift to everyone—to Allidians and humans alike."

She nodded, settling back in her chair.

"I'll be glad to have seen and heard it one last time before I go dance with the Twins."

She smiled then, but Allyndra began to cry. The old Mother came around the table and wrapped her in her arms.

"Now, now. Hush," she whispered. "You know this comes to us all one day. My time is near, and it has been a good life. Dry your tears—it will do no good to sing such a song with a voice cracked from weeping."

I remember Mother O'lathe doing the same for me, Allyndra thought, *when I lost my husband and children. When she named me Mother. Who comforts the Mother? Another Mother. May I be able to do so in my time?*

"It is time, Mother."

One of the attendants had brought her out of her reverie, and Allyndra nodded.

"Then let's go and meet our guests."

She descended the inner spiral ramp, looking down over the railing. One would never guess that these walls had once been scarred and blackened by smoke. Artists from every House, along with members of her own, had restored them—researching the old designs and carefully bringing them back to life. Where once a simple wall ornament had hung, there now stood one of the strange frames—the portal device—adorned with carved embellishments that helped it blend into the graceful architecture of the hall. The long tables had been cleared for the evening's celebration which would be held outdoors, beneath the warm High Summer skies.

She paused a few paces back from the portal and nodded to one of the daughters. The young woman stepped forward, touched the frame, and closed her eyes. The air before them shimmered— thinning, darkening—until a faint wind began to blow as the warmth of Allidia met the cooler air of Hulibri.

Through the portal appeared several figures bundled in heavy coats, surrounded by smaller ones—children, perhaps twenty in all. A man stepped through first, then beckoned to the others. The young ones followed, tugging back the fur-lined hoods of their handmade coats. Their eyes went wide as they looked around the grand hall.

Several daughters hurried forward, greeting them in English, reassuring them, and explaining that they would be cared for. The children relaxed, and the attendants led them away toward the guest quarters.

The man pushed back his hood, and Allyndra almost didn't recognize him. Beneath the thick beard and the deep lines of age, she saw the familiar face of Doctor Stephen Banks. He smiled and gave a stiff bow, hampered by the weight of his coat.

The other adult did the same, and Allyndra greeted her warmly.

"Captain Shelia—welcome. I'm glad to see you again and delighted that we'll have so many new students joining us."

Shelia smiled but did not curtsy. Her features, too, showed the touch of time.

"Thank you, Mother," she said, offering a small salute. "I'm already sweating in this coat, though. I'd forgotten how thick the air is here!"

She laughed, and Allyndra gestured for attendants to escort her to guest rooms and provide lighter clothing suitable for Allidia's climate.

Stephen had already shrugged off his jacket, though he still wore his coarse shirt, leather breeches, and heavy boots. He watched Shelia and the children disappear down the corridor before turning back to Allyndra.

"How are you, Allyndra? It's been a long time, hasn't it?"

"Indeed—ten years," she said warmly. "And how fare you and your colony?"

"Well enough," he replied with a weary smile. "A bit of chilled Blood Flower juice, and I'll tell you all about it—if you have the time."

"Always," she said, motioning to her attendants. "Daughters, please bring two cups of chilled Blood Flower juice."

The girls all but tripped over each other in their eagerness. Allyndra chuckled softly.

"I've said before—a little less formality would serve us well. But perhaps just a little is still needed."

She took a seat at a side table and gestured for Stephen to join her. He sat opposite her.

"So, Allyndra, what's the occasion tonight? The message said it was in honor of our first students coming here, but it also mentioned something special—some kind of entertainment?"

"That's right," she replied with a smile. "But it's more than that. It's been ten years since you first came here, Stephen. We've traded, exchanged, worked together—but truth be told, I simply missed you. And I'm not the only one. Do you remember Captain Hila'ar?"

"Oh yes," he said, chuckling. "A lively one. Is she still flying the *Wind Dancer*?"

"Yes, though it's a new ship now—larger, but still light and nimble. She said she'd never trade agility for grandeur. She's here tonight, and she sent a message for you. 'Tell that male who once flew with me that I wouldn't mind a dance or two—if such are on offer.'"

Stephen laughed heartily and slapped his knee.

"Well then, I'll try not to step on her toes—oh!"

He broke off as the two girls returned—one with a pitcher, the other with two brimming cups. They curtsied and retreated quickly.

Stephen took a sip and winced playfully.

"Sweet as ever. I always forget just how sweet it is—but still lovely. It reminds me of that night in the high peaks, in the hold of the *Wind Dancer*."

Allyndra smiled and nodded.

"So, Stephen—truly—how do you and the others fare? Feli'a tells me you're doing well, and that she's been working with you to give your people the same gift of regeneration we possess."

She sighed softly.

"I've come to think of myself as Mother not only to this House or this world—but to yours as well."

"That's true enough," he said, setting down his cup. "Life's harder, Allyndra—but damn, if I'm not fitter than I was ten years ago." He chuckled. "We travel with the herds and the waves of grain and berries. It means a lot of walking—though we've managed to domesticate some of the animals. Odd creatures. Everything there seems to have evolved an extra pair of limbs, and most of them look awkward as all get-out—but the hexadeer, as we've taken to calling them, are fast and gentle once they're used to you.

"There's no real agriculture. The seasons are too short. But some of our plants—and a few of the native ones—grow naturally in waves through the year. In a way, we've become more like the old Native tribes of Earth, migrating with the animals and the wild grains. It's a simpler life. Hard, yes—but people are stronger, healthier, and somehow happier.

"At the camps—or the semi-permanent settlements—we share everything. People talk again—really *talk*. There's music, stories, poetry. A sense of community that we'd forgotten. Oh, accidents happen, of course. But some of those semi-permanent bases we rotate between still have the medical facilities we brought with us.

"Feli'a's working with some of our scientists, trying to understand the biology of regeneration. Maybe we'll never match you, but we might get close. Some of the children die—it's hard— but maybe that's the world's balance, the due nature demands. Like your K'tareth in the sea."

He smiled faintly.

"As a doctor, it hurts to know I can't save everyone. But to see people living in harmony, connected again—it's worth more than all the machines we left behind."

"So you're learning balance with your world," Allyndra said approvingly. "That's good. We've decided the same—to study the old machines, yes, but not to rely on them. The way of the world still serves us well.

"But there is one exception. Warraquim—and to a lesser extent, Wussuru—will never hoard knowledge again. My vision now is that we are both *keepers* and *teachers*. That's why I asked for some of your younger generation to study here for a time."

"That sounds perfect," he said. "And of course, we'll welcome any of your daughters who wish to come to us. We'll make what accommodations we can."

He lifted his cup.

"To friendship—and to new paths forward."

Allyndra raised hers in return.

"To friendship," she echoed, taking a generous sip before setting it down.

"Well, I hope you'll enjoy the entertainment tonight. There'll be music, of course—but I've arranged something special: a water dance."

He grinned.

"I remember watching you long ago. Captain Hila'ar said you were exceptional. I suppose, being Mother of a House, you haven't had much time for that lately."

"I still practice whenever I can," she said. "We have the Artists' Guild here now, alongside all the other Houses. Still,"— she rose, smiling—"as you say, there never seems to be enough time. Be welcome, Stephen."

He stood too. Instead of bowing, he stepped forward and hugged her.

Surprised, she laughed softly.

"Less formality," she teased. "I did say that, didn't I?"

"Yes," he said, stepping back with a deep breath. "God, I'd forgotten how thick with perfume the air is here. I miss this world."

"I know," Allyndra said gently. "But Feli'a was right. It's best for you to walk your own path on your world—and we on ours. Still…"

She gestured toward the portal device on the wall.

"That lets us remain neighbors."

"Indeed," Stephen agreed, glancing down at his heavy clothing. "And as Shelia said, these things are starting to chafe. I'm sweating already. I hope there's still some of that fine linen around—I remember it from when I studied here."

"Of course," Allyndra said warmly. "Rest, refresh yourself, and be welcome, Stephen."

Her eyes sparkled.

"There's a gift waiting for you—from me to you. I hope you'll like it."

He gave a formal bow.

"A gift? I'm sure I will. Well then—tonight. Though I can't imagine what you'd give an old man."

"Tonight," she said with a mischievous smile. "You'll see."

She gave a graceful curtsy and turned to her attendants.

"Daughters, please see to my special guest."

The two Allidian girls dipped their heads and came forward to escort Stephen away.

***

The Twins had set, and all was in readiness. Chairs had been arranged along the beach, and guests were already gathering. Tables of food stood nearby—most dishes native to Allidia, with a few prepared especially for the humans from Hulibri.

The children of both worlds had discovered that play was play, no matter who—or what—you were, or which world you called home. They laughed, chased one another along the sand, and shrieked in delight.

In earlier days, such behavior would have been quickly discouraged, but when several daughters of the House moved to intervene, Allyndra had shaken her head.

"The old days are the old days," she had said gently. "Let's see if we can find a better path. Let them play—for soon enough, work will find them."

After that, she had quietly slipped away toward the House, unseen by most.

***

The mingling continued—talk, laughter, food, and music—until the first gleam of the Queen of Night's Promise appeared in the sky.

"It is time, honored guests," one of the daughters called out.

The daughters of Warraquim moved gracefully through the crowd, guiding everyone to their seats. Musicians from the House of the Artists gathered near the shoreline, instruments glimmering faintly in the reflected light as they prepared to play.

Then, as the Queen of Night's Promise stretched from horizon to horizon, a hush fell over the assembly.

A vast, silver arc—like a titanic rainbow—spanned the heavens, casting a soft brilliance across the ocean and land. The reflected light of the suns shimmered in waves across the beach. It was a perfect High Summer night: warm, clear, and touched by a gentle breeze. The sea was calm, the waves lapping softly against the shore, with only the occasional, lazy breaker rolling in.

Allyndra stood apart, watching the silver rainbow rise. It was her favorite moment—the time when the encircling rings of their world made the stars fade into soft twilight. She never tired of that sight, especially on such a balmy night.

The air was perfumed with the mingling scents of flowers—sweet, heady, drifting down from the gardens as the breeze moved from the warm land toward the sea. The night blooms, white and luminous, had opened in their containers all around, adding a faint radiance to the scene. The world itself seemed to glow under the light of the Promise.

The crowd had fallen utterly silent, faces turned toward the sea. Even the children grew still, settling cross-legged on the sand or curling up on woven mats as the first notes of music began to drift across the air.

From above, several Allidian women descended, wings glinting in the light. They hovered just beyond the surf, poised like living reflections of the stars that once shone above.

Earlier, Captain Hila'ar had found Stephen among the guests, and the two had embraced warmly.

"What's this?" she teased, tugging lightly at the shirt he wore.

"A gift from the Mother of this House," he said, showing her the garment—a fine Trellium-silk shirt that shimmered with shifting rainbows even in the dim light of the Promise.

"A rich present indeed."

She smiled and glanced toward the beach as the daughters began calling people to their seats.

"I had hoped for more time to catch up—but perhaps later."

"I would insist, *Mother*," Stephen teased.

She gave him a playful shove.

"No 'Mother'—I'm just a simple skyship captain."

"You are that," he said with a grin, "but you look after your crew as if you were one."

Before she could reply, one of the daughters approached and gestured for Stephen to follow. He was escorted to a seat near the front.

Captain Hila'ar drained the last of her cup and muttered with amusement, "Damn, a fine specimen of a male."

As she turned to find her place, an attendant wearing the sigil of Warraquim appeared and bowed.

"Mother, this way, if you please."

She followed and was led to the front row—right beside Stephen.

"Are you sure?" she asked with a wry smile.

"Yes, Mother," the attendant said simply.

Hila'ar took her seat and leaned toward Stephen.

"Why do I think Mother Allyndra had something to do with this?"

Stephen chuckled.

"If she did," he said, "I'm glad she did."

They had talked for a while about the old days—how the two Mothers had once flown him to the cavern entrance, how awkward and thrilling it had been.

"The male who flew," Hila'ar had teased, tugging gently at his beard in amusement.

As the dancers began to appear, she leaned closer and whispered, "This is the *hola o le matakin akaluah*—a little more formal than ordinary water dancing. It's the dance of wind and wave, a delicate balance of keeping one's feet just touching the water no matter how the wind drifts or the waves surge. It takes great skill not to be lifted or pulled under—to let the wings steady you while the waves try to sweep you away. The goal is to dance across the surface, catching the water with your feet but never losing balance."

Stephen told her that he was sure she could do it herself. She laughed softly so as not to disturb the performance.

"I can fly," she whispered, "but this takes years of practice—and very fine control. This old captain couldn't manage it then, and certainly not now."

They fell silent, watching as the women danced—feet brushing the wave tops, their long-practiced grace sending arcs of water spinning into the air to catch the silvery light of the rings above. Stephen sat utterly mesmerized by the movement, the music bright and fluid, a celebration of rhythm and motion. Then, as the song ended, the crowd erupted into applause, arms raised high as they clapped in delight. Stephen joined them, smiling broadly.

The musicians began another tune, slower now, rich with harmonies both joyful and melancholy. The notes tugged at the heart with a deep, aching sweetness.

Captain Hila'ar looked surprised. She leaned close again.

"*La'u meke nao nukou*," she murmured. "It means 'This song is my gift to you.' It tells of how one loves, loses, and yet carries hope—that love, in the end, returns. It's one of the most difficult dances there is. Whoever performs this must be someone very special."

As the melody deepened, a single figure descended from the sky, landing as delicately as a leaf touching a still pond. She seemed to stand upon the surface of the sea, her feet gliding with the rise and fall of the gentle swells. When the music returned to its opening refrain, the figure raised her arms toward the audience.

It was Allyndra.

Her voice rose, clear and strong, carrying across the waves. She sang as she danced, her movements fluid and luminous. Each sweep of her wings caught the breeze and the reflected light, casting silver arcs of spray that shimmered against the dark water. Her hair glinted with blue metallic streaks, and her eyes—like faceted sapphires—seemed to catch and hold the glow of the Queen of Night's Promise above.

"The Mother of Warraquim herself!" Hila'ar breathed, shaking her head in astonishment. "I remember her dancing years ago—it was beautiful then. But this…" She exhaled. "This is beyond anything I've seen, even from the finest artists."

Stephen nodded, eyes fixed on Allyndra.

"She's dancing from the heart," he said quietly, "not from form."

"That she is," Hila'ar agreed.

She listened a moment longer, then added, "The words—listen—they've changed. She's singing now of how the gift is the world itself. That love connects all living things—no, *all worlds.*"

She paused, smiling faintly.

"By the Twins, Stephen," she whispered, "I'd like to know how that beard of yours feels before dawn."

He turned to her, startled, then smiled back.

"And I'd like to know what a kiss from you feels like before dawn."

He took her hand and squeezed it gently. She turned back toward the performance, but her fingers remained entwined with his.

Mother Assura sat quietly, watching Allyndra dance, her old friend's song echoing through the night. We'ela was seated beside her.

"While I'm never as warm as I'd like to be these days," Assura murmured, "those words put a glow in my soul that warms me more than any fire."

We'ela reached over and patted her hand.

"Much has changed, Mother—and much remains the same."

"Indeed."

Assura's eyes glistened as she watched Allyndra balance upon the waves.

"I feel as though the gods themselves have guided us once again. The Aribabitru were meant to steer the future—and one of them still does, now as delicately as she balances upon the sea."

"There is wisdom in your words, Mother," We'ela said softly.

She turned back toward the waves.

Mother Assura closed her eyes as the final notes drifted over the water—and with that last, lingering chord, she passed peacefully into the arms of the gods.

Allyndra finished her dance with her arms raised high, one leg crossed over the other, balancing gracefully on a single foot that just brushed the waves. Her wings followed the rhythm of wind and tide as she lifted her face toward the heavens, smiling.

Above her, the Queen of Night's Promise stretched across the sky—no longer a reminder of loss, but a bridge, a symbol of connection.

Out of destruction, she thought, *something new has been built. It is not an end, but a joining.*

She closed her eyes for a moment and whispered a final prayer.

Twins bless that I have seen far enough ahead.

Bonus Chapter

THE TEARS OF PA'HOLE

It is said that once, long ago, Allidia was far greater than the scattered islands we know today. The story goes like this.

All of Allidia had once been a vast land—rich, green, and unbroken—its forests stretching from horizon to horizon, its rivers winding through valleys filled with song and light. But those days are gone, and this is how they ended.

The goddess Malina had a daughter, Pa'hole, who tended the forests, the flowers, and all living things within them. She was so beautiful that all the gods desired her, and many sought her hand. Yet Pa'hole favored none, for her heart belonged only to the wild and growing world.

Among those who pursued her was Polelyna, god of the deep caverns and hidden places beneath the earth. He did not take rejection kindly. Spurned and burning with jealousy, he vowed that if he could not win her love, he would take her by force.

Night after night, Polelyna crept from his shadowed domain, searching for her. Then, one evening, he found Pa'hole sleeping near the entrance of one of his caves. He seized her and carried her down into the depths—into the cold, dark chambers that were his realm.

Malina could do nothing, for her power did not reach where the light of the Twins could not shine. So she began to weep. She wept and wept, and her tears became rivers that swelled and flooded the land. The waters rose higher and higher until a vast sea spread across the face of Allidia.

The flood poured into Polelyna's caverns, filling the tunnels where he hid with his stolen bride. The waters rose until even he could not endure them. At last, he fled deeper into the earth, and Pa'hole escaped, climbing toward the light.

When she reached the surface and beheld the world, she cried out, "Oh, Mother—what have you done?"

For where there had once been endless forests and plains, there now stretched a boundless ocean.

"What has become of the creatures that roamed the land? All lost now beneath the waves!"

And Pa'hole wept. But her tears were not of water—they were of fire and living stone. Wherever her tears fell, new islands rose from the sea.

Malina looked upon her daughter and said gently, "All is not lost, child. Those who roamed the land I have given fins and gills, or wings to carry them above the waters. And I have saved the seeds of the lost forests."

Pa'hole planted those seeds in the soil of the newborn isles. They took root quickly and flourished, bursting forth in color and perfume. The creatures returned from sea and sky to the land, and life began anew.

She was content—but sometimes, when she remembered what had been lost, her tears would fall again. And each time she wept, a new island was born.

About the Author

ARIAN NIWL

Arian Niwl is the author of the following titles:

Man of the Lake

Queen of Night's Promise

Woman From the North